"Marry me, Thia..."

Luc threw one leg over both of Thia's and lay half on top of her, gently pinning her to the blanket, but she was oblivious to his weight. She was ignited by the fire of his kisses and the urgency of his caresses, until deep inside she was melting, burning with an unquenchable need.

But if Thia's desire for Luc was overwhelming, it was also frightening. With the last vestige of reason, she braced her palms against his chest and gasped, "It's too soon, Luc. Everything is happening so quickly. I can't think when you kiss me. Give me time—"

"Time won't change anything, Thia." His hands traced the curves from breast to belly to thigh in a hot, claiming caress. She bit her lip to keep from crying out her pleasure, but he felt the response that quivered through her and said, "Time won't change this...."

ROBIN FRANCIS
is also the author
of this title in
Love Affair

MEMORIES OF LOVE

Matthew Jonas didn't believe in good-byes. When he thought of all the people that had walked in and out of his life during his successful career as a journalist, he knew he would meet with some of them again. But he never expected to see Paige Cavanaugh.

Paige had met Matt eight years before. He was special to her—he was the first real love of her life. She had contacted him out of desperation—there was no one else for her to turn to, and he just had to help her. The realization that her worst fear might be true—the secret she had kept could be revealed—drove Paige to Matt for the answer she needed!

Season of Dreams

ROBIN FRANCIS

A Love Affair from

HARLEQUIN

London · Toronto · New York · Sydney

First published in Great Britain in 1985 by
Harlequin, 15–16 Brook's Mews, London W1A 1DR

© Robin Francis 1985

ISBN 0 373 16088 7

18-1085

Printed and bound in Great Britain by
Richard Clay (The Chaucer Press) Ltd,
Bungay, Suffolk

Chapter One

The ballroom of the Warwick Inn had been closed for more than two years. To Thia Sommers it smelled of faded flowers and secret dreams. But, she thought, it had lost none of its ambience.

Shortly after the inn's closing the furniture from the guest rooms had been repossessed. The Jackson County Historical Society had intervened in time to rescue the elegant period pieces in the ballroom from the auction block, but the ivory-damask settees that lined the walls were swathed in dustcovers and shrouded by perpetual twilight, as were the crystal chandeliers that blossomed from the ceiling like so many giant inverted mushrooms.

Assailed by memories—some bitter, some sweet, all of them poignant—Thia stood in the dusky patch of sunlight near the French doors, waiting for her sister, Celia, to find the circuit breaker. Outside on the terrace the balmy warmth of an early June evening tempted Thia to abandon the nostalgia of the ballroom for the relative safety of the grounds, but she made herself resist the temptation.

Eleven years ago the room had been alive with music and laughter, brightened by the youthful pastels of ball gowns. That school year Jim Croce had died in a plane crash, his "Time in a Bottle" depleted. Olivia Newton-John's recording of "I Honestly Love You" hit the top of the charts, and Billy Jean King and Bobby Riggs fought the battle of the sexes on the tennis court. The headlines blared of news about Vietnam, the antics of the Loud family, and the latest revelations of the Watergate hearings.

The in joke that spring had been that it took nine Americans to change a light bulb: one to replace the bulb, one to eulogize the old bulb, one to start an alliance against future light bulb changes, one to take the environmentalist perspective, one to take the women's perspective, one to take the gay perspective, one to give a seminar on the aesthetics of light bulb changing, one to pass out mushrooms, and one to videotape the event for public broadcasting.

The irony was that this joke had offered a fairly accurate summation of the times, for Thia's generation had come of age in a decade filled with crisis, confrontation, and consciousness-raising; with protest, polemics, and the feminist revolution.

But all that had seemed far removed from the Warwick Inn in Stratford, Oregon, where, secure in their innocence, the young folk had danced to the beat of a different drummer.

Careful not to stray into the shadows that ringed her pool of light, Thia walked ten steps this way, five the other. The lonely sound of her own footsteps accompanied her restless pacing, but she considered that an improvement over the silent echoes of the half-remembered melodies that had haunted her when she'd first entered the ballroom.

Why was Celia taking so long? Thia wondered. Turning on the lights should be simple enough, even for someone with her sister's limited knowledge of circuitry; yet it seemed like hours since Celia had disappeared behind the heavy velvet portieres at the far side of the dais.

Even as this thought surfaced, the wall sconces flickered on. Before Thia's eyes could become accustomed to the light, they went out again, but in the brief flare of brightness, she glimpsed the wraithlike figure of a woman approaching her. She started, then realized that the figure had been her own reflection in the French doors, and chided herself for allowing the visit to the inn to make her so jittery.

Her knees felt too watery to support her as she moved closer to the doors, and her hazel eyes were wide and stormy as she stared at her image in the glass. She studied the delicate oval of her face, with its dainty nose, pointed chin, generous mouth, and close-cut cap of finespun golden-brown hair, not from vanity, but because she felt a sudden need to confirm her own identity. She needed to reassure herself that she was not a shy, uncertain high school girl any longer. Despite her youthful appearance she was a mature, self-confident young woman of twenty-seven.

"Take it easy," she told herself firmly. "There's no reason to get uptight."

Thia might have convinced herself that she'd become invulnerable to the past, but just as she turned away from the French doors, she heard the rasp of wood against metal and an earsplitting thud, closely followed by a muffled oath.

"Celia?" she called anxiously. "You all right?"

"Everything's under control."

Celia's disembodied voice came from the darkness

behind the bandstand. She sounded perfectly calm, but Thia was still worried.

"What happened?" she called.

"Nothing much. I bumped into a chair and dropped the damned flashlight. Just a sec. I've almost got it...."

The lights came on again. This time they gave off a dim but steady glow, and a moment later Celia walked through the curtains onto the dais.

"Well?" she inquired expectantly, swinging her flashlight in a broad arc that took in the vast dimensions of the ballroom. "What do you think?"

Inwardly, Thia replied, *I think one of us is crazy, and I'm afraid it's me.*

Why had she let Celia con her into doing the flowers for the Founders' Day Dance? She had vowed to put the past behind her. She'd promised herself that never again would she get involved with one of Celia's causes, and the Warwick Inn was the last place she wanted to be.

If the circumstances had been different, Thia would not have hesitated to voice her misgivings. But Celia was smiling. Her face fairly shone with eagerness, and her green eyes sparkled. Even her ash-blond hair seemed to have regained its luster.

For the first time since her divorce from Ross Kilbourne, Celia was behaving like her charming, vivacious self, and recognizing that her sister was delighted to have been appointed Chairman of the Dance Committee, Thia could not bring herself to dampen Celia's high spirits.

"Well?" Celia prompted. "What about this ballroom? Isn't it super?"

"It's certainly—huge," Thia replied noncommittally, but Celia didn't notice her lack of enthusiasm.

While Thia looked on, she hugged herself as if she could not contain her elation and began dancing around the room, gliding and twirling to an imaginary waltz, her long blond hair floating about her shoulders like a creamy satin shawl.

"This floor is absolutely perfect for dancing! And will you look at that wallpaper. Isn't it gorgeous?"

The wallpaper was lovely, thought Thia, reluctantly admiring the panels of shimmering, gold-veined, pale-peach silk. And like the rest of the inn, it was in remarkably good condition.

"Think what it would cost to replace it," Celia cried. After a final graceful pirouette, she spun to a stop in the center of the dance floor. "Oh, Thia, doesn't this place bring back memories? Remember my Senior Prom?"

Thia nodded pensively. As a former homecoming queen, cheerleader, student council officer, and all-round most popular girl on campus, Celia had every reason to smile radiantly. Thia, on the other hand, had been a late-blooming wallflower. As an adolescent she'd found it hard to bloom at all in the shadow of her glamorous older sister, and her own smile was strained.

She had attended the Senior Prom her sister referred to only at their mother's insistence. Her escort had been hateful Cousin Vernon, and before the evening was over, he'd spiked the punch, propositioned one of the chaperones, and passed out in the cloakroom. Ten years after the fact, however, Thia could laugh about it.

"Frankly, Celia," she said lightly, "I wish I could forget your Senior Prom. Watching Cousin Vernon throw up for half the night was not the greatest experience of my life."

"Good heavens! I'd forgotten about that." Laughing, Celia crossed to one of the sofas. As she folded back the dustcover and seated herself, she remarked sympathetically, "Vernon always was the most awful jerk."

"Amen!" Thia joined Celia, perching on the arm of the sofa. "He used to tease me unmercifully—"

"That's because you got so upset, Sis. If you'd just ignored him, he wouldn't have bothered you nearly as much."

"Perhaps you're right," Thia agreed dubiously, recalling how, when she and Celia had been six and eight respectively, their much bigger cousin had tormented and bullied her into saying her full name. Thia happened to be short for Cynthia, and Vernon had derived some perverse pleasure from hearing her lisp, "My name ith Thynthia Thommers, and my thithter's name ith Thelia."

"Anyway," Celia said briskly, "all that's ancient history now."

"That it is, thank goodness. But I'll never understand how Mother could have thought Vernon would be a good influence for you and me."

"Well, he did go on to seminary."

Thia shook her head, marveling at this turn of events. "That's another thing I can't fathom. Don't get me wrong—I don't expect ministers to be uninterested in the opposite sex, but I do expect them to exercise a certain amount of discretion, and judging from the way Vernon groped poor Miss Brewster at the Prom, I wonder if he knows the meaning of the word."

Celia sniffed disdainfully. "If you ask me, Miss Brewster enjoyed his groping her."

"You've got to be kidding!"

"No, Thia, I'm serious. I know there's no love lost

between you and Vernon, but even you will have to admit that he isn't bad-looking, and he is a Sommers—''

Thia opened her mouth to protest, but Celia rushed on.

"Hear me out," she said soberly. "The family fortune might be gone, and you've made it clear that you consider it snobbish to rest on past laurels, but the Sommers name still carries a good deal of weight here in Stratford. And besides, Miss Brewster never did report Vernon."

"So maybe you're right," Thia allowed. "Maybe Miss Brewster got a charge out of his making passes at her. And maybe Mother's right too. Maybe reformed sinners do make the best saints. But even when we went to his ordination, I found it hard to believe that creepy old Vernon could have grown up to be a minister. Whenever I see him, I still expect him to pull my hair or drop a bullfrog down my dress."

"Thia! Must you be so graphic? You know I can't stand frogs." Celia gave a fastidious little shudder that underscored her dislike for such slimy creatures, and demanded, "How did we get started on this subject in the first place?"

"You brought it up, Celia. You mentioned the Senior Prom, and one thing led to another."

"Well, I assure you, I never wanted to discuss bullfrogs!"

"Then what did you want to discuss?"

"Brad Scofield." From her sister's dreamy smile, Thia guessed that Celia was lost in reminiscence about the boy who'd been Celia's date for the Prom even before she added, "I've been thinking about Brad quite a lot lately. He's coming to the dance, you know."

"That's a surprise," said Thia.

"Why do you say that?"

Thia shrugged. "Unless it's an election year, our illustrious congressman doesn't often visit his hometown. What's the big attraction?"

"Oh, Thia, don't be obtuse! The Stratford Centennial celebration doesn't happen every day—"

"Of course not. It happens only once a century."

Celia glared at Thia, annoyed by her irreverence. "I'll have you know that several well-known former residents are coming for Founders' Day."

"For instance?"

"Austin Cooke."

"The actor?"

"None other."

"I didn't know he was a native of Stratford."

"Technically he isn't, but he got his start at the Stratford Shakespearean Festival. And you'll be happy to hear that Mickie Lloyd has agreed to perform at the dance."

"Has she?" Thinking of the unassuming girl who had been her best friend from kindergarten through the sixth grade made Thia smile. "I wonder if Mickie's changed much."

"You'd know that better than I would. Haven't the two of you kept in touch?"

"Not really," Thia replied. "At first we wrote often enough to keep the post office hopping, but you know how it is. After a year or two we sort of tapered off, and now we just exchange Christmas cards."

"I see," said Celia. "Well, I haven't actually spoken to Mickie, so all I can tell you is that these days she's a brunette, and she looks quite stunning. But surely you've seen her pictures on her record albums."

"Yes, I have, but I meant has she changed inside."

Thia placed one hand against her bosom, near her heart, and Celia frowned contemplatively and asked, "How old was Mickie when her mother moved to California?"

"About twelve, I think," Thia answered.

"Then it would be a miracle if she hasn't changed. I mean, she's a big country and western star, and success usually does change people."

Thia couldn't help sighing, because chances were Celia was right. Mickie Lloyd's heart-tugging way with a ballad had brought her to stardom, and that degree of success must pack quite a wallop. And even if she hadn't become so successful, Mickie would have changed. Just as everyone had. Just as Thia had.

Thinking of the sloe-eyed temptress on Mickie's most recent album cover, Thia murmured, "I hope she's changed for the better."

"That goes double for me," said Celia. "The Dance Committee has an extremely tight budget, so I'm hoping to persuade Mickie to contribute her services."

"I suppose that means you'll ask me to contribute the nursery's services as well."

"That had occurred to me, but think of the publicity you'll get out of it, Thia. Think of the goodwill!"

"I already have." With another sigh, Thia glanced about the ballroom. "What I hadn't thought of was that you'd come up with acres of floor space that need decorating."

"The challenge will be good for you," Celia replied bracingly. "You've been a hermit far too long, dear. You can't spend the rest of your life talking to your plants, or whatever it is you do out at Grandma's, and this will help you get back into circulation. If you want to, you can use potted things—tree roses and azaleas might be nice. That way you can simply return them to stock after the dance.''

"Gee thanks, boss, I believe I will," said Thia. "And may I post a sign requesting people not to use the flower-pots as ashtrays or places to pour out their stale drinks?''

In the uneasy silence that followed her question, Thia acknowledged that her sarcasm had not been prompted solely by her concern for the welfare of her plants. The trouble was, Celia was right about her having become too reclusive.

It had been nearly a year since she'd opted to give up her job with a Portland public relations firm so that she could return to Stratford and take over the manage-ment of her grandmother's nursery and florist shop. Soon after her homecoming, Thia had become some-thing of a hermit, and while she'd let people assume that this was due to the demands of business, what really rankled was that half the town thought she was a failure because she hadn't managed to trap a husband yet, and the other half thought she'd come home be-cause she had failed at her chosen career.

Both of these charges were grossly unfair, and Thia had rapidly gotten fed up with being subjected to criti-cism and innuendo. Last January, to minimize her con-tact with the public, she had assigned Kate Mulholland to the florist shop, and since then she had concentrated almost exclusively on the nursery. As Celia so color-fully put it, she'd spent most of the past six months "vegetating" with her plants. But what Celia could not comprehend was that Thia had loved every minute of it.

Her life-style might not be glamorous, but she pre-ferred the tranquillity of the nursery to the clamor of the city. When she was tired, the vibrant greens of the foliage plants never failed to revive her, and she thought flowers were more brilliant and far more precious than jewels.

Her mother accused her of being a throwback to some obscure yeoman ancestor, and Thia countered that her grandparents could hardly be called obscure, and that they had founded the business. But she cheerfully admitted that she liked to work the soil. She loved the rich, loamy smell that pervaded the greenhouse, and she found the honest feeling of sweat upon her brow and dirt beneath her fingernails profoundly satisfying.

Only one thing marred her contentment with her cloistered way of life, and that was the knowledge that, sooner or later, she would have to confront her critics and show them that she had no intention of living her life by any rules but her own. But perhaps by now the speculation had died down. And if it hadn't, it was time she fought back. One way or the other, though, she should come out of her shell.

"Celia," she said quietly, "I told you I'd supply the flowers for the Committee and I will. But please, don't ask me to come to the dance."

"I won't," Celia promised. "You have my word on it."

"Fair enough," said Thia. "And would you answer one question for me?"

"If I can."

"If the Committee's funds are limited, why this place?"

"To begin with, when word gets out that so many local celebrities are going to be at the dance, we'll need the room."

"But there's the armory, and the high school gymnasium—"

"Both of which are about as tacky as they come!" Celia scowled and leaped to her feet. "I want this dance to be special, Thia. If I have my way, it's going to be the highlight of Founders' Day. I want it to be truly memorable, an occasion all of Stratford can be proud of."

Surprised by her sister's intensity, Thia rose and placed a calming hand on Celia's shoulder.

"I can appreciate your wanting all that, but isn't renting the Warwick ballroom a bit ambitious?"

"Not at all," Celia replied crossly. "The inn's new owner has been very generous. He's offered to donate the use of the ballroom, and that's a deal neither the armory nor the high school can match."

"New owner?" Thia repeated blankly. "Does that mean someone has finally bought this white elephant?"

"Go to the head of the class, Thia Sommers."

A rumbly baritone voice answered her question, and Thia's pulses raced erratically when she saw the man who had made the response. He was not terribly tall, and the conservative banker's-gray business suit he wore emphasized his spare, angular build, yet he gave the impression of strength as he stood just inside the French doors, studying her.

Thia returned his gaze. Celia poked an elbow in her ribs and whispered slyly, "Speaking of people changing for the better, how about him?" But still Thia stared at the man, openly trying to place him.

She saw that he had a swarthy, intelligent face with prominent cheekbones and a square, firm jaw. A single strand of coarse, dark hair had fallen across his broad forehead, the only thing about his appearance that seemed undisciplined. His voice was vaguely familiar, and there was something about his stance, some hint of tightly leashed power, that struck a responsive chord deep inside her, but it was not until he moved away from the doors, striding lithely toward Celia and her, that she recognized him.

She knew only one man who moved with that springy prizefighter's gait, treading soundlessly on the balls of his feet—

"Luc," she murmured. "Luc Domini."

A hot rush of color flooded her cheeks because she'd sounded giddy and breathless, but Luc attributed her embarrassment to her chance comment about the inn. Without relinquishing her gaze, he bowed slightly from the waist and remarked, "They say eavesdroppers never hear good about themselves, but in my own defense I must point out that one man's white elephant can be another man's tax shelter."

"You're the new owner of the inn?"

Thia's mouth was unaccountably dry, and her question had been barely audible. Luc leaned closer to hear her. Close enough that the tangy scent of his aftershave filled her nostrils. Close enough that she saw the shadowy line of his beard, and she wondered, irrelevantly, if he always shaved twice a day.

"Come again?" he said, and Thia moistened her lips and wished that she'd taken the time to freshen her makeup and change from her denim jumper and smock to something more flattering before her meeting with Celia. And why hadn't she done something about her fingernails?

Suddenly aware of how badly she needed a manicure, she jammed her work-stained hands into the pockets of her smock as she inquired, "Did you buy the inn as a tax shelter?"

"That's one possibility." Even as Luc spoke, he turned toward Celia. "Have you decided the ballroom will do?" he asked, but Thia scarcely heard him, and she paid no attention at all to her sister's reply.

Now that Luc had chosen to break the spell his unexpected appearance had cast, his bold black eyes had released Thia's hazel ones, but she continued to watch him circumspectly, appraising his hawklike profile from beneath the fan of her lashes.

Although he couldn't be much over thirty, harsh new lines curved between his eyebrows and bracketed the corners of his mouth. They spoke of shrewdness, while the sprinkling of silver in the dark hair at his temples lent a certain distinction to his rough-hewn features.

Even as a teenager, Lucian Domini had been fiercely proud, intensely ambitious, and oddly mature. He'd been knowledgeable beyond his years—Thia supposed "street wise" was the most accurate description for the kind of knowledge he'd possessed.

At almost nineteen, he'd been the oldest of the seniors at Stratford High School, while she had been among the youngest sophomores, but they'd been enrolled in the same Spanish and math classes. A natural leader, he'd been captain of the football team, and the yearbook had dubbed him a hunk because so many girls had had crushes on him and he'd had a reputation for being wild.

Quiet, retiring Thia Sommers had been as different from the tough, savvy Domini boy as day from night, yet they'd had one thing in common. Basically, both of them were outsiders.

Thia had been a loner because the other students had mistaken her paralyzing shyness for aloofness, but Luc had been one through choice. In those days he'd never had the money to buy tickets to movies and dances. He couldn't even afford Coke dates or club dues, and his pride would not permit his letting others pay his way.

Initially their mutual loneliness had drawn them together, but it was their differences that cemented the bond between them and made them friends. They complemented each other. Luc was a cynic and she a romantic. He helped Thia keep her feet on the ground and prevented her going off on tangents, and she brought softness and laughter to his life.

No one else understood their alliance. At the time even Thia wasn't sure what Luc saw in her. She was aware that the other girls in her class were envious, but she hadn't realized that her sister was jealous of Luc's interest in her until Celia informed their mother that Thia was seeing him.

Predictably enough, Denise Sommers was horrified. She forbade Thia's having anything to do with "that fast Luc Domini." In return, Thia declared that Luc had always behaved like a perfect gentleman with her and that she intended to go on seeing him with or without her mother's permission.

The battle lines were drawn. Although Denise had anticipated a display of her younger daughter's independence, she hadn't reckoned with Thia's becoming impertinent. She was stunned by Thia's defiance, but she remained adamant. Thia might see Luc as a diamond in the rough, but she saw him as being uncouth, and to Denise Sommers this was one crime that was unpardonable.

It was only after endless arguments that they'd reached a compromise, and Thia had agreed not to meet Luc outside of school.

In the months that followed, part of Thia wished she hadn't made this bargain with her mother, but mostly she felt protected by it. Luc continued to treat her like a sister, but there was an aura of danger about him that she found tremendously exciting and more than a little frightening. In many respects he seemed as exotic as a creature from another world, and one day, much to her astonishment, Thia discovered that Luc thought she was exotic too.

The truth dawned when she complained about the curfew her mother had imposed, and Luc told her, "Maybe you don't think it's an asset, Half-Pint, but a guy like me would give his right arm to always know what to wear and what to say and which fork to use. So what if your mother's overprotective? Being a lady is as natural to you as breathing, for Chrissake, and you should thank her for teaching you the social graces, 'cause I can tell you one thing: They're hard as hell to learn if you're not born with 'em."

At the time Thia hadn't known how to respond to Luc's reprimand, but now she silently qualified, *Hard as hell, perhaps, but certainly not impossible!* Not for a man as determined as Luc Domini.

Judging by the impeccable cut of his suit and the courtly bow he'd given Celia and her, Luc had acquired the urbane polish he'd always admired, yet Thia sensed that his urbanity concealed a hard core of ruthlessness. . . .

This disturbing thought brought Thia back to the present. She dragged her gaze away from Luc and saw, with some bemusement, that her sister was smiling into Luc's eyes, brazenly flirting with him. It became obvious that Celia had made a unilateral decision to hold the Founders' Day Dance at the inn when she said, "I can't tell you how much this will mean to the Committee, Luc."

"Don't mention it," he replied.

"Oh, but I must, and I'm sure the rest of the Committee will want to thank you personally. I realize it's short notice, but we're meeting tomorrow night and I'm having a little get-together afterward. If you're free, I'd adore for you to stop by—in fact, I insist that you join us."

Luc's grin warmed the cool, dark depths of his eyes. "Very well, Celia, if you insist."

"Marvelous! Then I'll expect you about eight thirty."

Luc nodded. "Do you still live on Madrone Lane?"

"Since my divorce." For a moment, Celia looked touchingly forlorn, then she brightened. "Of course your wife is included in my invitation. I'd just love to meet her."

"Sorry I can't oblige, but I'm not married."

Celia's glance roamed over Luc thoughtfully as she said, "I should have known you're not. You have the look of a bachelor."

"What look is that? Do I have a loose button or a hole in my sock?"

"You know you don't." By now Luc was openly amused, and Celia dimpled engagingly and tucked her hand into the crook of his arm. "I'm not sure I can put it into words—"

"Please try," Luc drawled. "I find this fascinating."

"Then we're even, because I find you fascinating, Luc."

Having made this confession, Celia lowered her eyelids with a demure flutter of lashes, and Thia bit her lip to keep from breaking into a grin.

She had always known that her sister was an accomplished flirt, and she understood Celia's tendency to overdo it lately. After her divorce, it wasn't surprising that Celia needed proof that men still found her desirable. But much as Thia sympathized with her sister, this reluctant wanton routine was too much. She cleared her throat to get Luc's and Celia's attention and quietly made her good-byes.

"If the two of you will excuse me," she said, "I'll be leaving now."

"But you've hardly looked at the ballroom," Celia protested, "and you haven't seen the lobby or the powder room."

"That's all right," said Thia. "I've seen enough."

She started toward the French doors, but as she tried to step around Luc, he caught hold of her arm. The heavy fabric of her smock separated his fingers from her skin, but she felt electrified by his touch. His urgency was almost palpable as he asked, "Will I see you tomorrow evening?"

"No. I'm not on the Committee."

She tried to free her arm, but Luc's grip tightened and Celia hastily explained, "She's only doing the flowers."

"And I don't live at home anymore," Thia finished.

Although she stared pointedly at Luc's hand on her arm, he did not let her go until Celia added, "Naturally, Thia, if you'd like to join us, you'd be more than welcome."

"Thanks. Perhaps I will."

Now why did I say that? Thia wondered. She had fully intended to decline Celia's invitation, and instead she had virtually accepted it.

"We can go together, Thia," Luc said smoothly. "I'll stop by for you about eight."

How could she argue with him when he used that confident, no-nonsense tone? When he favored her with one of his rare, disarming smiles? It was all she could do not to rub the spot where his fingers had fastened around her arm. Beneath the sleeve of her denim smock her flesh felt sensitized, and her skin tingled with awareness.

"Eight will be fine," she agreed, and Celia went slack-jawed with disbelief.

"What's your address?" asked Luc.

"It's in the phone book, under Sommers Nursery."

Thia wanted to run, but as she waved good night and left the ballroom, she saw that Luc was staring after her, his eyes hooded and unwavering. She forced herself to walk sedately until she had left the terrace. Then her pace quickened until, at last, she gave up the pretense of composure and sprinted the final thirty yards or so to her van.

Dismayed by her loss of control, she climbed into the van and sat slumped over the wheel, berating herself for acting like a foolish teenager.

Why should her heart skip a beat at the thought of seeing Luc Domini tomorrow night? What had gotten into her? And, dear God, what had she gotten herself into?

Chapter Two

Half an hour later, his business with Celia Kilbourne concluded, Luc left the inn to return to his motel on the northern outskirts of Stratford. He drove by reflex, automatically guiding the Porsche along the steep, winding road to the valley below, recalling the first time he'd seen the quaint southern Oregon town.

He'd been fifteen then, and instead of driving a sleek sports car, he'd ridden down Main Street on the back of his father's rattly old pickup. He'd seen the lights wink on along Stratford's broad avenues and gracious tree-lined boulevards, and he'd experienced a sense of homecoming.

They'd driven around the plaza and past the Elizabethan theater where the Shakespearean Festival was staged. They'd taken a detour through the beautifully wooded park, and he'd seen the shoppers and theater-goers pausing to drink from the mineral-water fountains. He'd seen the gemlike lake where a pair of swans held court, and the peaks of the Siskiyou Mountains towering against the sky, and the houses nestled into the pine-covered slopes of Mount Grizzly, and he'd known instinctively that someday he would live in one of those houses.

That night he'd declared his independence. "I wanna settle down, Pop," he'd announced. "It's okay by me if you wanna leave when pear season's over, but I'm staying right here. I wanna be part of this town. Someday I'll be respected by everyone in it."

His father had laughed at him for being a dreamer. "Damned if you're not just like your old lady," Giles Domini had sneered. "She always wanted to come back here too. Made me feel like a pile of crap, the way she looked down her snooty nose at me. You'd of thought she was a regular Miss Gotrocks instead of just a poor relation, the way she carried on about that highfalutin family of hers. I told her they wouldn't have anything to do with her. Not those bastards. They wouldn't give her the time of day. She saw to that when she took up with me. But she couldn't face it."

Giles had paused to take a swig from his bottle of muscatel; then he'd set the bottle down, balancing it carefully on the uneven planking of the porch, and lumbered to his feet. His expression was menacing as he snarled, "Your mother never did learn her lesson, boy. Not to the day she died. But if I have anything to say about it, you will!"

When he'd seen that Luc was not impressed by his threats, Giles had hit him once or twice, called him a coward because he wouldn't fight back, and gotten drunk—not necessarily in that order. But that was nothing new, and Luc had never been swayed by his father's logic, nor by his beatings.

After that night he had weighed everything he'd done. The value he'd placed on any accomplishment was directly proportional to how much closer it brought him to his goal.

He'd gone out for the high school football team with

an eye to a college scholarship. He'd stopped growing at
five feet ten, but he was compact and better coordi-
nated than the bigger players, and his speed and agility
had given him an edge as a running back. That had
been good enough for his high school coach, but it
wasn't enough to make believers of the college scouts.

Disappointed but more determined than ever to further his education, he'd arranged for early graduation
and enlisted in the Army. He'd thought that once he
was discharged he could go to college on the G.I. Bill.
The army recruiter had guaranteed him assignment to
the foreign language school at Ford Ord and a tour of
duty in Germany, and Luc had reasoned that a couple
of years in Europe would turn him into a sophisticated
man of the world.

Instead, after basic he'd been shipped to Nam, and
six months in the jungles and rice fields had taught him
to cover his tail and watch out for punji sticks and various other booby traps. He'd buried the last of his illu-
sions somewhere in the Mekong Delta and left the
Army older than his years. Too old for college.

At the age of twenty-two, bitterly aware of the odds
against his gamble succeeding, he'd attended a public
auction where, for a fraction of their original price,
he'd bought a broken-down earth mover and road
grader.

A year later, with cool objectivity, he'd decided to
take another risk. He'd scrounged up some financial
backing and parlayed his newly acquired contractor's
license and the antiquated construction equipment into
the real estate development firm he had founded. The
same objectivity allowed him to cut nonessentials and
calculate costs to the nth degree, so that Domini Developers, Inc., consistently was awarded the contracts on

which it bid. Within five years of its inception, the firm had become a power to be reckoned with in the building industry.

Throughout this meteoric rise, Luc had been guided by the clear vision of the kind of future he wanted. His colleagues, even his most rabid competitors, often remarked upon his ability to remain poised under pressure, but it was vision that enabled him to see desirable high-rise offices and condominiums where others saw urban blight, to see a profitable shopping mall where others saw only a swamp. It was vision that made him an effective spokesman with the environmentalists who had opposed one or another of the company's proposed projects. And ultimately, it was vision that had brought him back to Stratford.

Through all the false starts and blind alleys, the town had remained one constant in his plans. The only other constant was Thia Sommers. She didn't know it yet, but she had always been a central figure in his dreams. If she chose to, she could give substance to his vision.

Years ago, when he'd first met the teenaged Thia, he had seen the promise of passion in the tender curve of her mouth. He'd looked at the budding contours of her body and seen the warm and loving woman she would become. And after seeing her tonight, he knew he'd been right.

Just the thought of her clear hazel eyes and honey-gold skin filled him with longing. His need for her had become an aching emptiness that was both emotional and acutely physical....

A No Vacancy sign flashed by on his right in lurid red neon, and Luc realized that he had driven past his motel. He muttered an oath, and as he pulled into the left-turn lane and doubled back, he remembered the guarded way Thia had studied him and told himself that he must take it slow and easy, one step at a time.

To win Thia's favor, he was prepared to court her family and friends as well as Thia herself, but above all else, he must not lose his cool.

Hard as it was to be patient now that his objective was in sight, it would not do to rush matters.

The following evening Thia seemed delicate as a flower in her jonquil-yellow sundress. As Luc walked beside her across the lawn to her mother's house, she looked as if she had materialized from his dreams, and to reassure himself that she was flesh and blood and not a figment of his imagination, he placed one hand on the smooth bare skin of her back.

He was careful to keep his touch light and not at all suggestive. The barely perceptible movements of his fingers were affectionate rather than sexual, yet he felt her tremble slightly and knew that she was attracted to him.

He wanted to shout with triumph. He wanted to take her in his arms. He wanted to forget about Celia's get-together and carry Thia off to some quiet, private place and make love to her, but in the end he allowed himself only to feel cautious optimism.

Relax, he told himself sternly. *Your plan's gotten you this far. Stick to it.*

Thia's steps lagged as they neared the front door, and he saw that she was fiddling with the clasp of her handbag.

"Relax," he said softly. "Everything's going to be all right."

Thia nodded absently and reached for the doorknob, but Luc stopped her, taking her hand in his.

"Celia told me you've caught a lot of flak since you decided to take over your grandmother's nursery, but you can't let it get to you. Whenever people get critical, try to consider the source."

Thia sighed and met his gaze. "I realize you're trying to be helpful, Luc, but the problem is that the most critical people are my friends. That's why the criticism hurts so much."

Luc heard the aggrieved note in her voice. He saw the accusing "Et tu, Brute?" look in her eyes, and said, "My advice only made things worse, didn't it?"

"Yes, frankly, it did. It implies that I can't cope—and maybe I can't. But if I can't handle the situation, I won't need you or anyone else to point it out to me."

"In that case, would it help if I told you that, by rights, I'm the one who should be nervous? After all, it's not every day I beard the social lioness of Stratford in her den."

"It doesn't help much," Thia returned gravely, "although I think my mother would love it if she knew you think of her as the queen of Stratford society."

Luc's glance left Thia's to wander over her body, lingering on the soft rise of her breasts beneath the camisole bodice of her dress.

"Well then," he said, "would it help if I told you how lovely you look this evening?"

A sunny smile chased the clouds from Thia's hazel eyes. "Now that helps more than you'll ever know!"

To show her gratitude, she turned her palm confidingly toward his. His hand was large and callused, and she sensed the strength in the long, blunt-tipped fingers that engulfed her own, yet as Luc drew small circular designs on the back of her hand with his thumb, his touch was surprisingly gentle.

The admiration in his eyes lifted her spirits, but his light, repetitive caresses gave her the confidence to return his compliment, and she said, "I don't know why I should be worried about attracting unwanted attention. It's obvious that you'll be the center of interest, Luc. You're especially handsome tonight."

Luc brushed a nearly invisible speck of lint off the lapel of his blazer, and it occurred to Thia that he was genuinely concerned about making a good impression on her mother. He fingered the knot in his necktie, and Thia said, "Your tie's perfectly straight. Truly it is. You look as if you'd just stepped out of an ad in *Gentlemen's Quarterly*."

Luc shook his head wryly, half in denial of her flattery, half with self-mockery, but his lopsided grin told Thia that her commendation had pleased him. They were still smiling at one another and holding hands when Denise Sommers suddenly opened the front door.

"Why are you standing out there on the steps, Cynthia?" she inquired coolly. "Are you trying to make up your mind whether you want to stay?"

Without waiting for an answer, Denise flung the door wide and moved aside to allow Luc and Thia entrance, and as she led the way along the hall toward the living room, she went on reproachfully, "I didn't believe Celia when she told me my long-lost daughter was honoring us with her presence tonight."

"But as you see, Mother, here I am," Thia replied evenly. "You remember Luc Domini, don't you?"

"Who?" Denise turned around and studied Luc, finally peering at him through the spectacles that were suspended from the pearl-studded chain around her neck. At last she snapped, "Of course I remember him.

Worrying about you and your sister hasn't done my sanity any good, but I'm not senile yet!'' She gave Luc a last hurried once-over and informed him, ''I'm happy to see that you've improved with age, young man, although when one thinks about it, you couldn't have gotten any worse.''

Having rebuked Thia and damned Luc with faint praise, Denise continued along the hall, and Luc's steps slowed so that he trailed some distance behind Thia and her mother.

Because his own mother had died when he was very young, in the old days he'd never understood why Thia should complain about the way her mother tried to organize her life, but now he did. Denise's overbearing attitude explained a lot, and her home filled in the remaining blanks.

On the outside he'd noticed nothing unusual about the house, except that it was smaller than he'd remembered. It was a classic two-story Colonial, much like the others on the block. But the inside was gloomy and strangely cheerless, and the air in the hall was stuffy enough for Luc to wonder if Denise Sommers suffered from a fresh-air phobia.

As he pried his wilting collar away from his neck with a cautious forefinger, he thought, *How does she stand it? Living here must be like being wrapped in cotton batting.*

Just inside the door to the living room Denise paused, and her expression underwent a remarkable transformation. In the wink of an eye her petulance vanished and she went from long-suffering mother to charming hostess. She looked at least ten years younger once she'd fixed a regal smile on her lips, and her smile became less artificial by the second as she waited for the others to notice that the guest of honor had arrived.

"Well?" Thia whispered to Luc. "What do you think of your social lioness now?"

Startled by the change in Denise, Luc answered slowly, "She didn't pull any punches, I'll give her that. Apparently she doesn't like me any better now than she did when I was in high school."

"Please, Luc, don't think that," Thia murmured. "Mother's upset, but it's me she's angry with. She didn't welcome you properly, but you are welcome."

As if to illustrate how welcome he was, Celia rushed at them, her hands outstretched in greeting.

"Luc!" she cried. "I'm so happy you could make it." She was laughing and animated, very much her old self as she dragged Luc into the center of the room and called gaily, "Attention everyone! Our man of the hour is here."

Celia waited until the odd assortment of guests had interrupted their conversations to look at the late-comers before she introduced Luc to the assembly, beginning with the portly, middle-aged man on her right. "Lucian Domini, this is Hogarth Jantzen—"

"We've met," Luc broke in tersely. "His bank handled the financing on the inn." Then, realizing how curt he'd sounded, he added, "It's a pleasure to see you again, Mr. Jantzen."

"Call me Hoagy, won't you?" Jantzen gave Luc a well-oiled Ivy League smile. "It's not dignified, I know, but I like to think of myself as a friend and neighbor first, and a banker second."

Recognizing that the loan officer's primary concern was for the future deposits Domini Developers might bring to the bank, Luc inclined his head politely and turned to the elderly couple standing next to Hogarth Jantzen.

"Les Aitcheson," said the man, vigorously pumping Luc's hand. "And this is my wife, Hannah."

Before Luc could reply, a feisty, ginger-haired matron spoke out. "I'm Cassie Bennett, young man. My husband and I own the acreage adjoining the inn, and I for one would like to know exactly what you're going to do with the property."

"Just now, Mrs. Bennett, we're waiting for the results of feasibility studies," Luc replied affably. "We're considering several alternatives, but I'll certainly keep you posted. When our plans are more definite, you'll be among the first to know."

Cassie Bennett's raddled, pug-dog face fell into more amiable lines. She fired another question at Luc, but Thia could not follow the rest of their exchange. A number of other guests had formed a circle around them, and Don Gallagher's wide shoulders had cut off her view of Luc. Before she could find a better vantage point, Don's wife, Cheryl, cornered her, armed with the latest batch of snapshots of their children.

For the next fifteen minutes Thia looked at the pictures Cheryl shoved at her. Initially she tried to keep track of Luc and, at the same time, make appropriately enchanted comments about how tall Don, Jr., had grown and how adorable baby Jennifer's toothless grin was, but she soon discovered that admiring the Gallaghers' offspring required all of her concentration.

Just when she began to feel as if her smile were permanently frozen in place, Cheryl proudly disclosed that she and Don were expecting again, and Thia's eyes brightened.

"Congratulations!" she exclaimed. "When is the baby due?"

"In January." Cheryl patted her slight tummy bulge,

which was almost unnoticeable beneath the calico prairie skirt she wore. "Donald wanted to wait another year. He's doing very well in his practice, but he says even doctors can't afford to have three children in college at once nowadays and we have to think of the future. Then he found out his sister is pregnant again, and he changed his tune in a hurry."

Thia knitted her brows, trying to make sense out of this bit of information. "I'm afraid I'm a little slow on the uptake tonight," she said. "What does Don's sister's pregnancy have to do with your having another child?"

"This is her fourth, Thia."

"So?"

"So we can't let Ralph and Janine get too far ahead of us." Nodding complacently, her mop of dark curls bobbing about her forehead, Cheryl began gathering up her snapshots. Almost as an afterthought, she added, "By the way, sweetie, as long as the subject's come up, if you don't get going soon, you'll be out of the race entirely."

With that parting shot, Cheryl went off to show her photos to Hannah Aitcheson, leaving Thia fuming speechlessly and wondering how anyone could look upon marriage as if it were a contest and motherhood as some sort of sweepstakes prize.

She and Cheryl had grown up together. She'd known Don Gallagher since high school. Both of them had always taken pride in being trendsetters. They had always been competitive, but until this moment Thia hadn't realized the extent to which they had allowed their competitive spirit to dominate their lives. Evidently competition dictated even the size of their family.

Thia stewed over Cheryl's goading remark for the

rest of the evening, mentally searching for a snappy comeback. Typically, however, she didn't come up with a suitably cutting retort until she and Luc had left the party and were almost back at the nursery.

"Quantity is no substitute for quality! That's what I should have told her."

The moment the words were out, Thia suppressed a groan and clapped her hands over her mouth, but it was too late. Taken aback by her outburst, Luc said sharply, "What was that?"

She had no choice but to tell him about her encounter with Cheryl Gallagher, but she was relieved when he found her explanation entertaining. He even suggested another approach she might have taken.

"You could have encouraged Cheryl to stick with it; just keep on having babies till she and Don get it right."

"Now why didn't I think of that?" said Thia.

"Probably because it's hard to think at all when someone's sniping at you," Luc replied quietly. "Is that why your mother's angry with you? Because you haven't married?"

"No. Celia's the one my mother raised to be a happy homemaker. I'm supposed to be the up-and-coming career woman, and Mother hasn't forgiven me for quitting my job in Portland. Now and then she sends me a magazine or newspaper article about some lady tycoon, just to remind me what a disappointment I turned out to be."

Thia did not add that Denise had decided long ago that, in all likelihood, her younger daughter would never marry. The whole idea of Thia's career had been her mother's, and Thia's biggest mistake had been playing along with Denise in a misguided effort to win her approval.

"What kind of work did you do?"

"I was in public relations."

He raised a quizzical eyebrow at her.

"You're surprised by that, aren't you?" said Thia.

"I'll admit it's not a field I'd expect you to choose. You seem so—reserved."

"You're right. I'm not a raving extrovert, but it wasn't myself I was publicizing. Sometimes I think the entire episode was an attempt on my part to compensate for not being more outgoing."

"Were you any good at it?"

"My boss seemed to think so. He kept giving me more responsibility and bigger and better accounts. And as long as a client had something positive to promote, I did very well at it."

The headlights of the Porsche had picked out the signboard marking the lane to Sommers Nursery. As Luc braked to make the turn into the drive, he nodded as if he had anticipated her response and inquired, "Why did you resign?"

"Several reasons." Thia waited until Luc had pulled into the cul-de-sac near the house before she went on. "To begin with, I was assigned to whitewash a politician who'd gotten caught with his hand in the public till. I won't mention any names, but the more I found out about the man, the less likely it seemed that I'd be able to find any redeeming qualities in him. I mean, I scratched the surface of a petty crook and found a major felon. He'd taken bribes and rigged elections, he was guilty of conflict of interest—the whole bit."

"So you couldn't find anything positive to promote," said Luc.

"Well, to be fair, his private life was decent enough. He had a lovely family and he was devoted to his children. But once I'd gotten involved with his campaign, I learned a lot about the way he operated, and the more I learned, the more I felt that if I sold him to the voters, I'd be an accomplice to his crimes."

"Then it became a matter of ethics."

"That's it exactly, Luc. If you can see that, why can't my mother?"

Thia stared at Luc wide-eyed, clearly hoping that he could provide the solution to the riddle Denise Sommers posed, but he only smiled and reached in front of her to open her door. While he climbed out on the driver's side, she stepped out on hers, and together they walked toward the house.

She had forgotten to leave the porch light on, and the front windows were dark, but even the darkness couldn't disguise the fact that the gray-shingled bungalow needed a coat of paint. Despite its air of genteel shabbiness, however, it looked cozy and welcoming. To Thia, it had always seemed like home.

"This is another reason I resigned." Her gaze was fixed on the house, but even without glancing at Luc, she sensed he understood that she was referring to all of her grandmother's property: to the five acres of gently rolling foothills, to the greenhouse and garden shop, to the machine shed and smaller outbuildings. "I've always loved this place, so when Gran decided to move to Arizona, she gave me first crack at it—"

"And you jumped at the chance to come home."

"You understand that, too!"

"That's because I've always looked forward to the time when I could make my home in Stratford."

There was a moment of silence while Thia searched for her latchkey. As she unlocked the door, she said,

"Is this the time, Luc? Are you planning on staying here permanently?"

"I'd like to," Luc answered. "If things work out as I hope they will, I'll certainly stay on."

He followed Thia into the parlor and studied the room curiously while she moved about, switching on lamps and opening windows to catch the cool night breeze off the mountains.

He had thought the cottage would be much the same as it had been in Thia's grandmother's day—ultrafeminine and decorated in pastels. Instead he saw pine-paneled walls, a hooked rug in shades of brown, cream, and rust, and oatmeal tweed upholstered pieces.

At first he was puzzled by the lack of frills and furbelows, but on second glance it became apparent that the use of neutral colors and simple furnishings was intentional. The subdued decor provided a pleasantly unobtrusive background for the flowers that were scattered about the room. In jugs and pots and vases, bouquets of daisies and roses and less common varieties of flowers he couldn't identify bloomed flamboyantly and perfumed the air.

"May I take your jacket?" Thia asked.

Luc hesitated until he saw that Thia had kicked off her shoes. Then he grinned and took off his blazer. By the time she had hung his jacket away in the guest closet, he had loosened his tie and rolled up his shirtsleeves. He might have been astonished at his informality if he hadn't felt so much at home.

Strange, he thought. Although he'd hardly touched Thia, he was keenly aware of the reciprocal tension between them. He hadn't expected to feel so comfortable now that they were alone....

"Would you like a nightcap?" Thia inquired. "I can offer you wine or ginger ale or coffee—"

"Coffee will be fine, thanks. I—uh—because of my father's problem with alcohol, I rarely drink anything stronger."

Thia nodded. She had noticed that Luc hadn't touched the vodka and tonic her mother had pressed upon him at the party.

In the kitchen he lounged against the counter and watched her start the coffee brewing. Without the high-heeled sandals she'd been wearing, she was smaller than he'd realized, and her diminutive stature made him feel protective. He remembered his old nickname for her. Half-Pint. She hadn't grown any taller, but she had definitely matured in other ways.

Last night she'd worn some sort of coverall, and while the dress she was wearing tonight displayed the fine, honeyed skin of her shoulders and upper back, it was fitted only at the waistline. It left most of her body to his imagination, but now and again the gossamer-light material of the sundress clung to the ripe contour of a breast or the curve of a hip, and when she turned, the soft, gathered skirt floated about her shapely calves and hinted at gracefully tapering thighs.

She reached for the sugar bowl and creamer on a shelf high in the cupboard, and he marveled at how narrow her rib cage was, how tiny her waist. His hands ached to span it.

She went onto her tiptoes and arched her back, straining to retrieve a tray from the top shelf of the cabinet, and her posture allowed him a tantalizing glimpse of the delicate undercurve of her breasts, of her neatly rounded derriere....

"I can't quite reach the tray, Luc. Could you give it a go?"

Luc's hand was unsteady as he undid the second button on his shirt. "Sorry. I was too busy enjoying the view to recognize that you needed help."

His voice was unsteady too, and when Thia glanced at him over her shoulder, his lazy grin told her that she was the view he'd been enjoying.

She smiled self-consciously. A lovely tinge of pink crept into her cheeks, but she didn't turn away from him. Her breath had lodged in her throat, and she was incapable of moving.

Luc's eyes roved over her, darkening and widening as they returned to her breasts. Beneath the fiery ardor in his eyes her nipples grew saucily erect, tenting the gauzy cotton lawn of her camisole. She knew that Luc saw this, knew that he saw the hectic pounding of her heart, and she acknowledged that she was excited by the speculative way he was looking at her.

Time seemed to stand still. Luc came toward her and she watched him approach as if in slow motion, registering the most minute details of his appearance. The same strand of hair had fallen across his forehead, and she saw the confidence in his smile, the determined angle of his jaw, the proud set of his shoulders.

He reached her side and removed the tray from the shelf easily, and as he set it on the counter she saw the way his shirt molded the well-defined muscles of his chest. She saw the smooth bunching of his biceps and the smattering of fine dark hair on his forearm. Now that he stood so close to her, she could feel the heat he exuded. She felt his urgency, and when she met his eyes, she saw the desire written there.

Once again his gaze traveled over her features, finally

settling on her mouth. He touched her hair, smoothing his palm over the cap of silky, golden-brown waves as if he must memorize its texture, and she sensed that he was struggling to keep his emotions in check.

"Your hair is different," he mused.

"It's shorter. Do you like it?"

"Very much. The gamine look suits you."

Honesty compelled Thia to protest that she was too subdued to be gamine, but Luc's touch and the warmth of his smile were wreaking havoc with her pulse rate. She couldn't speak, and she could not bear the excruciating intimacy of the moment, but when she would have looked away from him, his hand cradled the base of her skull while his fingers curved around the nape of her neck. His thumb found the wildly racing pulse at the base of her throat, then slid along her chin, tilting her face toward his.

Acting on impulse, she pushed the stray lock of his hair into place. A perplexed frown ruffled the smoothness of her brow as she said, "Your hair is different, too."

"Is that why you had trouble recognizing me last night?"

When Luc spoke, she tasted the spicy warmth of his breath, and she outlined the bridge of his nose, straight now where once it had been broken.

"No," she replied. "It's your nose—"

"I had surgery to correct the deviated septum a few years ago. While they were at it, they fixed the bump."

A slight turn of his head flattened her palm against his cheek. She felt the scrape of his bearded jaw as slowly, sensuously, he brushed his lips against the sensitive skin of her inner wrist.

It seemed unreal that they could be speaking of in-

consequentials when the way he was looking at her
made it clear that he wanted to make love to her.

He is making love to me, Thia told herself. *With his
eyes. In his thoughts...*

"Does the nose job make that much difference?"
asked Luc.

"Not really."

Her voice sounded hollow and far away. Somehow
Luc's arms had enfolded her, and she swayed against
him weakly. He bent his head so that his mouth was
only a whisper away from hers, but when he would
have closed even that tiny gap, she found the strength
to turn away.

His lips grazed her cheek as he whispered, "What's
wrong, Thia? Are you involved with someone else?"

"No, I— It's just—" She heard the revealing quaver
in her voice and gave up trying to explain her reaction,
but Luc would not be put off.

"You're trembling all over, honey," he persisted.
"Are you afraid of me?"

"I'd be a fool if I weren't!"

Luc chuckled and rubbed his chin against her temple. "Why? Am I moving too fast for you?"

"You're making my head spin," she answered breathlessly.

"Great! That's the general idea."

"I already knew that. What I'd like to know is why,
Luc. Why are you doing this?"

"Do I have to have a reason?"

"If anyone else asked that, I'd say no. But with
you—yes. I think you do have a reason."

Luc laughed deep in his throat. "Don't you think
you're making too much of this, Thia? After all, what's
a kiss between friends?"

"You never tried to kiss me before."

"I wanted to, though. Almost as much as I want to kiss you now."

Luc gently traced the outline of her lower lip with his forefinger before she managed to free herself and take a step or two away from him.

"What else do you want, Luc?"

"Come off it, Thia. We're both adults. You have to have a fairly good idea what I'd like to do right now."

"Yes, but I don't know why."

Smiling sardonically, Luc answered her question with one of his own. "Don't you know how desirable you are?"

Her eyes searched his, measuring the validity of his response, as she said, "I wasn't being coy, Luc, and I wasn't fishing for compliments. What I want to know is why you're putting the rush on me. Why have you come back to Stratford?"

"You already know the answer to that, Thia. There's the inn—"

"Luc, if I believed your only business here was the inn, I wouldn't have bothered asking."

"Okay, then. You want the truth, so here it is." Luc inhaled deeply and squared his shoulders. "*You're* the reason for my visit to Stratford, Thia Sommers. I've come back for you."

"For me?" she said faintly.

"That's right, and as long as I've told you that much, you might as well know that my intentions are strictly honorable." Without inflection, as dispassionately as if he were talking about the weather, Luc added, "You see, Thia, I intend to marry you."

Chapter Three

After Luc's flat pronouncement it seemed anticlimactic to sit with him in the kitchen, drinking the coffee she'd made, but that was what Thia did. Although they talked, afterward she had no recollection of what they had discussed.

The following morning she made her delivery of cut flowers to the florist shop later than she usually did so that she could talk with Kate Mulholland. Thinking that Kate, with her down-to-earth Midwesterner's point of view, might be able to make sense of the events of the previous night, Thia filled her in on what had happened between Luc and herself quickly, without digression, but once she had finished telling Kate about Luc's claim that he had returned to Stratford to marry her, she concluded lamely, "The rest of the evening passed in sort of a blur."

"I can see why," Kate remarked tartly. "Lordy, but I do appreciate a man who knows his own mind. That's why I married Ken."

In the eight months that Thia had known the Mulhollands, she'd grown accustomed to Kate's laughing at Kenny's chameleonlike changes of opinion. There was rarely any resentment or ridicule in Kate's jokes about her husband, and once she had admitted indulgently, "The joke's on me, because I knew perfectly well what Kenny was like when I married him."

Soon after Kate had begun working at the florist shop, she had explained her attitude to Thia, saying, "I love my husband dearly, but there have been moments when his waffling made me want to scream. The truth is, he's just a big, overgrown kid. He isn't ready to settle down, and maybe he never will be. So if I'm going to stay married to him—and I am!—I have two choices. I can either laugh about his immaturity or cry about it, and life's too short to cry for what Kenny can't give me when he gives me so many of the things I do want."

Thia had often wondered if Kenny Mulholland knew how lucky he was to have found a wife as tolerant and undemanding as Kate. In spite of Kate's momentary bitterness she wondered as much now, as Kate returned to the topic of Luc Domini.

"You must have said something when he proposed to you, Thia."

"It wasn't a proposal—"

"Okay, okay. Let's not get into a hassle about semantics—not when I'm dying to hear what you said to him."

Her color high, Thia replied, "I think I said, 'Just like that?' or something equally moronic."

"And how did Luc react?"

"He said naturally it wouldn't be just like that. We'd see each other, get reacquainted—"

All at once Kate's blue eyes were dancing mischievously behind the huge, owlish lenses of her glasses, and Thia interrupted her narrative to declare, "It's not a laughing matter, Kate."

"Of course it isn't, Thia. It sounds really serious."

Despite Kate's hurried agreement, Thia recognized that her friend was having a hard time keeping a straight face. Kate's lips twitched suspiciously, and although she hunched over the invoice on her desk and bent her head, trying to cover her amusement by ducking behind her bright auburn hair, Thia saw her smile.

Scowling, she demanded, "Did I say something funny?"

"It's not what you said, it's what you didn't say. You didn't turn Luc down, did you?"

"Well—no. No, I didn't. In fact, I'm having dinner with him tonight."

"That's a relief."

"Why a relief?"

Kate grinned at her, no longer attempting to hide her laughter. "In the time I've known you, you've been such a homebody that I've been afraid your feminine instincts might atrophy from lack of exercise. Trust them, Thia. They won't let you down."

"Won't they?" Thia shook her head, wondering if her friend was speaking from experience. "I wish I could be as sure of that as you are."

Kate studied her over the rims of her glasses. "Look, if it's a pep talk you need—"

"It wouldn't hurt."

"All right, then. Listen up while I remind you that, from certain things you've said about Luc Domini, it's obvious that you've been more than halfway in love with him since you were a teenager. In the months I've known you, you've talked about him often enough for me to feel like he's an old friend, which leads me to believe that you still have a soft spot in your heart for him. Granted it's been a long time since you've seen him, but so what?''

Leaning back in her swivel chair, Kate settled her glasses more squarely on her small, pert nose and regarded Thia sternly. "Good Lord, Thia! Circumstances being what they are, you can't hope to get away with saying 'Why, Mr. Domini, sir, this is so sudden!' ''

Kate pursed her lips and batted her lashes, and her impression of a prim Victorian miss brought a shaky smile from Thia.

"But in a way it *is* sudden. And my feelings aren't the issue. Just now it's Luc's feelings I'm concerned about.''

"Seems to me he made his feelings clear when he proposed to you, Thia. What more do you want?''

"It wasn't a proposal—''

Kate threw up her hands in mock surrender.

"Really it wasn't,'' Thia persisted. "Luc didn't ask me to marry him. He simply stated his intentions.''

She had spoken as if her very life depended on Kate's acknowledging this fact, and Kate replied solemnly, "I'm not sure that the distinction amounts to anything, Thia. Frankly, I think you're splitting hairs, but just for the sake of argument, let's say you're right. Let's assume that Luc doesn't love you. That still leaves one question. If he doesn't care for you, why would he want to marry you?''

"I don't have the answer to that one, Kate. Not yet. But sooner or later I will.''

"And when you have it, what will you do? Do Luc's motives make that much difference?''

Before Thia could formulate an answer to this question, a knock at the street door reminded them that it was past ten o'clock and that they hadn't yet opened the shop for business. Kate went off to admit the day's first customer while Thia finished checking the invoice against her morning's delivery. It took her much longer than it should have to complete the task, because thoughts of Luc kept intruding.

Did he see her as a lover? she wondered. Maybe he had decided a wife would be an asset to his business. Or maybe, because the Sommers name was synonymous with a certain social prominence in Stratford, she represented nothing more than a status symbol to him.

And if she discovered that Luc didn't love her, would it make a significant difference?

Thia bit her lip as she confronted the disturbing truth that she might marry him anyway. Part of her was afraid that it wouldn't make any difference at all. But another part—perhaps the major part—was even more afraid that it would.

The morning had gotten off to a frustrating start, and things did not improve as the day progressed.

Thia drove the five miles from town to the nursery without incident, but on her arrival at the garden shop she learned that Duffy Langtry, the elderly retainer who had helped her grandparents establish the business and stayed on to teach her some of his vast knowledge of horticulture, had not showed up for work. A phone call to his home revealed that Duffy might not be in for several days.

"It's his rheumatism again, Miss Sommers," Duffy's daughter Velma irritably explained. "If I'd had my way, Pa would've quit his job when your Grandma left. A man his age shouldn't be doing that kind of work in the first place. He's out in all sorts of weather.... It's just not right."

"No, it isn't," Thia sympathized. "I've tried to get your father to slow down, believe me I have. He promises to take it easy, then the minute my back is turned, he's out spraying the orchard stock or loading sacks of fertilizer."

"Pa always says he'd rather wear out than rust out."

Velma Langtry sounded somewhat less aggrieved now, even proud of her father's obstinacy, but that didn't stop Thia's feeling guilty as she expressed her hope that Duffy would soon be out and about.

Lord knew she hated being dependent on anyone. Something inside her rebelled at the idea that she couldn't make it on her own, and she wished she were prepared to force the old man into retirement. But a lifetime of farming and work as a nurseryman had made his advice invaluable. He was a walking almanac, chockful of information about plants and seeds and soil types and equipment, and he'd been a godsend to Thia. If she hadn't had him to rely on, the nursery would not have survived the first few months of her management. She knew this, just as she knew that other employees might come and go, but dedicated as he was, Duffy would never willingly quit his job. But she also knew that Duffy's doctor had advised him to move to a milder climate.

Given a little more time—maybe by the end of the summer—she'd have acquired enough expertise to run the nursery without his assistance, and once she felt confident, she would give him as healthy a bonus as she could afford and her undying thanks for his help and send him on his way. But at this point, much as she disliked admitting it, she wasn't ready to go it alone. Not just yet.

Thia realized that Duffy's attack of rheumatism was as

much his fault as hers. The day before he had sneaked off and transplanted half a dozen dwarf apple trees before she'd found out what he was up to and put a stop to it. Despite this, however, and despite her resolution to dispense with his services in the fall, she still felt pangs of guilt as she glanced through the day's mail.

For the rest of the morning she busied herself with answering letters and writing out checks. The phone rang occasionally, and Penny Burgess, the salesclerk, came into the makeshift office that was tucked away in the back corner of the garden shop to make several price checks, but everything went smoothly until early afternoon, when Thia left the office to inspect a recent planting of Pfitzer junipers. As she had anticipated, the early summer heat wave had taken its toll, and the shrubs needed watering. She had just finished adjusting the sprinklers when Celia came tripping along the path through the greenery, cautiously picking her way to avoid soiling her shoes.

"Heavens! Look at you. It must be a hundred degrees in the shade, and here's my baby sister hard at work." To emphasize how hot the day was, Celia fanned herself with the white straw clutch bag she carried. "It's inhuman, Thia. If you have to be outdoors, you should at least wear a hat."

Celia's voice lilted, and she looked as carefree as a butterfly in her immaculate white piqué dress, but as she drew nearer Thia saw that the tip of her nose was pink, her mascara was smudged, and her eyes were red rimmed from weeping.

To the best of Thia's knowledge, only one thing could induce Celia to leave the house with her makeup less than perfect, and she said, "You've had another run-in with Mother."

"How did you guess?" As soon as the words were out, Celia held out one hand as if to ward off Thia's response and said shortly, "Don't answer that. I guess it's pretty obvious that Mother and I have been at each other's throats ever since Ross and I separated. She's always taken his side against me."

"I know she can be difficult, Celia—"

"Difficult!" The cadence of Celia's fanning quickened. "You don't know the half of it, Thia. Lately she's getting to be downright impossible."

"Only because she's concerned about you."

"Well, she has a funny way of showing it! This morning she—she— Oh, Thia, I've absolutely had it with her!"

Outraged tears had welled into Celia's eyes. She was shaking with fury, and she held her purse so tightly that her nails dug into the loosely woven straw. Thia would have given her a consoling pat on the shoulder, but Celia recoiled at the sight of Thia's earth-stained gardening gloves, and Thia let her arm fall back to her side.

"What happened this morning?" she inquired.

"The usual. We fought over whether to have orange juice or cranberry juice for breakfast, then during breakfast we fought about who should wash the dishes, and after breakfast we fought about whose turn it was to do the grocery shopping. From there Mother got into really heavy-duty nagging. According to her, I'm a tease who flirts with everything in pants—Thia, she even called me man crazy!"

This accusation had some foundation in fact, and Thia had to suppress an urge to laugh. Her voice wobbled a bit as she replied, "Cheryl Gallagher must have gotten to her."

"What does Cheryl have to do with this?"

"Maybe nothing, Celia, but you know how deprived Mother feels because she has no grandchildren."

"How could I not know? She's done everything but take out an ad."

"That's right," said Thia. "And last night Cheryl was doing her earth-mother bit, showing everyone pictures of the kids and really rubbing it in that she's pregnant again. That could account for Mother's bad mood."

"Sure it could," Celia agreed facetiously. "Or maybe the moon's in the wrong phase, or her feet hurt, or she's tired after the party—"

"It's possible."

Celia tossed her head angrily. "For Heaven's sake, Thia! Spare me your philosophy and don't make excuses for her. Mother and I have never gotten along for more than five minutes running. That's something I faced ages ago, and it's time you faced it too. No matter how hard I try, nothing I do pleases her."

"I'll admit she's always been a fussbudget, Celia, and it's certainly not her most appealing trait, but she does have your best interests at heart, and she doesn't mean anything by it. If the chips were down, she'd back you against anyone—including Ross Kilbourne."

"You've been out in the sun too long," Celia replied somberly. "You say Mother has my interests at heart, and I think she's possessive and overprotective. You say she's a fussbudget, that she's worried about me, but I think all she cares about is appearances. Ever since Daddy ran off with that secretary of his, she's been so damned concerned about what people will think of her and her 'darling little girls' that she'll stoop to just about anything to preserve our image."

If Celia had asked her opinion, Thia might have described their mother's defensiveness more strongly. She believed that Denise was overcompensating; that her chip-on-the-shoulder attitude since their father had left was evidence that she hadn't cared about anything. But Celia didn't ask, so she restricted herself to saying, "You're terribly angry, Celia. You don't really mean that."

"Yes, I do. I married Ross because Mother seemed to want it so much, and was she satisfied with that? No! You can bet your sweet life she wasn't. She had to pry and meddle until Ross couldn't take any more of her interference, and now she blames *me* for failing as a wife."

Celia's voice rose shrilly as she went on, "It's just not fair! She preaches to me that I have to learn to accept responsibility. She talks a great game, then she turns around and treats me like a child. I'm almost thirty years old, and she treats me as if I were about ten! And today she had the nerve to read my mail. She actually opened a letter that was addressed to me—"

"It can't have been intentional, Celia."

"So Mother said, but she read it, Thia!" An unbecoming flush mottled Celia's fine, creamy complexion. "My very own personal, private letter from Brad Scofield, and she deliberately read it!"

Thia removed her gardening gloves slowly, pulling them off one finger at a time, stalling while she tried to come up with a plausible explanation for Denise's behavior. Finally she ventured, "You know Mother's anxious to see you resolve your differences with Ross—"

"She should have thought of that before she drove him off," Celia interjected hotly. "After what he's done to me, I wouldn't have Ross Kilbourne on a silver platter. Not if he were the last man on earth. Not if he got down on his knees and *begged* me to forgive him for walking out on me."

"Wait a minute, Celia. I thought you were the one who walked out."

"Well, I wasn't." For a moment, Celia pressed her lips together, horrified by what she had revealed. Then she glared at Thia and snapped, "I never should have married Ross. He's just like Mother—impossible to please. He constantly criticized the way I kept the apartment, and he was always saying that I spent too much on clothes. God, but he was stingy! Did I tell you he took away my credit cards?"

Thia couldn't help smiling at this complaint. Glancing at Celia's expensive designer dress, she inquired, "Did you spend too much?"

"I suppose I did, but I only wanted to look my best for him. Is that so wrong?"

"No, of course it isn't. But maybe you could have gotten by with a little less till Ross's practice was better established."

"I would have, except..." Celia faltered into silence and blinked back tears.

"Except what?" Thia prompted gently.

"The only thing about me Ross never found fault with was my looks. And it's not as if I didn't warn him ahead of time. When we first started dating, I told him straight out that I'm no good at budgeting, and he knew long before the wedding that I can't cook and that I'm a lousy housekeeper. He said none of that mattered, that I could learn—"

"You could if you put your mind to it," said Thia.

"I tried to, Sis. Really I did. But I'm so disorganized,

and Ross is so blasted capable!'' Celia's shoulders drooped defeatedly. "He made it through medical school with a perfect average, and the doctors at St. Michael's, where he did his residency, respect him, and the nurses admire him, and his patients think he's some kind of god. I always felt inferior to him, but after we'd been married a few months, I began to feel totally incompetent. It seemed to me that the only things I had going for me were that I could look pretty and that I pleased him in bed.'' Celia's voice broke as she finished, "For a while I thought that would be enough, but it wasn't.''

"You're being awfully hard on yourself, Celia. Lots of people have trouble balancing checkbooks, and cooking and cleaning are no big deal. If you want to learn to keep house, you can.''

"What's the point?'' Celia replied dispiritedly. "I've already lost Ross.''

"It sounds to me as if you still love him.''

"That's the worst of it, Thia. I do.''

"Then why are you here? Why don't you go up to Eugene and see Ross and tell him how you feel?''

"Because I just can't,'' Celia declared vehemently. "I wish I could, but I can't. Not after the cruel things he said to me. Did you know he told me to grow up?''

"But if you love him—''

"The point is, I'm not sure Ross loves me anymore. That's why I wrote to Brad and invited him to the Founders' Day Dance.''

Confused, Thia shook her head. "I'm afraid I don't understand.''

"Don't you see, Sis? Mother's kept in touch with Ross, and he's always been a teensy bit jealous of Brad, so I thought if Ross heard that I'm going to be seeing

Brad, he might be jealous enough to make the first move."

"Correct me if I'm wrong, but is the gist of what you're saying that you're making a play for Brad to get to Ross?"

"That's it!"

"And Mother was supposed to do her bit by keeping Ross informed?"

Celia nodded earnestly.

"Then why in the world are you upset over her reading Brad's letter? Isn't she playing right into your hands?"

Celia stared at Thia, dumbfounded. Annoyance chased uncertainty across her face as, at last, shrugging off Thia's arguments, shrugging off her own inconsistencies, she replied, "I suppose she was, but it's the principle of the thing that counts. She's forever prying and snooping, and I'm not sure how much longer I can put up with her invading my privacy."

Thia frowned.

"Doesn't that make sense?" Celia demanded.

"I'm afraid it does," Thia conceded grudgingly. "But what are you going to do about it?"

Celia's eyes shied away from Thia's. "For openers, I've decided to look for a place of my own."

"Have you?" Thia exclaimed delightedly.

"You approve?" asked Celia.

"Yes, I think it's a terrific idea."

"Well, I'm glad you feel that way, because I'm going to need your help."

Now that it was too late to backtrack, Thia recognized the purpose of her sister's visit and her heart sank. "My help?" she echoed woodenly.

Celia nodded. "I'd like to move in with you, Thia—

just temporarily, mind you. I'd only stay here till I get on my feet financially. Naturally I'll have to find a job."

That, thought Thia, was easier said than done. In college Celia had taken a mishmash of liberal arts courses that had sharpened her skills as a conversationalist and left her well-informed but untrained for anything specific. And although she had done some volunteer work, she had never been gainfully employed.

That was one strike against her to begin with, and the second was that these were lean economic times. And even in the best of times jobs were scarce in Stratford. It would take nothing less than a miracle for Celia to find anything that paid more than minimum wage, and it would take another miracle before she'd manage to save any of her salary for a move to her own place.

Thia barely made ends meet herself. Not two months ago she'd had to replace most of the irrigation system, and even before that she had been plowing most of her income back into the business—not that the business made that much profit to begin with. Furthermore, she had never found her sister easy to live with. If Celia and Denise were too much alike to be compatible, Celia and Thia were too dissimilar.

Celia was a night person. She came to life after sundown just when Thia began to wind down. Thia enjoyed having a certain amount of solitude—she needed it to recharge her energies—while Celia seemed out of her element when she wasn't surrounded by friends.

Yet in all good conscience, how could Thia deny her sister's request?

"You realize how small the house is?" she inquired cautiously.

"I know you don't have much room," Celia answered, "but I promise you'll hardly even know I'm around."

Thia sighed as another argument occurred to her. "Mother's not going to like your moving out."

"That's her problem," said Celia.

"What if she solves it by spending a lot of time here?"

"I'll worry about that if it happens," Celia countered. "Please, Thia, say yes."

How can I say no when I think she's doing the right thing by making a bid for independence? Thia wondered. *How can I turn her down when she's looking at me so hopefully?*

"You're sure you want to do this?"

"Positive," Celia answered firmly.

"Well, then—"

Thia got no further than this before Celia's face lighted up and she cried, "You won't regret it, Thia! Not for a moment."

Her objective won, Celia hastily arranged to move into Thia's spare bedroom the next weekend. Evidently she'd given some thought to her chosen course of action, because she added, "Maybe I'll even have a job by then."

Thia derived some encouragement from Celia's optimism. As she walked Celia to her car, she told herself, *Maybe this time Celia really does intend to get her act together.*

Before Celia left, she inquired casually, "By the way, how did you and Luc hit it off last night?"

Seconds ticked by while Thia tried to frame an answer. Then, opting for nonchalance, she offered a half-truth.

"We got along fine."

"Will you be seeing him again?"

"Yes, I will," Thia replied evenly. "As a matter of fact, we're having dinner together tonight."

Celia's eyebrows shot up. "Are you?"

"Why the surprise? If you recall, Luc and I were always friends."

"Friends, yes, but somehow I never thought of the two of you dating."

"Neither did I."

"Do you think he's heard about my divorce?" asked Celia.

"Yes. That is, I'm sure he must have. Didn't you mention it the other night?" Celia *had* mentioned it, hadn't she? "Why do you ask?"

"No reason." Celia climbed into her car and started the engine, but before she drove away, she got in one last dismaying comment. "Thia," she said absently, "don't you think it's funny that Luc should ask you out when it's me he's always had a crush on?"

"It's very funny," Thia replied flatly. "In fact, it's practically a cosmic joke."

"Then why aren't you laughing?" asked Celia.

Thia had no answer for that one. She shook her head and returned Celia's wave and watched as her sister's sedan turned onto the county road at the end of the lane and disappeared. She went back to her work in the greenhouse, but for the rest of the afternoon her mind kept repeating Celia's question along with a few of her own.

Silently, she asked herself, *Why aren't you laughing, Thia Sommers?*

Last night the man she'd carried a torch for since high school had said he wanted to marry her. Tonight she had a date with him. Wasn't that cause for celebration? Wasn't it an opportunity most women longed for? Wasn't it the stuff dreams were made of?

Certainly she had dreamed of it often enough. But now, as she tried to envision what it might be like to be married to Luc Domini, she realized that there was a wide divergence between fantasy and reality.

In her fantasies Luc's feelings for her had gone beyond infatuation. They had gone beyond desire. He'd fallen hopelessly, helplessly, irrevocably in love with her.

In reality it seemed that Luc's reasons for wanting her to be his wife were practical ones. He was attracted to her physically, and she was flattered by his interest, which made the idea of marrying him tempting. But she also resented Luc for the uneasiness he'd created.

She'd had more than her share of feeling self-conscious as an adolescent. She hadn't liked being insecure at sixteen, and she didn't like it now, and she had to admit that she was more than a little alarmed by Luc's proposal. Especially after hearing Celia's tale of woe.

Hadn't Celia's marriage foundered because she and Ross had nothing in common but sexual compatibility?

And suppose her dream became reality? What if she and Luc were to fall madly, passionately in love with each other? Would she rejoice then, or would her misgivings multiply?

So it went all afternoon. The list of questions seemed endless. But try as she might, Thia could not come up with any definitive answers. And she still wasn't laughing.

Chapter Four

Some of the same questions were running through Thia's mind that evening as she prepared to go out with Luc, but a relaxing soak in a tub of fragrant, almond-scented water helped her put her doubts in perspective.

After a day of strenuous physical labor she routinely pampered herself a bit, but tonight she carried the indulgence further than usual, slathering her face with moisturizer and adding an extra measure of perfumed oil to her bath. She let the soothing emollients work their magic before she reached for the soap and loofah, lying back in the tub with her eyes closed until her thoughts grew tranquil and the tension left her body.

Both Celia and Denise predicted that constant exposure to the weather would make Thia's fine-grained complexion as tough as old shoe leather, but so far she had escaped that fate. The truth was that she had been blessed with the kind of wholesome, golden-brown skin that never tanned or burned no matter how long she stayed outdoors.

Her hands, however, were an entirely different matter. As she scrubbed one slender arm, she examined her fingernails. For the past two days she had been careful to wear gloves, and she thought she saw some improvement. Her hands looked smoother, and the blister at the base of her thumb had healed. It helped that she'd given herself the long overdue manicure, but it would take weeks, maybe even months, before the calluses disappeared.

The water had grown chilly and she let the tub drain, then turned on the shower to shampoo her hair. Thanks to her dawdling, by the time she left the bathroom she had only fifteen minutes to dress and apply her makeup, and she hurriedly slipped into her clothes, luxuriating in the satiny coolness of the lace-trimmed teddy next to her skin, in the sensuous way the silk batiste of her skirt swirled about her legs and rustled with her slightest movement. The sound made her feel terribly feminine and a trifle wicked.

It had been a long time since she'd had a date; so long that she couldn't recall precisely when she'd last gone out with a man. But not for lack of offers.

In her first couple of years in Portland, Thia had learned to play the singles game, and she'd played it well. She'd even enjoyed it. Then, gradually, the novelty had worn thin and she'd begun to realize that the men she was dating were interchangeable and that the round of bars and parties was pointless. Finally she'd decided that the popularity she had envied so much as a high school girl was not all it was cracked up to be, and after that she'd dated infrequently.

Tonight, though, she felt excited. The prospect of seeing Luc had brought a rosy glow to her face, and she used cosmetics sparingly. A subtle blending of eye shadow accented her hazel eyes; a miserly amount of mascara dramatized her naturally long, thick lashes; a hint of blusher highlighted her cheekbones; a touch of frosted-plum lip gloss called attention to her mouth and toned with the muted violet of her shirtdress. She stepped into frivolous, strappy sandals and she was ready.

Thia looked poised and confident when she opened the door to Luc, and she responded without missing a beat when he complimented her on her appearance. She returned his praise, thinking that the gray-plaid sport jacket and open-collared shirt he was wearing suited him better than a business suit and tie.

They talked easily, reminiscing about old times, during the drive along the meandering back road that led to Pete's Hideaway. The restaurant was spacious and swank, elegant and intimate, with individual booths that were screened by luxuriant foliage plants. Thia wondered how long the plants survived in such dimly lighted conditions. She made a mental note to find out who supplied them, and that was her last rational thought.

During dinner, every time Luc smiled at her, every time he glanced her way, her excitement mounted. She ate every morsel of her sauerbraten without really tasting a bite. Yet when Luc ordered Sacher torte for dessert, she did too.

"I like a woman with a good, hearty appetite," said Luc. He was lounging comfortably in his chair, and his comment seemed nonchalant, but his deep-set eyes reflected the warmth of the candle flame. Thia was aware that his eyes were communicating on a deeper, more personal level than his words even before he teased, "I read somewhere that a healthy enjoyment of food is a sign of lustiness in bed."

"Is that so?" she inquired soberly.

Luc nodded, and she met his gaze without wavering as she ate the last of her dessert. Impulsively, she added, "It can also indicate a hard day's work and a skipped lunch."

"Or all three?" Luc challenged.

"Or all three," she agreed.

Luc leaned forward in his chair, studying her intently while the waiter removed their plates and refilled their coffee cups. When they were alone again, he remarked in a bland, insinuating tone, "Unless my eyes are deceiving me, you're wearing next to nothing under that dress, Thia mia."

Thia did not even try to respond to this observation. The best she could do was replace her cup in its saucer without spilling the coffee.

"Obviously you have no need to diet," Luc went on, "so why did you skip lunch?"

"Celia paid me a visit, and there went my lunch hour," Thia replied huskily. She paused to take a sip of water before she elaborated on her reply, telling Luc about her sister's decision to move out of Denise's house the following weekend. Now that Luc had given her the perfect opening, she ended by saying, "Celia asked me if you knew about her divorce, and I told her I thought you did. You had heard about it, hadn't you?"

"Yes," said Luc, answering her question much as she had answered Celia's. "Why do you ask?"

"Well, I thought—"

Struck by how much she might be revealing, Thia hesitated. She shifted uneasily in her chair, and Luc gave her a coaxing smile.

"It's just—Look, there's no tactful way to say this—"

"Whatever it is, Thia, out with it."

"All right, then. Here goes." She inhaled deeply. "When we were in high school, didn't you have a crush on my sister?"

"Wow! That's a long time ago. Of course, most of the guys were wild about Celia, and I've always thought she was pretty, but if my feelings for her went any deeper than admiration, I honestly don't remember it." Frowning thoughtfully, Luc added, "It's interesting that you should mention it, though."

"How do you mean?"

Luc shrugged, but there was a hint of tension about him that made the movement of his shoulders far from casual. It was as if he were getting ready to pounce.

"After twelve years," he said quietly, "even if I'd been crazy about Celia, would it make any difference to us?"

Is there an "us"? Thia wondered. Uncertain how to respond, she averted her eyes, and Luc went on, "So far tonight, I haven't said anything about our marriage. Have you wondered why?"

"Yes!"

Luc chuckled at her impassioned response, and she glared at him, vexed by his amusement.

"Go ahead and laugh," she said crossly, "but can you blame me? I've been on tenterhooks all evening, waiting for the other shoe to drop—"

Luc reached across the table and placed a silencing finger on her lips.

"I don't blame you at all, because that's how I hoped you'd feel. Fact is, I'm encouraged by it. After the way I jumped the gun, the most I could hope for was that you'd be intrigued enough to see me again, but it never entered my mind that you might think you're not my first choice."

With his forefinger, Luc outlined her mouth. He touched the curve of her cheek and the hollow of her temple, where the skin was so translucent that he could see the fragile tracery of fine, blue veins. Her delicacy made him feel uniquely protective, and as he withdrew his hand, he said simply, "Not only are you my first choice, Thia, you're my only choice."

Luc had left a hot, tingling sensation wherever he'd touched her, but unsettled as she was by his caresses, Thia was even more disturbed by how desperately she wanted to believe him.

Was she his first—his only—choice? she wondered. And if so, why?

Luc Domini was compellingly attractive, intelligent, dynamic, financially successful, and undeniably sexy. He embodied the kind of potent masculinity most women found irresistible. Over the years he must have been the target for all sorts of seductive come-ons. He must have known any number of women who'd have jumped at the chance to be his wife. No doubt he'd had affairs with more than a few of them. So why had he chosen her?

"Why me, Luc?" she asked coolly.

For long moments Luc only stared at her. Then he smiled mechanically, cryptically. He got to his feet with a curious abruptness and signaled to the waiter for the check.

"Come with me, Thia," he said, holding out his hand to her. "There's something I want to show you."

Thia had lived in Jackson County most of her life, but she was familiar with Ramsey Slough only by reputation.

The town had been built by one of the lumber companies that had prospered several decades before, and for as long as the postwar housing boom had lasted it hadn't been too unpleasant a place to live. In recent years, however, with the market for forest products becoming more and more severely depressed, the town had changed.

Now its public image was one of grinding poverty. It was destitute, desperate, and derelict, and whatever lawlessness occurred in the area was likely to happen in "the Slough." The neighborhood was a hotbed of family fights and drunken brawls, and even stabbings were not uncommon.

Thia stared out the car window, wide-eyed, trying to take it all in as Luc drove down a seedy commercial street lined with card rooms, adult book stores, massage parlors, and sleazy hotels, and turned onto a rutted dirt road on the northeastern fringe of the industrial district.

They passed the abandoned lumber mill with its rusted teepee burners and moldering heaps of sawdust, and the Porsche jounced over the railroad spur that ran into the mill yard before Luc braked and pulled the car onto the shoulder.

There were no street lamps, and when Luc turned off the headlights it was very dark. The night air was stagnant and thick with the odor of burned cabbage—a remnant of the mill's dried-up log pond. Somewhere in the distance a dog barked, then yelped as if someone had kicked it, and was silent. Despite the seasonable warmth of the June evening, Thia shivered.

Luc retrieved a flashlight from the glove compartment, and as he climbed out of the car, the overhead light came on, throwing the bones of his face into prominence. His features seemed all planes and angles, so rigid, so masklike that they might have been carved from stone.

"Watch your step," he cautioned as he handed her

out of the car. It was the first time he'd spoken since they'd left the restaurant.

The heels of Thia's sandals sank into the loose, gravelly soil as she stepped onto the roadside, but she was so intent on trying to make out her surroundings that she never thought of the damage to her shoes. She peered into the darkness beyond the beam of the flashlight and saw a row of shacks huddled close together along one side of the right of way. They were gray and squalid and cheerless. Most of them were deserted, and the shack Luc led her toward appeared to be even more dilapidated than the rest. Thia clung to his arm as they walked toward the sagging front stoop.

Before they went inside, he swept the flashlight across the narrow front yard. Here and there a clump of rank weeds poked ragged heads through the hard-packed earth, but other than that the yard was barren.

"Nothing ever would grow here," Luc remarked. His low-pitched voice held an ineffable sadness. For a moment he seemed touchingly young and vulnerable, but in the next moment he opened the front door and quipped, "Welcome to the wrong side of the tracks, Miss Sommers."

"Is this where you used to live?" Thia inquired.

Luc nodded and shone the light around the small front room. It was littered with rubbish, and brambles trailed through the rough-planked flooring. The walls were papered with newspapers, and cobwebs hung like dirty laundry from the rafters. A heavy layer of grime covered every surface.

"I had no idea," she murmured. Impossible as it seemed, the inside of the cabin was even worse than the outside.

"No, of course you didn't," said Luc. "No one did. I used to be ashamed of living here."

"But you're not anymore."

"No. Not anymore. Not for some time."

While Thia remained standing near the open door, Luc wandered to the far corner of the room and began scanning the columns in one of the newspapers. Evidently he was searching for a specific article, and after several minutes had gone by, Thia asked, "Should we be here, Luc? Wouldn't the owner object?"

Without interrupting his search, Luc replied, "I'm the owner, Thia. I bought this place a few years ago to remind me of my humble origins."

"You don't sound humble."

Luc swung around to look at her. "Very astute, Miss Sommers. I am proud of what I've accomplished."

"And of your 'humble origins'?"

"Yes, dammit!" Luc trained the beam of the torch on her. "Is there any reason why I shouldn't be?"

The light blinded Thia, so she couldn't see Luc's face. His tone was so harsh that she regretted challenging him, but she was also determined not to let him see her timidity. Slowly, with as much spirit as she could muster, she answered, "No, except that there is such a thing as reverse snobbery."

Luc laughed at her rejoinder, and the rich, rumbly evidence of his restored good humor was oddly comforting.

"Okay," he agreed flippantly, "so I'm not Saint Luke, but before you find me guilty of the crime of arrogance, I hope you'll consider that this place was a step up for my Dad and me. Since most of our wages went for cheap booze, we were accustomed to much less—"

"Stop it, Luc! I wasn't judging you."

"Weren't you? You could have fooled me."

Embarrassed, Thia hastily apologized. "You're right. I suppose I was making judgments, and I'm sorry if I've offended you. It's just that there's something about being here that makes me feel defensive."

"Funny," said Luc. "It used to have the same effect on me."

He turned away from her and resumed his search, and within a matter of moments found what he'd been looking for. "Here they are," he muttered, intent on reading the articles.

"What, Luc?"

"Come see for yourself."

When he motioned to her to join him, she responded automatically, moving through the darkness toward him as eagerly as a moth drawn to a flame. And when she reached his side, he draped an arm about her shoulders and directed her attention to the clippings he'd found.

Her own face leaped off the newspaper, and she realized the stories were about her.

Thia shook her head with disbelief and studied the articles in detail. There were three of them in all, and the first one included a picture that had been taken during a recital her ballet class had given when she was twelve. It showed several dancers *en pointe,* but she was in the foreground in her tutu and tights, looking frisky and coltish but hardly graceful and not at all happy. Her hair was skinned back into a tight topknot, and her expression was tragic, her eyes round and startled.

"The other girls were smiling," Luc observed softly, close to her ear. "Why were you so solemn?"

"As I recall, the flashbulb surprised me," Thia

answered evasively. "Besides, my head hurt from that awful hairdo, and I never did like performing."

"What about this one?" Luc inquired.

A subdued groan escaped her as her gaze fell upon the second newspaper photograph. It showed her on the tennis court at thirteen, squinting into the camera after the junior doubles tournament at the country club. This time her hair was pulled into a single long braid, and she looked shy and leggy, all awkward elbows and knees. Beside her stood Hoagy Jantzen, holding a huge loving cup....

"That trophy's about as big as you were," said Luc. "Is that why you were scowling?"

"No. I was upset because my partner and I had just lost our match."

"The others are smiling."

Now, seeing the picture as Luc must, sheltered by the protective curve of his arm, Thia could smile too. "So they are," she said. "But their mothers weren't trying to make excuses for them because they weren't in top form."

"And your mother was?"

Thia smiled ruefully. "She still is."

The third picture was a snapshot that had been taken on the occasion of her fifteenth birthday, just as she was preparing to blow out the candles on the cake. Her cousin Vernon lurked behind her, smirking and leering, while she was frowning.

"Heavens, Luc! Wherever did you get this one?"

"I bought it from Vernon."

"You bought it?"

"That's right." Luc grinned and pulled her closer to his side. "Paid him fifty hard-earned cents for it. But tell me, why did you look so gloomy at your own birth-day party?''

Thia laughed. "Probably because Vernon had just pinched me.''

The Stratford *Courier*'s typically small-town, chatty account of the birthday party was taped beneath the snapshot, and she had finished reading it before she realized that the other papers lining the wall dated from the generation preceding hers and Luc's. Yellowed and brittle with age, some of the newspapers went back even further.

She glanced questioningly at Luc. She sensed that he was watching her intently, and she wished that she could see his face. As if he'd read her mind, he said, "The article about the recital was in the paper the day my Dad and I arrived in Stratford.''

"And you saved it all these years?''

"Yes," Luc replied without inflection. He indicated the spot where they were standing. "My bed used to be here, and for three of those years the pictures of you were the first thing I saw in the morning and the last thing I saw at night. I don't know if I can explain why they meant so much to me—hell! I'm not even sure I understand it myself. But I hope this convinces you that you're my first and only choice—''

"I'm convinced," Thia said.

And she was, although she still had no idea why Luc had chosen her. Coming to the shack with him and see-ing the pictures and the newspaper clippings had raised as many questions as it had answered, and she was lost in thought while Luc drove her home.

Had the photos aroused his sympathy? she won-dered. Had he pitied the awkward little ballerina? Had the unhappy birthday girl touched his heart?

No, she decided. That was highly improbable. Luc was the most complex man she had ever met, and although he had collected the articles about her and bought his former home, she never thought of him as sentimental. It seemed much more likely that, in his drive to success, she was the carrot, the symbol of the respectability he hoped to attain, while the shack was the stick that goaded him onward.

At last, because each of the articles had stressed her family's social prominence, Thia confronted the possibility that, given Luc's pride, he very well might have been turned on by the Sommers name.

Did she represent a foothold on the social ladder? Had he been attracted by her obvious shyness? Had it made her seem attainable? Was she nothing more than a means to an end?

For all her uncertainties, when they had arrived at her front door and Luc took her in his arms, this time she didn't try to avoid his kiss.

He smoothed the silky tendrils of hair away from her temples and studied her face in the shadowy glow of the porch light, and for a heart-stopping moment she thought he might be comparing her features to those of the young Thia in the photographs. Then, smiling, he cupped her head between his hands so that she couldn't turn away while he found her mouth with his, and after one taste of his mouth, she didn't want to turn away.

Luc's lips brushed hers almost tentatively at first, feathering gently from side to side in a soft, testing sort of kiss, and she was incapable of resisting. Of their own volition, her arms slipped inside his jacket and wound about his waist to draw him closer while his hands caressed her shoulders and wandered over her back, molding her softness to him. He parted her lips, deepening his possession of her mouth, and in the instant she felt the sweet stroking movements of his tongue, she abandoned herself to sensation.

Somehow Thia had always known that Luc's kiss would be like this. Seeking and yielding, demanding and giving, at the same time velvety soft and rough with desire.

She felt the supple play of muscles beneath the fine fabric of his shirt and realized that some hidden part of herself had always known that his body would be hard and urgent, that she would melt beneath the searing heat of his ardor, that his embrace would leave her shaken and devastated, buffeted by the wake of undiluted passion.

His hands spanned her waist and caressed her sides, promising delicious intimacies without actually touching her intimately, finally coming to rest just beneath her breasts. She trembled with anticipation, waiting for him to claim her breasts, wanting his touch, longing for it. His mouth enticed, his tongue explored and provoked, but his hands only tantalized, and his control was maddening.

Was he waiting for some sign from her? Some indication that she wanted him to touch her?

If she leaned away from him ever so slightly, if she arched her back the tiniest bit, his fingertips would come into contact with her breasts.

She willed him to move his hands that last fraction of an inch, but much as she yearned for greater intimacies, she dreaded where they might lead. She wished she might stay in his arms forever. She wanted him to kiss her again and again, wanted to make love with him more than she had ever wanted anything, but some feeble residue of sanity cooled her response and kept her from making the move that could end only in seduction.

Luc must have sensed her hard-won restraint, because he ended the kiss. She felt his lips move as his mouth skimmed across her cheek, and she knew that he was speaking to her, but the pounding rush of blood through her ears drowned out the sound of his voice.

"What?" she murmured. "Did you say something?"

He covered the sensitive skin at the side of her neck with kisses and she shivered uncontrollably.

"I asked if you're free tomorrow night."

"No, I'm not," she answered breathlessly. "I'm having dinner with the Mulhollands."

Luc raised his head to look down at her, and she chattered on uneasily. "Do you know them? Kate manages the florist shop—"

"And Ken's a free-lance writer," Luc finished.

"Then you've met Kenny?"

"We've spoken on the telephone. I agreed to see him tomorrow morning for an interview. He wants to do a piece on me for the *Courier*. Is he any good?"

"He's first-rate—when he wants to be."

Between brief spurts of industry, during which he did odd jobs and wrote an occasional newspaper or magazine article, Ken Mulholland loafed and meditated. He called this "trying to find himself," and because of his recurring identity crises, he and Kate had lived in ten different states in as many years.

Thia said none of this to Luc, of course, but it seemed she didn't have to. Either Kenny's reputation had preceded him or Luc had read a lot into her answer, because Luc smiled wryly and returned to his original line of inquiry.

"How about Saturday?" he asked.

"You've forgotten Celia's moving in."

"No, I haven't forgotten. I thought you might be able to use an extra hand."

"It's kind of you to offer—"

"But?" Luc prompted.

Thia sighed. "I really think it would be best if Celia and I had the day alone."

"Sunday then," Luc said firmly.

His arms circled her waist, pressing her thighs against his, and her breath came in shallow, ragged gasps. Unsure of her voice, Thia nodded.

For a moment longer Luc held her close. Then he put her away from him, and she moved dazedly toward the door. As she stepped inside, he said, "Till Sunday, Thia mia."

"Yes, Luc," she replied faintly. "Sunday."

Chapter Five

Thia had dinner with Kate and Kenny Mulholland once a week. Shortly after Kate had begun working at the florist shop, Thia had discovered that both Mulhollands were gifted amateur chefs, but she'd had supper with them several times before Ken and Kate had learned that one of Thia's hobbies was collecting recipes. After that they had agreed to cook—and eat—their way around the world.

They'd started by perfecting the specialties of northern Italy, and from there they had progressed to Swiss, Viennese, and Eastern European cuisines. With the occasional detours they made—preparing Peking duck and celestial three-color soup for Chinese New Year, and borscht, piroshki and blini to celebrate Russian Easter—they believed they could complete their kitchen circumnavigation in three to five years. In the meantime they had the compensation of some spectacular meals together.

Thia and Kate willingly conceded that Kenny was the most accomplished cook. His skill in the kitchen surpassed Kate's and was far superior to Thia's, but aside from the modifications he introduced, each of them tried to make the dishes they prepared as authentic as possible.

Sometimes they got together at Thia's place, sometimes at Kate and Kenny's, and while the menu might be formal, the atmosphere would invariably be relaxed and casual, with the three of them pitching in to prepare the menu they'd planned the previous week.

But that Friday was different.

Normally, Kenny was too preoccupied with eating to do much talking, but after one day in Luc's company both his huge appetite and his usual sleepy-eyed look had deserted him. His rumpled, lived-in face was animated as, filled with enthusiasm, he talked about the interview.

From things Kenny let slip, it soon became evident that Luc had spent a good part of the morning pumping him for information about Thia, and she became increasingly edgy. By the time they started on the veal paprika, Kate had noticed Thia's agitation.

Kate tried to change the subject. Glancing about the room, she said, "I've been thinking of stripping the woodwork and refinishing it. That might make this kitchen brighter. But then again, maybe it's too big a hassle. What do you think, Kenny?"

"Seems like a lot of bother since we only rent the place, but whatever you want to do is fine with me, dear."

After this reply he immediately launched into another anecdote about his meeting with Luc, and he continued singing Luc's praises while Kate served the raspberry torte.

It was not until they were lingering over coffee that he ran out of superlatives grand enough to describe Lucian Domini.

"I've got to tell you, Katy," he said, "Luc's one of the most extraordinary men I've ever interviewed."

Thia tossed her napkin down and countered, "Sounds to me as if he's the one who did the interviewing."

Kenny frowned, but before he could answer her charge, she turned to Kate for confirmation. She was startled to see that her friend was staring at her in a way that seemed to ask, "Who rattled your cage?" and she went on more calmly, trying to justify her reaction.

"From what you've said, Kenny, I gather you gave Luc your whole life history—and Kate's. You told him about all the cities you've lived in, not to mention the apartments. You gave Luc a thorough rundown on where you went to school and on every job you've ever had, and most of the ones Kate's had. You even gave him a blow-by-blow account of your stint in the Army."

"Luc's been in the Army too," said Kenny. "It's only natural that we should compare notes."

"Compare notes! Is that what you call repeating things I've told you and Kate in confidence?"

"You're exaggerating, Thia."

"Not by much. For Heaven's sake, Kenny! You told Luc about my decision to retire Duffy Langtry, and I haven't even had the chance to talk with Duffy about it yet. How's he going to feel if it gets back to him? What if he hears about it from a third party?"

"He won't," said Kenny. "If there's one thing I'm sure of, it's that Luc would never betray a confidence."

"Kenny's right, Thia," said Kate. "Your secrets are safe with Luc."

"You met him too?" asked Thia.

"Yes, I did," Kate replied. "We only talked a few minutes, but I'm positive you needn't worry. I agree totally with Kenny's assessment of Luc." With a smile at her husband, she finished, "He truly is a very special man."

Thia had thought she might buy some time, and perhaps a bit of objectivity, by not seeing Luc for a couple of days. Now she realized she had been outmaneuvered. With the Mulhollands acting as if they were Luc's own private cheerleaders, she knew she'd been outflanked and outwitted. But what troubled her most of all was that she really didn't mind.

Saturday arrived, and with it, Celia. It didn't take long to unload the bags and boxes from the small trailer she'd rented, but Thia wondered if she would ever become accustomed to sharing her home with her sister.

When Celia had disappeared into the guest room to unpack her designer wardrobe from her designer luggage, Thia wandered among the movers' cartons that threatened to crowd her out of the living room and prayed for divine intervention.

"Let Celia find a job soon," she silently petitioned. "But if she doesn't, please, Lord, give me patience."

That evening Denise paid them a visit. She said she'd come by to deliver a few items Celia had overlooked, and she also brought Thia several magazines.

Now that Celia had taken the first steps toward self-reliance, she seemed to have forgotten her many quarrels with Denise. While they gossiped over their teacups, Thia leafed through the magazines her mother had given her and found that Denise had marked one article documenting the rising fortunes of four alumnae of the Wharton School of Business.

You Can Have It All the title proclaimed, and the photographs of the women supported this contention.

Ten years after graduation, each of them had achieved unqualified success in her chosen career. Each was attractive, interesting, and glamorous. They appeared to have everything going for them, but Thia was struck by how dissatisfied they were with their personal lives beneath the surface gloss.

Three of the four had been through at least one divorce, and the fourth was quoted as saying that she'd been engaged several times, but in the end she'd decided that marriage would be incompatible with her ambitions. "I wouldn't have it any other way," this woman said, yet Thia thought that, all in all, the underlying message was one of loneliness.

The next day, while she and Luc picnicked on the shore of Emigrant Lake, she told him about the article. He listened attentively, as if he sensed how distressed she was by the story, and she finished by inquiring, "Do you think it's possible for anyone to have it all?"

"No," Luc answered succinctly.

"Why?"

"Because human wants are insatiable, Thia. The more a person has, the more they demand."

"In other words, life's a no-win proposition."

"Oh, I wouldn't say that. It's just that I think it's only human to find struggle more stimulating than success."

Thia sighed heavily.

"Depressing, isn't it?" said Luc.

"Yes, it is."

"Then why did you bring it up?"

"Darned if I know," said Thia. "Maybe it's just that I wish I could have been born a hundred years ago, when people were more dependent on one another. I mean, they had to work out their differences and pull together in order to survive."

A smile played about the edges of Luc's mouth. "You wouldn't have liked it, Thia. Not for long. In those days, women didn't get to choose the kind of role they wanted to play—"

"They weren't subjected to the stress that goes with having that kind of freedom either."

"Neither were men," said Luc.

"I know." She sighed again, this time wistfully. "Things were so much simpler then, Luc. Expectations weren't so high. Lately, whatever I do, I know I'm going to disappoint someone—maybe myself most of all. But what really bothers me is that I can't enjoy the good things that happen because I'm waiting for something equally bad to offset them."

"Welcome to the club, honey."

"Does that mean I'm not alone?"

"If it's any comfort to you, no, you're not. From what I've seen, anxiety is the equal opportunity ailment of the self-employed." Pausing, Luc grinned and added, "Or maybe it's a sign of the times or a symptom of maturity. But whatever it indicates, pessimism has its advantages. Once you've accepted the possibility that disaster can strike at any moment, failure's easier to handle."

"I can't imagine your ever taking failure lightly, Luc."

"No?" Luc's grin broadened and he tossed her an apple from their picnic basket. As he rummaged through the basket and dug out another apple for himself, he said, "If you take your mistakes too seriously, they can stop being temporary setbacks and turn into full-fledged defeats. And anyway, sometimes you learn more from your failures than you do from your successes."

"That sounds very much like my grandmother's philosophy."

"It should. She's the one who taught it to me."

"I hadn't realized you know her."

"Sure I do," Luc affirmed. "When I was a little kid, my mother used to tell me that everyone in Stratford knew Elvira Sommers. She's practically an institution, Thia. Then, when my dad took off, your grandmother gave me part-time work doing odd jobs around the nursery. We still keep in touch—exchange an occasional letter and talk on the phone every few months, that sort of thing. She's the one who told me you'd come home."

Startled by this disclosure, Thia studied Luc covertly as he eased into a half-reclining position on the blanket. Only when he had made himself comfortable, propping one elbow on the spongy carpet of pine needles and lying with one lithe, muscular leg stretched out and the other jackknifed, did he bite into his apple.

It was another swelteringly hot day, and before lunch they had gone for a swim to cool off. Afterward they had chosen a picnic site shaded by tall cedars and firs, and Thia had slipped into her light cotton beach wrap, but Luc wore only brief swimming trunks and the towel he had draped around his neck.

He might have a heavy beard, but his broad naked chest was surprisingly smooth and hairless, so that his slightest movement called attention to the powerful rippling of muscles beneath coppery skin as fine and flawless as oiled silk. There was a hard, sensual beauty about him that made even the act of eating an apple seem suggestive and erotic.

Electrified by the sight of him, Thia bit into her own apple, unconsciously mimicking his gestures. She chewed absently, watching as if mesmerized while he took another bite. And another. And another.

She noticed the way Luc cupped the apple in his palm, the way his long tapering fingers curved around the firm uneven sphere, the way his arm flexed as he lifted it to his mouth. She saw his strong white teeth sink into the rosy skin and thought how very dark his complexion looked by contrast with the pale, tender flesh of the fruit. She saw the flick of his tongue as he licked the juice from his lips, and the way his throat worked as he swallowed, and by the time he threw the core to a waiting blue jay, she felt that Luc had consumed her resistance to him as surely as he had consumed the apple. She felt that he had stripped away her defenses and penetrated to her core, and in that moment she knew that if he were to crook his little finger, she would fall into his hands as easily as ripened fruit drops from its tree.

Even worse was that the thought of falling into Luc's hands excited her. It excited her so much, she was afraid that if she didn't stop looking at him soon, she might actually throw herself into his arms.

Somehow Thia managed to tear her gaze away from him, but she made the error of focusing on her own partially eaten apple. She stared at it vacantly, without really seeing it. Instead her treacherous memory replayed vivid images that recalled Luc's sensuality, and she remembered Thursday night and their tender farewell on her front porch; the feel of his body against hers, the warmth of his mouth as he'd kissed her, how desperately she'd wanted him to touch her—

"Do you really want that?"

Luc's softly voiced question jolted Thia out of her reverie, and she rubbed the back of one hand across her forehead, swamped by confusion.

Had he read her mind? Did he know how much she wanted him?

"If you don't, I'll finish it," Luc said hopefully, patting his flat belly.

Seconds passed before it dawned on Thia that he had been referring to the apple.

"All right. It's yours."

A sweet lassitude possessed her. Her voice was throaty, and her arm felt languid and heavy as she handed the fruit to him. Luc's fingers brushed hers as he accepted her offering, but even that fleeting contact ignited a primitive shockwave of desire that spread like wildfire through Thia's veins.

Had Luc felt it too?

She risked a glance at him and saw that he must have shared her response. He examined the apple thoroughly, deliberately seeking the spot her lips had touched, and when he found it, he bit into the fruit slowly, carefully, as if he were savoring the taste of her mouth, as if he were feasting upon her.

Would he be as slow and deliberate as a lover? Would he be thorough and greedy, relishing every touch, savoring every moment? Would he be insatiable? Inventive? Uninhibited?

Her desire had escalated to the point that Thia was certain that Luc must be able to detect the hunger in her eyes, and the certainty made her feel naked and exposed. Again she looked away from him, this time concentrating on tying the belt of her wrap so that it concealed more of her bikini-clad body.

But her awareness of him grew. The few feet that

separated them seemed charged by his magnetism. The silence between them seemed to crackle with an exquisite tension that promised undreamed-of pleasures. She couldn't bear not looking at him. She couldn't bear the distance between them. She couldn't bear the silence. She had to say something. Anything—

"It's—uh, it's awfully warm, isn't it?"

The instant the words were out, Thia wished them unspoken. How inane! she thought. And worse than inane, her stammer revealed her nervousness. She was relieved when Luc made no reply.

"Did you say your mother told you about Stratford?" she tried again.

"That's right. She was born and raised here."

Luc's low-pitched drawl was gentle as a sigh, yet as vibrant as a caress. He shifted his weight slightly, crossing one leg over the other, and Thia was conscious that his movements brought him closer to her. Although she wasn't looking at him, her senses were so keenly attuned to him that she could envision the watchful tilt of his head, the burnished width of his shoulders, the length of his hard-muscled thighs. Her hands were clenched about the belt of her robe, but mentally she was stroking his warm, supple skin, and every time she inhaled, she breathed in his subtle, sun-washed scent.

"She married my father when she was just sixteen," Luc went on in the same quiet tone, "and her family disowned her."

Under the bombardment of sensory impressions, Thia's mind was muddled. She shook her head to clear it and swallowed hard to ease the dryness in her throat.

"Her family?" she repeated dully.

"She was a Jantzen."

"Then you're related to Hogarth Jantzen?"

"We're second cousins," Luc said brusquely.

Thia studied a pine cone that lay near the edge of the blanket as she ventured, "You don't much like him, do you, Luc?"

"No, not much."

"Do you mind if I ask why?"

"Well, naturally I resent the way the Jantzens treated my mother. She died when I was seven, but even when her parents knew her illness was terminal, they didn't contact her, and I guess some of my anger spills over onto Hoagy. But besides that, I've always mistrusted loan officers who put on that phony folksy act. In my opinion they have all the integrity of a turnip, and about that much intelligence."

Thia dumped a handful of twigs about the pine cone and piled them into place, burying the pine cone, symbolically burying her response to Luc.

"It sounds as if you're speaking from experience."

"I am," said Luc. "When my business was getting off the ground, I dealt with a guy a lot like Hoagy, and he smiled all the while he was turning down my loan application. It was frustrating as hell trying to do business with him. Not because he didn't recommend the loan. I was undercapitalized and I understood why the bank considered me a poor credit risk. But I didn't appreciate some unimaginative clown poking fun at my plans."

"At least you had the last laugh," Thia said softly.

Luc chuckled. "So I did, thanks to your grandmother."

"Why thanks to her specifically?"

"She cosigned a loan for me."

Thia nodded thoughtfully. Her grandmother had cosigned a number of notes, and not all the debtors had paid off their loans. That was one reason the nursery was in hot water financially. But until now Thia hadn't known that Luc had benefited from Elvira Sommers's largesse.

Obviously Luc was very grateful to her grandmother. Was that why—

"I know what you're thinking." Luc's statement disrupted Thia's train of thought and she looked at him coolly.

"Do you?" she asked.

"Oh, yes."

Luc's fingers closed around her wrist. With a single effortless tug, he pulled her off balance and tumbled her onto the blanket beside him. He cushioned her fall with one arm angled beneath her, so that she found herself lying with her head on his shoulder, staring into the unfathomable depths of his eyes.

"You're wrong, you know," he said gruffly. "I didn't propose to you out of gratitude to Elvira."

"You didn't propose to me at all," Thia returned stiffly.

Luc frowned. "Didn't I?"

"No, you didn't. You only said you'd come back to Stratford to marry me."

"In that case, I'd better rectify my oversight here and now." For a moment a roguish grin lifted the corners of Luc's mouth and glinted in his eyes. Then, with a swiftness that took her breath away, he sobered and said, "Will you do me the honor of marrying me, Thia Sommers?"

His self-confidence was maddening. "I'll think about it," she snapped, but Luc was undaunted by the chill in her voice. His hands roamed over her, one molding itself to her hip, the other sliding beneath her robe to explore the burgeoning swell of a breast, and when her body went slack and yielding in his arms, he whispered, "While you're at it, think about this, too."

She inhaled sharply, but before she could object to his arrogance, he captured her lips in a playful, biting kiss that suddenly became hard and possessive, then altered again as they clung together open-mouthed, tongues touching and twining, invading and withdrawing, darting and sweetly dueling in an intoxicating liquid fusion of desire.

Luc threw one leg over both of hers and lay half on top of her, gently pinning her to the blanket, but she was oblivious to his weight. He twisted his hips against hers in a grinding, circular motion that let her feel the virile thrust of him against her thigh, and she responded joyfully, hugging him to her fiercely, quickening to his tempo.

She was soft to his hardness, and she kindled to the fire of his kisses and the urgency of his caresses until deep inside she was melting, burning with an unquenchable need that only he could satisfy.

But if her desire for him was overwhelming, it was also frightening to want him so badly when she had so many questions about his motives. With the last vestige of sanity, she braced her palms against his chest and gasped, "It's too soon, Luc. Everything is happening so quickly. I can't think when you kiss me. Give me time—"

"Time won't change anything, Thia." His hands traced the curves from breast to belly to thigh in a hot, claiming caress. He touched her intimately, and she bit her lip to keep from crying out her pleasure, but he felt the response that quivered through her, and said, "Time won't change this."

She hesitated for the space of a single pulse beat before she tried to pull away from him, and brief as it was, that hesitation told Luc how much she wanted to capitulate. Thia saw this in his knowing smile, in the flinty determination in his eyes.

"You're pretty damned sure of yourself, aren't you?" she muttered.

"Why does that bother you?" Luc demanded.

"I—I don't know," she answered weakly.

She was lying and both of them knew it. As if to reassure her, Luc framed her face between his hands and planted a tender row of kisses from her temple to her lips.

"If I seem calculating," he murmured against her mouth, "maybe it's because I've wanted you for so long."

"And do you always get what you want?"

"Yes," Luc answered simply. "Always."

Chapter Six

The Founders' Day Dance Committee was scheduled to meet at Cassie Bennett's farm on the last Wednesday in June. As Celia prepared to leave the house that evening, she said, "I'd like to give the others a progress report about the arrangements you're making for the flowers."

"Is that a hint?" asked Thia.

"You betcha," Celia returned.

"Oh." Thia felt herself starting to blush and hurriedly went on. "I meant to get to the plans this week, but I haven't had the time."

"No, you haven't," Celia teased, "what with Luc giving you such a rush."

"We've been looking for an apartment for him, but now that he's decided to lease the Kirby estate—"

"Has he?" Celia broke in eagerly, and when Thia nodded, she exclaimed, "Some people get all the breaks! I adore that old place. It's utterly loaded with history, and it oozes potential."

"It's not definite yet," said Thia. "Hoagy Jantzen is executor of the estate, and it depends on what sort of terms he and Luc can work out."

"Knowing Luc, I'm sure he'll bring Hoagy around. But tell me, Sis, will Luc be redecorating?"

"He hasn't said. The place is pretty run-down, though, so I imagine he will if he signs the lease."

"Well, if he does, I hope you'll steer him my way. I've been thinking of setting up shop as an interior designer."

This latest scheme of her sister's was news to Thia, but it came as no surprise. While Celia hadn't found a job yet, she religiously checked the Help Wanted column and made the rounds of prospective employers, and she hadn't let her lack of success discourage her. At least not noticeably. Each time she was told that she didn't have quite the skills an advertiser was looking for—or the experience, or the attitude—Celia came up with a rationalization that implied that the job was not suited to her rather than the other way around.

"The truth is, I'm overqualified," Celia would say. Or "Filing tax forms all day would be deadly dull."

Just that afternoon she had come home from an interview with Don Gallagher's office manager practically sputtering with rage. She had walked into the living room shrieking, "I've never been so insulted in all my life!"

"Why, Celia? What happened?" asked Thia.

"Nothing unusual," Celia answered indignantly. "Just Fran Cullen acting like her own snotty self. She started out by claiming that I don't know the first thing about office procedures. That got me so upset that I flunked the typing test, and to add insult to injury, Don had the nerve to say that my knowledge of medical terminology was too limited to be of any use to them."

Flinging her handbag onto a lamp table, Celia demanded angrily, "Can you believe it? Why, Ross and his friends could talk rings around Don Gallagher in their sleep, and I never had the slightest bit of difficulty following their conversations."

"I'm sorry your interview didn't go well." Thia steadied the lamp Celia's purse had nearly upended and watched her sister uneasily, fearing for the safety of the furniture if Celia threw anything heavier than her handbag. She was relieved when she saw that the unpredictable Sommers temper had abated as quickly as it had flared.

With a negligent shrug, Celia perched on the sofa and slipped off her shoes. "Oh, well," she said. "It's probably just as well Fran didn't hire me. Can you see me taking orders from her?"

Thia laughed at this suggestion, and Celia joined in. Although Thia didn't say so in as many words, she couldn't see Celia taking orders from anyone, and while she deplored her sister's refusal to face reality, she admired Celia's chutzpah.

Now, as Celia collected her notebook and carryall, Thia promised, "I'll try to have some sort of plans worked out before your next meeting."

"That'll do." As Celia headed for the door, she gave Thia a meaningful smile and added, "With the way Luc's been monopolizing your time, I guess it will have to. Which reminds me, where is he tonight?"

"He had to make a trip to Portland."

"Oh?" Celia paused in the doorway. "Business or pleasure?"

Thia smiled ruefully. "Business, of course. A meeting with his board of directors."

"Of course," Celia agreed after a momentary hesitation. "Luc is all business, isn't he, Thia?"

"No, Celia. Not quite all."

"But more than you'd like?"

"Perhaps," Thia answered evenly, but inwardly she flinched at the accuracy of her sister's insight. And long after Celia had left, she prowled about the living room, tormented by Celia's chance comment.

Luc had always been determined, but now, at times, he seemed driven. And although she believed that he wanted her, she couldn't help thinking that he would have proposed marriage even if he hadn't found her physically appealing.

As Thia paced from the fireplace to the desk, she asked herself whether Luc had given any thought to the contributions she might make to his business, and her answer was an immediate, unequivocal "Yes!"

Certainly Luc's reaction to the Kirby place demonstrated that, as far as he was concerned, practical considerations outweighed other matters.

Only last night they'd toured the grounds and walked through the lovely old house, and while she had delighted in the beautifully tended herb garden and the ivy-trailed, dusky-rose brick walls and the gracious bay windows, Luc had remarked that there would be ample off-street parking along the horseshoe drive. While she had rhapsodized over the elegant staircase, the handsome woodwork, the roominess of the bedrooms, he'd said only that the location would do and that the place should be big enough for entertaining clients and business associates.

If Luc could look at such a charming home and see it only as a proper setting for negotiating contracts and finalizing deals, didn't that prove that his business interests were all-important to him?

Reluctantly, Thia admitted that it did.

Yet he'd kept the pictures of her, and the newspaper articles. He'd virtually made them into a shrine.

But was it she Luc idolized, or his own ambition?

And why should it matter to me at all? Thia wondered. But even as she asked herself this question, she felt a hurtful germ of conviction take root inside herself, and she knew that it mattered because she had fallen in love with Luc.

And she realized something else, as well.

The next time Luc asked her to marry him, she would say yes. The decision was out of her hands, but if she had cared for him less, or if he'd cared for her more, it would have been easier to accept. As things stood, however, her sense of helplessness bordered on despair.

Thia wished she had someone to talk with. Preferably Kate.

She sat at the desk and dialed the Mulhollands' number, but there was no answer. Stymied, she stared at the phone and tried to think of someone else who might advise her.

If her mother's judgment had been more sound than her own, she would have called Denise. But Denise's bias that Thia should be her career-oriented daughter would color any advice she could give and render it invalid.

Thia thought next of her sister. Celia would understand. She would even sympathize because it seemed apparent that both of them had inherited their mother's luck in love—all of it bad!

But Celia was at her Committee meeting, and Thia needed someone to confide in now, before her anxiety grew out of reasonable proportion. She needed to talk to someone wise and objective and reliable. Someone who knew Luc—

"Of course," Thia cried. "I should have thought of Grandmother immediately."

She quickly dialed Elvira's number in Arizona, but she allowed her grandmother's phone to ring only twice before she broke the connection.

If she spoke to her grandmother now, she'd sound silly, overemotional and overwrought. She'd sound exactly the way her mother and Celia sounded in some of their least attractive moments, and this was a trap she had always sought to avoid.

Maybe it would be better to take some time to regain control of her emotions, to put her fears in writing....

Without further delay, she found the stationery in the top desk drawer and began composing a letter to her grandmother, writing hastily, almost feverish in her need to put all her concerns down on paper. Her pen flew across the page, leaving a wild trail of words that amounted to a silent plea, a visual cry for help.

The first draft was almost illegible and more than a little garbled, and she crumpled the paper and stuffed it into one of the pigeonholes at the back of the desk and began again, revising and organizing her thoughts as she went.

Thia was still writing when Celia came home from her meeting. She was so intent upon the third version of her letter that she hardly noticed when Celia gave up trying to get her attention long enough to say good night and went to bed.

It was after eleven before Thia was satisfied with what she had written. When she glanced at her wristwatch and saw how late it was, she wondered if her watch might be running fast. As she checked it by the kitchen clock, it dawned on her that she had been listening for the phone to ring all evening, waiting for Luc to call.

She took her time folding the letter into an envelope

and addressing it, and when that was done she had to look for a stamp. After that she disposed of the wadded pages that protruded from every slot in the desk and testified to her earlier state of near panic. She tidied the living room and freshened the water in the flower vases and fluffed the sofa cushions.

Finally, at eleven thirty, she locked the front door, turned off the lights, and went to her own room, disheartened because Luc hadn't called.

Luc still hadn't called by Friday evening, when the Mulhollands came for dinner. Kate and Kenny talked nonstop and laughed at trifles, and during the meal Kenny announced that his article on Luc was slated to appear in Sunday's paper. With undisguised pride he said, "I don't mind telling you, Thia, I think it's the best thing I've ever done."

Aside from this, he and Kate were careful not to mention Luc, but Thia was not in a festive mood. She was relieved when her friends left early.

After that inauspicious start, Thia spent the weekend barricaded in her office, catching up with the end-of-the-month billing and working out a plan for turning the Warwick Inn ballroom into a Victorian garden, complete with fountains, a wishing well, and a vine-covered arbor.

Some of that was too costly to be practical, but she had an assortment of portable fountains and some plastic pools in stock. If Celia could find a volunteer to build a ramp and a small platform, she also had several roll ends of artificial turf that would transform the incline into a grassy slope and lily pond. And if they had a carpenter with sufficient skill, they might even rig up a moon gate or a humpbacked bridge over the pond.

With that as a foundation, if she added some greenery and a lot of fuchsias and ferns planted in hanging
baskets, which had the decided advantage of being less
accessible to drunks and careless smokers, *voilà!* the
main entrance to the ballroom would resemble a path
through an old-fashioned garden: romantic, impressive
enough to please Celia's discriminating eye, and best of
all, recyclable.

Thia became so engrossed with making lists and
drawing up the plans, it was Sunday evening before she
thought about reading Kenny's article on Luc. She had
just begun scanning the day's paper, looking for it,
when Celia wandered into the living room. Yawning
hugely, she curled up at the opposite end of the sofa.

"I'm bushed," she declared.

"Where have you been all weekend?" asked Thia.

"Mother and I drove over to the coast. How about
you?"

"Working mostly."

"On a gorgeous day like this?"

"'Fraid so, but I got the bills out and I finished the
plans for decorating the ballroom."

"Hey, that's terrific! When do I get to see them?"

"Whenever you'd like. They're on the dresser in my
room."

Revitalized by this information, Celia sprang to her
feet and started toward Thia's bedroom.

"If you're looking for the story on Luc," she said,
"it's on the front page of the *Stratford Today* section."

While Celia pored over the plans, Thia found the article. Although it covered half the page, it didn't take
long to read. Even if she hadn't been involved with
Luc, Kenny's concise, vigorous reporting would have
made her feel as if she were personally acquainted with
his subject.

With bold, sure strokes he detailed Luc's checkered background. He outlined the vagabond boyhood spent mostly in migrant worker camps, with an occasional stopover in a big-city tenement. He described Luc's footloose, irresponsible father—always on the lookout for a free lunch, for a handout or a hand up, frantically searching for the ticket to the big time that somehow never materialized, embittered by his failure so that he ended his life seeking oblivion in a bottle.

Never once did Kenny resort to overstatement or sentimentality, but Thia felt his compassion, and his restraint made her painfully aware of Luc's growing desperation over his father's increasingly destructive behavior. Disappointments were inevitably followed by bouts of violence, but ultimately the ugliness the young Luc witnessed and the deprivation he endured helped forge his sense of destiny.

Kenny went on to recount Luc's years in the military. He highlighted several of Luc's more profitable business ventures, and with this "poor boy makes good" ending completed his sketch of a dynamic young man on the move.

The article had captured all of Luc's independence. It made him seem tough, single-minded, unstoppable. Yet at the same time Kenny had captured something else in Luc's character: an elusive, perhaps illusive, vulnerability.

Maybe I'm reading something into it that isn't there, thought Thia. It could be Kenny's vulnerability coming through.

With a pensive sigh, she folded the paper and laid it aside.

"Well?" Celia inquired. "What do you think of Kenny's article?"

"It's a fine piece of writing. He told me he considers

it the best thing he's ever done, and he might very well be right."

Celia nodded. "What surprised me is that he really made me feel Luc's loneliness."

"So you noticed it too," Thia murmured.

"How could I miss it?" Celia laughed shakily. "It made me want to cry."

"Me too," Thia said with quiet intensity. "Oh, Celia, me too."

On Monday Thia received a note from her old school friend Mickie Lloyd. Postmarked Indianapolis, the message read, "The bod's here on tour, but the spirit's in Stratford. I'm looking forward to a hot time in the old town on Founders' Day, kiddo. Can't wait to see you."

Thia also received a much longer letter from her grandmother. Elvira Sommers wrote:

Dearest Cynthia,

How typical of you to ask for my advice as you did, by putting your concerns about Luc's proposal in writing rather than simply picking up the phone. I'll wager you even copied your letter over so that you could keep your display of emotions to a minimum.

Forgive me if that sounds hard-hearted, my dear, but you've always been inclined to discount your feelings. And it isn't necessary. As your friend Kate told you, you have excellent instincts, and I urge you to trust them.

After this opening, no doubt you're wondering why I'm writing when I might just as easily have telephoned you, but the explanation is simple. If we spoke, I'm afraid you'd maneuver me into saying more than I intend to say, and I'm convinced that you should discuss your concerns with your mother. If you give her half a chance, I promise that you'll be pleasantly astonished by how understanding she can be. You may not know it, dear, but Denise needs to be needed, and you need to learn to rely on others.

Self-sufficiency is a trait you and Luc have in common. I applaud that, and your generosity, but I dread thinking of what your future will hold if one of you doesn't develop a bit of selfishness.

You see, Cynthia, I believe that you've already made your choice, just as Luc has made his. I believe you're going to marry him, and if there's one thing life has taught me, it's that love is mostly a matter of give and take. By that I mean that before one can truly give love—without question, without reservation—one must be willing to take it.

Elvira went on for another page or so before she closed, but basically she was bringing Thia up to date on her activities. She had added a postscript, however, and it read:

In your letter you asked two direct questions, and here are the answers. Yes, my darling granddaughter. Although he'd probably fight like the devil to deny it, Luc most definitely does need love. And, never fear, the two of you will always have problems. Everyone does. Trouble seems to be the price you pay for love, and you don't need to go out of your way looking for it. It will find you. So take some advice from a veteran of more than fifty years of marriage, and don't waste your energies worrying about the things you can accept.

Thia smiled as she tucked the letter into the pocket of her smock, along with Mickie's note.

"Thanks, Gran," she murmured. "That's all I needed to know."

Chapter Seven

The heat from the greenhouse struck Luc as forcibly as a blow. Just inside the doorway he stopped to peel off his tie and suit coat and loosen his collar. He was unbuttoning his shirt cuffs when he heard a strident oath from somewhere above his head.

Guided by the sound of the voice, he glanced upward and saw Thia, barely visible in the lush growth of the bougainvillea, which had been trained along one corner of the glass roof to provide shade for the sun-sensitive plants. She was clinging precariously to the woody brown trunk of the vine while her dangling feet scrabbled to find a toehold on the top rung of a teetering ladder.

"Dammit, Penny! Can't you hold it any steadier?"

"Don't you take that tone with me, Thia Sommers," the middle-aged woman at the bottom of the ladder replied testily. "I'm doing the best I can."

Penny looked as though she might have said more, but a sharp, cracking sound came from the crown of the vine just then, and the trunk dipped ominously.

Thia clutched at the trunk and squawked with terror, and Penny gritted her teeth and threw all her weight against the ladder. Luc saw her legs buckle with exer-

tion and her shoulders twitch with the strain of trying
to balance her unwieldy burden, and he dropped his
coat and rushed to help.

When he reached over Penny's head and righted the
ladder, the salesclerk looked at him as if he were the
answer to a prayer, and once Thia's toes had made contact with the top rung and found a safe purchase, Penny
gave him a grateful smile.

Now that the immediate danger had passed, Luc saw
that Thia was fumbling with the latch on one of the
manual vents in the ceiling, trying to open it.

"This damned thing is solid rust," she grumbled,
following her complaint with a string of epithets that
brought a scandalized gasp from Penny.

"Thia!" she cried, her face bright with embarrassment. "Wherever did you learn that kind of language?"

"I read it on the wall in the ladies' locker room at the
country club," Thia retorted sourly. She swore at the
latch again and gave it another push, and this time it
slid back. "Finally!" she muttered. She swung the vent
back as far as it would go and, after fixing it in place,
started cautiously down the ladder.

Her voice settled into a more melodious range as she
said, "Thank goodness that's the last one. You wouldn't
believe how hot it is up there. I'm about to suffocate."

She looked it, thought Luc, taking in her flushed,
dust-streaked face and tangled hair. Because of the
heat, she wore only shorts and a halter top, and while
the skimpy garments might have protected her from
heat prostration, they hadn't kept the bougainvillea
branches from tearing at her soft skin.

His concern mounted as she clambered down the
ladder and he saw that her arms and shoulders were

covered with angry-looking welts and a network of small, livid scratches.

She seemed to sense his presence before she actually saw him, for all at once, midway to the floor, she stopped and slowly turned to look at him.

"Hello, Luc," she said coolly. "When did you get back?"

Her voice was calm and uninflected, but he saw the sudden leap of pulses in her throat and grinned at her.

"By the look of things, just in time," he answered dryly.

He held his hands out to her, silently offering to help her down, but she ignored his offer and resumed her descent.

What she hadn't reckoned with, however, was that Luc would insist upon helping her. As soon as she was within reach, his hands fastened about her waist. He felt her tense. He saw her hands tighten on the sides of the ladder and knew that she would have tried to wriggle out of his grasp if they'd been alone. But Penny Burgess was there, a round-eyed audience of one, avidly watching this bit of byplay. At last Thia let go of the ladder and allowed him to lift her down, but when he set her on the floor, she glowered at him so ferociously that it became obvious, even to Penny, that she resented Luc's help.

Wondering why Thia should be offended by the interest of such an attractive man, Penny scolded, "Heaven only knows what might have happened if Luc hadn't come along when he did."

"Yeah," Thia retorted with patent insincerity. "He's a regular knight in shining armor." Luc squeezed her waist punishingly, and confronting Penny, she suggested sweetly, "Let's try the fans now, shall we? Before the plants bake in this heat."

"Sure thing," Penny replied. Her curiosity was aroused, and she might have tarried and tried to figure out exactly what was going on between Luc and Thia if she hadn't seen the storm warnings in Thia's hazel eyes. But she had seen them, and deciding that discretion would be the better part of valor, she bustled away before things really began to get hot.

Luc took advantage of Penny's departure by giving Thia a quick, hard kiss on the mouth, but she managed to keep her lips stiff and unresponsive beneath his, and when he released her, he asked with some bemusement, "What's going on?"

Thia knew what Luc meant. She knew he was asking why she hadn't returned his kiss, but she was in no mood to be cooperative. Purposely misinterpreting his question, she said, "The cooling system's on the blink, and the repairman can't service it till tomorrow."

As she answered, she stepped away from Luc, putting a distance of several yards between them. He would have pursued her, but when he noticed her combative posture, he stopped, mystified by her hostility, and she stood with her hands on her hips, tapping one sneakered foot, waiting until the fans came on and Penny was safely out of earshot. Then she demanded, "Why didn't you call?"

"You said you needed time to think," Luc answered laconically.

"If I'd said I craved chocolates, would you have given me a candy store?"

Luc's expression hardened. He'd been working sixteen-hour days so that he could steal some time to be with her. He was hot and tired and hungry, and his temper was on a dangerously short fuse. He'd had to wrestle with the urge to call all week, and instead of appreciating his consideration for her feelings, Thia was obviously spoiling for a fight. Shrugging mentally, he decided to oblige her.

"If I thought that a candy store was what you really wanted, yes, I damned well might!"

"So you went away for a week and didn't call me once," Thia said curtly. "Tell me, Luc, don't you think that's overdoing it?"

He frowned repressively and moved closer, but Thia held her ground, pleased because her salvo had found its mark.

"Thia," he said evenly, "it's too hot to fight. But even if I felt like fighting, I wouldn't want to argue with you."

Infuriated by his condescension, Thia scowled. "Well, that's just dandy, because I don't want to argue either. I merely want to make the point that you apparently have no sense of proportion."

Through clenched teeth, Luc conceded, "Perhaps not about you, but I have enough sense to recognize that you have trouble saying what you mean."

Drawing herself to her full height, Thia inquired shrilly, "Are you implying it's my fault?"

"What, Thia?" Luc shot back. "I don't even know what the hell we're fighting about."

Thia stared at him mutely, dismayed, her anger defused by this counterattack.

How do I answer that? she wondered. *How can I accuse Luc of making me care for him too much? How can I tell him that I'm scared to death he doesn't care enough?*

Her fury ebbed, leaving her feeling drained, bewildered, defeated. Seeing this, Luc draped his arm about her shoulders and gave her a hug that was more consoling than loverlike. He had not forgotten about her injuries, and he was careful not to hurt her, but she winced and he murmured a quick apology.

"Truce?" he said gruffly.

Thia nodded and leaned against him. She looked so pale and shaken that he wanted to comfort her, yet she was also delectably disheveled, and he wanted to make love to her. And when he thought of what might have happened if he hadn't come along in time to steady the ladder, he wanted to shout at her never to take that kind of risk again.

Wisely, though, he decided to forgo all of these things—for the moment.

His hand shook as he pulled out his handkerchief and wiped away the smudge of soot that dotted the end of her nose. As he pocketed the handkerchief, he dropped a kiss on the spot he'd just cleaned.

"Come on," he growled. "Let's go up to the house and take care of those scratches."

Twenty minutes later Thia sat on the padded bench in front of her dressing table while Luc applied antiseptic to the scratches on her back.

His touch was soothing, yet oddly exhilarating. After a refreshingly cool shower, her still-damp hair was tucked into one towel and her body was swathed in another, which she had fashioned into a sarong, and at first Luc's hands felt hot enough to scorch her water-chilled skin. But as they gradually warmed her, she felt herself relaxing, lulled by his gentle ministrations.

"Lower the towel a little, will you?" he said. "I can't quite reach all of the scratches."

Without giving his request a second thought, she loosened the fold of terry cloth at her bosom so that the towel slipped almost to her waist in back, and Luc began applying the cream to an especially sensitive spot beneath her shoulder blades.

"Ouch," she complained mildly. "That smarts."

"Sorry. You've got a nasty bruise here." He stroked the medicine on more gingerly than before. "All right now?"

"Mmmm," she murmured, swaying into his touch to guide his hand to another bruise. She heard Luc's ragged intake of breath and glanced at him in the mirror. "Is something wrong?"

"Nope. This tube of ointment's about had it. That's all."

"There's a new one in the medicine cabinet. I'll get it."

"No, don't move." Before she could get to her feet, Luc gripped her upper arms, urging her to remain seated, enforcing his directive with unwarranted strength, and Thia wondered fleetingly if he found her near nudity disturbing.

No, she thought, studying his reflection, *that's absurd.*

The towel was more modest than her bathing suit. It was even more concealing than the shorts and halter she'd been wearing in the greenhouse, and Luc hadn't seemed the least bit disconcerted while she'd worn them. He wouldn't meet her eyes because he was concentrating on squeezing the last dab of medicine onto his palm, and that's all there was to it.

Stop imagining things, she told herself firmly. Besides, worrying required too much effort, and the warm random patterns Luc was tracing on her back had sapped the last of her energy. As he continued the massage, working at the tight knots of tension at the nape of her neck, a peculiar lethargy stole over her. Thia's eyelids drifted shut, and she went bonelessly limp beneath his hands.

But Luc's next question made her wonder if he might have seduction on his mind after all.

"Where's Celia?" he asked.

Thia's head jerked upright, her eyes opened wide, and she encountered his gaze in the mirror. Making light of her turbulent emotions, she smiled and wrinkled her nose at him.

"Why do you ask? Are you afraid I might corrupt your virtue?"

"Not at all," said Luc, completely deadpan. "I know I can rely on you to be honorable, Thia. It's just that I'd like to know how much time we have."

"Why?"

Luc answered with an eloquent lift of an eyebrow.

In a small, prim voice, she said, "My back feels fine now. Surely it won't take you much longer to finish—"

"That depends." Luc spoke in a slurred, silky drawl, but the uncompromising jut of his chin told her that he would not be distracted from his question. "Where's Celia?" he repeated.

Thia fidgeted uneasily. "Playing tennis."

"Then I take it she hasn't found a job yet."

"No, not yet."

The towel had slipped lower over her bosom, exposing a nearly indecent expanse of the rounded rise of her breasts. She tried to hitch the terry cloth higher, but that only called Luc's attention to her plight. His hands froze, fingers splayed across her shoulders, while his glance strayed over the flawless honey-gold slopes with a hot-eyed languor that seemed to strip the towel away.

Thia couldn't tear her gaze away from the couple reflected in the mirror. It was as if she were watching Luc and herself in a dream, and her voice was breathy with excitement as she murmured, "She's thinking of starting her own business."

"Who is?" Luc inquired absently.

"Celia. Jobs are so scarce—"

"Why are you whispering?"

"Why are you?"

Luc shook his head and smiled. His dark eyes were beguilingly soft, but his grip on her had tightened until his fingertips dug into her skin. For several seconds after he lifted his hand to unwind the towel from her hair, the imprint of his fingers remained clearly outlined on her shoulder. He tossed the towel across the foot of the bed, and his strangely disjointed movement freed Thia from her inertia.

She tilted her head back to look at the flesh-and-blood man rather than his mirror image, and slight as it was, this simple shift of focus added a compelling new dimension to her perceptions.

A sudden rush of sensory impressions overwhelmed her. The awareness of textures and shadings and scents was captivating. Where before she had felt the pressure of Luc's hands upon her, now she was conscious that Luc had left his suit coat and tie in the living room. He had rolled back his shirt-sleeves and loosened the top buttons of his shirt, and the smooth dusky skin at the base of his throat shone with a fine film of perspiration.

She was conscious that only the lightweight fabric of Luc's trousers separated his thighs from her naked back, and she could not distinguish between his spasm of anticipation and her own uncontrollable trembling.

The air in the room was permeated with the musky odor of desire. It shimmered with passion. Her skin tingled as an enervating wave of heat swept through her.

It left her weak and dizzy, and when she closed her eyes, she saw a psychedelic spectrum of color.

She realized that Luc had pulled her to her feet and was embracing her from behind, holding her close against him so that his hands were free to caress her breasts. Her pulses leaped wildly, and when she opened her eyes, the dazzling colors still zigzagged in front of them.

"I feel so funny, Luc," she murmured brokenly. "I feel as if I'm on a high."

He nipped delicately at her earlobe and traced its shell-like convolutions with the tip of his tongue. His warm breath fanned her skin as he countered, "You feel beautiful. Wonderful. Perfect."

Velvet, she thought. *His voice is rich brown velvet.*

Her hands clutched the towel to her bosom convulsively. "Do you suppose there was something wrong with that ointment?"

"No, my lovely golden girl." Luc laughed deep in his throat and nuzzled the side of her neck. "I think everything's very right—or it will be if you'll just let go of that towel."

She met his gaze in the mirror and saw that one of his hands had settled over both of hers, urging them to relax their grip.

"From what I've seen of you, your skin is the color of honey," he went on thickly, "and I've got an irresistible urge to know if you're the same sweet color all over."

Drugged by his nearness, Thia allowed her hold on the towel to slacken. She half turned in his arms and raised one hand to touch the crease between his eyebrows, lightly smoothed a fingertip over the lines to erase them. She followed the bridge of his nose to his mouth, and for an instant her hand hovered indecisively in midair. She wanted to trace the sensuous curve of his mouth, but in the second she hesitated, she lost her nerve.

Thia's arms fell to her sides, and Luc hurriedly dispensed with the tuck that kept her makeshift sarong in place. In less than a moment the towel had whispered down the length of her body to the floor, and Luc's gaze wandered freely over the perfection he'd unveiled.

"Beautiful," he crooned. With his hands on her waist, he turned her so that they stood face to face. "My God, but you're lovely!"

He breathed the praise huskily, almost reverently, for it seemed inadequate for a woman so exquisitely formed. She was small, yet delicately voluptuous, and her skin had the fine creamy translucence of a pearl.

And she was his! He knew it, and he exulted in the knowledge.

Slowly, as if he had all the time in the world, his hands moved to cup the fullness of her breasts. As his thumbs drew provocative, feathery designs over the proud coral peaks, teasing them to tautness, he observed hoarsely, "You're not quite the same color all over."

Luc's admiring appraisal of her body had fanned the flames of Thia's excitement even before he'd touched her, and now his lips found hers with an impatience that matched her own, and as she opened her mouth to receive the soft invasion of his tongue, desire flared out of control.

Thought was impossible. Resistance was impossible. Restraint was impossible. She could only savor his touch and the taste of his kisses and abandon herself to the riotous, glorious, primitive need he had created within her.

With shaking hands she worked at his shirt buttons, eager for the feel of him, and when she had undone the last button, his arms closed about her and crushed her tight against his chest.

"You taste like honey too," he marveled, and they kissed again, their mouths seeking and sampling, hungrily feasting, almost devouring in their urgency.

While she fumbled with his belt, with the zipper and snap on his trousers, baring his body for her pleasure, his hands played over her body in a series of bold, fiery caresses, lingering to explore the undercurve of her breasts, the hollow of her waist, her gracefully rounded thighs and the shadowy valley between them, finally molding themselves to her derriere and lifting her onto her tiptoes, fitting her hips possessively to his.

Thia was only vaguely aware that Luc had lifted her completely off her feet until he toppled her onto the bed. Even as he peeled off the last of his clothing, she drew him down beside her. She seemed to see him through a roseate haze, but when her arms opened wide to enfold him, she discovered that in other ways her senses had never been more acute.

The brush of hands, the moist glide of lips, the silky friction of naked flesh with naked flesh, the hushed voices and ragged breathing, the sound of hearts racing in unison, were like an aphrodisiac that bound them together in a single volatile need. Their limbs entwined and suddenly they were tangled together, straining to be even closer, laughing and kissing and touching as joyfully as children.

But there was nothing remotely childlike about the hard masculine body that covered hers, pressing her into the mattress. She ran her palms over his rugged shoulders, along the sinewy ridges of muscle at either side of his spine, and when her hands found his sleek, taut buttocks, she rejoiced in his maleness.

His stubbly chin grazed her breasts, and the rasp of his beard against her skin excited her beyond endurance. She reveled in the sensuous abrasion of his tongue as he coaxed her nipples to tender points, in the hotly persuasive hands that knew exactly where to touch her to give her the most delicious pleasure, in the mouth that demanded her response and gave her ecstasy wherever he kissed her.

And he kissed her everywhere, touched her everywhere, explored every part of her and made it his own. Desire escalated. It quickly became explosive; immeasurable and undeniable.

"Honey," he sighed as he entered her. "Sweet as honey."

In a voice rough with passion he whispered endearments and described the ways he wanted to make love to her, but his movements were measured and gentle, allowing her body time to conform to his, and his control delighted and tormented her.

Her body writhed feverishly beneath the intimate burden of his weight; wanting him, needing him. She wrapped her legs around his waist and arched her hips to his, inviting him to bond them together.

"Please," she gasped. 'Please, Luc."

He supported his weight on his elbows and held her face between his hands, and she stared into the dark, liquid depths of his eyes.

"What, sweetheart? Tell me what you want."

"More. I want more...."

Her voice failed her, and she mouthed the supplication soundlessly, but Luc read the plea on her lips. He saw the invitation in her eyes and he plunged deep, so that he was enveloped by her softness. And then, with a hoarse cry of triumph, with intoxicating kisses and wild caresses, he gave her delights she'd never dreamed existed. He gave her everything she'd ever wanted.

Chapter Eight

Although Thia never accepted Luc's proposal in so many words, after that afternoon of lovemaking her doubts seemed irrelevant. For a long time they lay in each other's arms, their bodies nestled together, heads on the same pillow.

Speaking in whispers, Luc confided in her. He told her of his hope and plans for the future, and she felt an intimacy with him, a oneness that she had never felt with anyone else. She felt a closeness that was more than merely physical, and she knew that in the act of giving him her body, she had also given her vows. Her fate was sealed.

In some mystical way her new receptiveness must have communicated itself to Luc, for both of them understood that she would marry him.

By the time Celia arrived home that evening, Thia had arranged a light supper of salads and cold cuts on the dining-room buffet. Celia's eyes lit up when she saw the frost-beaded pitcher of iced tea, and she paused to pour herself a glass and drink half of it before she wandered into the kitchen, looking for Thia.

Holding the chilled glass against her perspiring forehead, she called, "This is just what I needed. You're a lifesaver, Sis. It's hot as Hades..."

She trailed into silence when she saw that Luc was with Thia, sitting on a stool behind the breakfast bar, shirtless but totally at ease, while Thia spread some sort of cream on his back.

With a haste that betrayed her nervousness, Thia asked, "How was your tennis match?"

"We lost. I had the rotten luck to draw Cheryl Gallagher as a partner, and her mind wasn't on the game. All she can talk about is natural childbirth."

While she spoke, Celia studied her sister and Luc and wondered what Thia had to be nervous about. Then she saw the droplets of water that glistened in Luc's dark hair and in Thia's wispy curls, and she chided herself for being overly suspicious.

"Been swimming?" she inquired.

"No," Luc replied.

He was completely unscathed by the speculative gleam in Celia's eyes, but Thia started and dropped the tube of ointment. As she bent over to pick up the medicine, Celia moved farther into the room, stopping when she saw the scratches on Luc's shoulders.

"Heavens!" Celia exclaimed. "You look as if you've tangled with a wildcat."

"I did," Luc said with a grin.

Thia turned brick red and dropped the tube of ointment again, and as she picked it up the second time, Celia saw the condition of her sister's back.

"For goodness' sake," she drawled, tilting her head to one side. "What on earth have the two of you been up to?"

Belatedly it occurred to her that Thia looked as if she didn't know whether to throttle her or run out of the room to hide her embarrassment.

"Oh my God!" Celia cried as comprehension dawned.

Her own face grew warm as she recognized the extent of her blunder. "Please, forgive me. I'm not usually so dense about these things. If I'm interrupting anything, just say the word and I'll leave."

"No, Celia. Stay." As if he'd guessed that Thia was about to take flight, Luc slipped his arm about her waist. "Your timing couldn't be better. In fact, it's perfect."

Celia stared at him incredulously, and Thia muttered, "Speak for yourself, Luc."

Chuckling, he tightened his arm about Thia's waist, anchoring her securely to his side. For as long as he was the only unembarrassed person in the room, he had the upper hand, and he intended to make the most of it. He felt like crowing, but he managed to confine himself to a contented grin as he said, "Thia and I would welcome your opinion."

"My opinion?" Celia echoed.

"About what?" Thia asked sharply.

"Come on, honey. Don't be coy." Luc winked at Thia, attempting to placate her, but she repeated, "About what?"

Please, Luc, don't do this, she silently pleaded. *Don't tell Celia just yet.*

Perhaps it was selfish not to want to share her newfound happiness with anyone but him, but the unspoken commitments they'd made, their feelings for one another, were so tenuous, so fragile and new, that she wanted them to remain private, at least for a little while. She wanted a quiet time to savor the knowledge that she would be Luc's wife. She wanted to hug their secret to herself and anticipate spending the rest of her life with Luc.

It became apparent that Luc had misinterpreted her silent message. He must have mistaken her reticence for shyness, because his grin slowly broadened, and he said, "I'd like Celia's advice about our wedding, of course. What else?"

"Wedding!" Celia stared at Thia with open astonishment. "Does that mean you and Luc are getting married?"

"That's right," Luc answered. "I hope you approve."

"Oh, I do," Celia said. "I most definitely approve. It's just that this is such a surprise. Thia's never been at all interested in marriage—"

"Maybe not before, but she is now," Luc cut in.

"I wish," said Thia, "that you two would stop talking as if I'm not here."

Her irritation evaporated when Luc gave her a heart-melting smile and murmured, "Sorry, sweetheart."

"Have you told Mother?" asked Celia.

Thia shook her head. "You're the first to know."

"Then this calls for a celebration." Smiling, Celia saluted them with her glass of iced tea. "Have you set the date?"

"Not yet," Thia replied grudgingly.

She averted her eyes, and when her gaze fell upon Luc's scratches, her blush deepened. Until twenty minutes ago they had been too busy making love to concern themselves with anything practical. Earlier, while they'd showered, Luc had teased her affectionately about the marks she'd left on his skin, and she had retaliated by teasing him because he'd neglected to dry his back after his shower.

"There are times," she'd declared, "when I think you don't believe in anything you can't see, including your own backside!"

"Drives you wild, doesn't it?" Luc replied with a leer. "C'mon now, confess."

Thia had made a face at him, and in reprisal he'd lunged at her; and before she had been able to elude him, he'd lassoed her with his towel and dragged her close against him, and in the moment their damp, naked bodies collided, both of them had forgotten about getting dressed.

They hadn't forgotten how little time they had, though. They knew that Celia could return at any minute, and they'd made love with one eye on the clock, fervently, with a haste that intensified their excitement, and afterward they had hurried into their clothes and prepared supper. But even then they'd kept up an almost constant barrage of kisses and touches and occasional quick embraces, so that the languorous afterglow of love had not faded.

But if she was woefully unprepared to come back down to earth, Luc had made the transition easily, and Thia found that she resented his sudden shift from the romantic to the matter-of-fact.

Her spirits had plummeted, and she felt depressed and slightly disoriented. She listened with a growing sense of unreality as he and Celia discussed churches and music and flowers and caterers.

If either of them had asked her, she would have told them she preferred a simple civil ceremony, because a big church wedding seemed so complicated. Just for starters, her mother might insist that Vernon officiate, and she didn't even want to invite her cousin to the wedding. He might be a changed man, but she still did not like him.

Luc and Celia's debate went on and on, and Thia

wanted to shout at them to stop it, but she couldn't force the words past the lump in her throat. Her spirits sank even lower, and they hit bottom when Luc said, "Unfortunately, I'm going to be pretty well tied up with business till the end of September. We've decided to lease the inn to a health-spa chain, and that means I'll have to wait till remodeling is underway before I'll be able to get away for a honeymoon."

"How about the first Saturday in October?" Celia inquired. "Would that give you enough time to get things squared away?"

"If there aren't any snags," Luc replied.

"Then to be on the safe side, maybe we'd better make it the middle of the month," Celia suggested.

Luc nodded, and Thia felt bereft because he had removed his arm from about her waist and withdrawn behind an expressionless mask. His attitude was impersonal and businesslike as he watched Celia leaf through the calendar. Finally she uncapped a Day-Glo marker, drew a bright-red circle around Saturday, October thirteenth, and laughingly inquired, "You're not superstitious, are you?"

"No." Luc grinned and shook his head. "Not about dates anyway."

"Well, I am," Thia asserted so vehemently that Luc and Celia looked at her as if she had taken leave of her senses. "Oh, not about the thirteenth," she went on more calmly. "You might think it's hopelessly sentimental, but I'd like to at least be consulted about the date of my own wedding."

Celia's face was stricken, and even Luc had the grace to look sheepish. Both of them started to apologize, but Thia rushed on, speaking directly to him.

"The fall just happens to be one of the busiest times of year at the nursery, so if the wedding is any time before Thanksgiving, you'll have to honeymoon without me."

Horrified, Celia exclaimed, "Surely you're not going to insist on working here after you're married?"

"Naturally she is," said Luc.

"You bet your sweet life I am," Thia declared, and silently qualified, *if* I can keep the business solvent that long. *If* I can manage to stay afloat without Duffy Langtry's assistance.

She glanced at Luc, and when she saw the tender amusement in his eyes, her annoyed scowl warmed to a tentative smile. She leaned over to whisper, "I love you, Luc," and give him a quick kiss on the ear, only to have him brush her aside as if he were brushing aside an insect.

This reaction was not at all what she would have expected from the man who was capable of marathon kissing sessions in the bedroom, but after a brief moment of hurt, she realized that he must dislike public displays of affection, and she decided not to take the rebuff personally.

She had intended to promote the kind of ceremony she wanted, but then she remembered the confidences he'd shared with her. Did he hope to repay some of his social obligations with a formal wedding and elaborate reception? Did he want to impress his colleagues? And if he did, was that so very wrong?

No, Thia told herself. Because the rituals weren't important. What mattered were the pledges they would make to one another.

Having arrived at this conclusion, Thia decided that

for the time being she would forget her other demands and try to negotiate a more convenient date.

"Any objections to the end of November?" she asked Luc softly.

"Only one," he replied.

"Which is?"

"I'm a patient man, Thia mia, but I'm not that patient. I don't like waiting so long to marry you. Not when I've already waited half my life."

"But you will wait." Somehow, Thia felt certain of that, even before Luc nodded gravely and said, "If I have to."

She didn't actually ask him how long he was prepared to wait, but he continued as if she had posed the question, saying, "I'll wait just as long as it takes, sweetheart. If I have to, I'll wait till hell freezes over and we have to hobble down the aisle a step ahead of Old Nick himself."

The following week was a busy one. Thia and Luc saw each other only in snatches and had almost no time alone. Luc managed to make it to the Friday-night dinner with the Mulhollands, but even then the pressures of business forced him to leave early.

His schedule was filled with laying the groundwork for the remodeling at the inn, and his days and evenings were given over to reviewing bids from various subcontractors and appointments with the owners of the properties neighboring the inn.

Much as Thia wished he would set aside an hour or so to be with her, she couldn't fault his concern for the public image of Domini Developers—not with her insider's knowledge of public relations. And besides, she had her own problems to contend with.

Duffy Langtry's arthritis had flared up again, which meant that she was doing double duty at the nursery. And to make matters worse, her floral designer left without giving any notice at all. She and Kate extemporized, filling in as well as they could, but the additional hours imposed a hardship on both of them.

After one especially trying day, Thia told Celia, "If I don't find another designer soon, I'm afraid Kate will quit too."

"Why?" Celia asked. "Has she said something about leaving?"

"No, she hasn't even complained. But she puts in long hours without the extra work load."

"I thought you'd had a good response to your ad," said Celia.

"We've had at least a dozen applicants. The trouble is, none of them has had any experience arranging flowers. Kate claims they can't tell a tulip from a daffodil, and I don't know where I'm going to find the time to train anyone. Lately there aren't enough hours in the day as it is."

"How about giving me a crack at it?"

Taken aback by her sister's proposal, Thia stared at Celia. After a long silence, she said, "That's odd. I could have sworn you just asked for a job."

"I did," Celia returned. "Your ears aren't playing tricks on you, Thia. I give you my word, I'm completely serious about this."

"I can see that you are, but I don't understand why. You must realize that I can't afford to pay much."

Celia shrugged. "Let's just say that I've lowered my sights a bit."

"Quite a bit, I'd say."

"Have it your way. The thing is, I've been job hunting for a month now. Long enough to figure out that with my limited skills, I can't realistically expect to earn the kind of salary I'd like. But I'm also aware that I have certain things going for me—"

"I know you do, Celia."

"I'm good with people," Celia went on crisply, as if Thia had argued the point, "and I have an eye for color and proportion. And although I hate grubbing about in the nursery, I do adore flowers. With a little experience, I think I could be a damned good floral designer, besides which, I'm willing to try almost anything. You could interview people for a year, and not find anyone as willing as I am."

Thia sighed. She didn't doubt her sister's willingness, but she did question her perseverance. And with good reason. When they had been children, how often had Celia thrown herself into some new endeavor only to lose interest when the going got rough?

Of course, it was possible that this time Celia would carry through. She seemed very conscientious about fulfilling her obligations as chairman of the Dance Committee, and she hadn't let her lack of job offers discourage her, and those were hopeful signs.

Everyone's entitled to the chance to prove herself, Thia reminded herself, and despite her lackluster track record, Celia was no exception.

"Okay," Thia said cautiously. "I'll concede that you're willing, but what guarantee do I have that you won't change your mind after the first month? I mean, we're not talking about some high-powered career here. As I said a minute ago, the hours aren't the greatest, and the pay's lousy—"

"I'm not saying I'll stay on forever, but I'd be as

permanent as anyone you could hire off the street, and I promise that when I do give notice, I'll stay long enough to train my successor. So what have you got to lose, Thia? I'm your sister, and I may be taking advantage of that, but that's the only advantage I'm taking.''

Thia waved one hand dismissively. "That goes without saying, Celia. I never thought you'd give the job anything less than your best. If you want to know the truth, I'm afraid that if I agree to your working for me, I'll be the one taking unfair advantage.''

"Well, don't be. I can look out for myself.''

Can you really? Thia wondered. *And if you can, do you honestly want to look out for yourself, or are you still hoping that Prince Charming will come riding out of the sunset on his snowy-white charger and rescue you from a life of independence?*

While Thia tried to come up with the answers to her questions, Celia gave her something else to think about.

"Before you make up your mind," she said quietly, "I wish you'd consider this. For the past few weeks, you've been helping me, and you haven't asked for anything in return. Now I have an opportunity to repay your kindness, and I think you should let me return the favor.''

"No one's keeping score, Celia. It's not necessary.''

"It is for me. Look, Thia, I know you're proud. I know you don't like to feel indebted to anyone. But I have my pride too, and even if it goes against the grain to let me do this for you, I think you owe it to me.''

It did go against the grain. Thia was surprised to realize how much. But personal feelings aside, Celia's argument seemed irrefutable. And finally, although she remained unconvinced that the arrangement would work out, Thia agreed to give her sister a trial.

Although Thia and Luc had arrived at the point of making wedding plans, Luc didn't feel the full impact of their engagement until the afternoon he picked up Thia's ring from the jewelry store. He was writing a check to pay for the diamond when all at once, right there in Paul Searle's showroom, he was struck by the awareness that within a few months Thia would be his wife.

Damned if it's not really happening, he thought. *We're actually getting married!*

His signature wavered drunkenly across the bottom of the check, and he glanced at the jeweler, hoping that Mr. Searle hadn't noticed how shaken he was.

The twinge of anxiety passed as quickly as it had overtaken him, however, and in the next instant he could scarcely contain his elation. He felt as tough and triumphant as he had as a kid when he'd scored the winning touchdown at the homecoming game.

He wanted to laugh and clap the jeweler on the shoulder and tell the man how lucky he was. He wanted to tell the world what a charmed life he led.

Instead, he gave Mr. Searle a dopey grin as he handed him the check. He pocketed the ring and said good day and left the store with a spring in his step. But when he reached the sidewalk, he spotted a sign in the shop window that proclaimed, "A diamond is forever."

Panic returned as he admitted to himself that, aside from lovemaking, he didn't know the first thing about being a husband.

What will she expect of me? Luc wondered. *Whatever*

she expects, can I give it to her? And what if I can't? Is love enough to keep us together till death do us part, or have I been kidding myself all these years?

Chapter Nine

On the Sunday before the Founders' Day Dance, Luc and Thia had dinner with Denise. Luc had made reservations at the Stag and Hare, the Olde English pub and restaurant that was Stratford's most exclusive, and Thia prepared for the evening carefully.

She needed all the confidence she could muster, because she was worried that her mother might create a scene.

It would not have been the first time Denise had resorted to a show of temperament to get her own way. Years before, out of jealousy, rage, and sheer orneriness, she had used precisely those tactics with Thia's father. But as it turned out, on this night Thia's fears were groundless.

Once they were seated at their table, Thia relayed Celia's regrets for not being able to join the party, and Denise accepted her older daughter's apologies graciously.

"How's Celia working out as your floral designer?" she asked.

"She's a natural," Thia replied enthusiastically. "She has a flair for design, and she's terribly conscientious, which is why she couldn't be here tonight. She asked me to tell you that since she has to get up with the sun, she's taken to going to bed with it too."

Denise shook her head with wonderment. "That doesn't sound at all like the Celia I know, but I must say I find it encouraging."

While Thia puzzled over her mother's remark, wondering if Denise had deliberately goaded Celia into striking out on her own, Denise concentrated on Luc. After some preliminary verbal sparring, during which each of them took the other's measure without once overstepping the bounds of propriety, Luc commented that he'd heard that Denise was president of the Historical Society.

"Cassie Bennett told me that you're responsible for saving the inn," said Luc, and Denise agreed that she had staved off efforts to tear down the building almost singlehandedly.

This led to the discovery that they had a common interest in preserving the pioneer heritage of Stratford, and after that they got along amazingly well; so well that Thia couldn't help thinking that her engagement ring might have prompted her mother's atypical amiability.

Luc had given her the ring only the night before. The blue-white, emerald-cut diamond was large enough to impress, yet not so large as to seem gaudy. With its simple white-gold setting, the ring was in perfect taste, but Thia felt self-conscious about wearing it. Its elegance seemed out of place on her capable hand, and every time she looked at the stone, she wondered whether it symbolized Luc's affection for her or his own success.

If Luc had consulted her, she would have told him all she wanted was a wedding band. She rarely wore jewelry, and she was inclined to be careless with the few pieces she owned. She'd lost count of the number of earrings she'd misplaced, and she was too afraid she might lose the engagement ring to relax while she was wearing it. But Luc hadn't bothered to ask, and he'd presented her with the jeweler's box so proudly, grinning like a kid on Christmas morning, that she couldn't bear disappointing him.

She had accepted the ring, she hoped gracefully, and she supposed that, given time, she would become accustomed to wearing it. In the meantime she felt horribly petty for questioning Luc's motives in giving her such a costly bauble. And it didn't help that when she had confided in her sister, Celia had exclaimed disgustedly, "Come off it, Thia! I wish I had your problems, and so would most women."

Thia readily acknowledged that Celia had a point. Having been given so much, she was annoyed with herself for wanting Luc's love as well, yet she couldn't seem to turn off her skepticism.

And so, although she was happy that Luc had won her mother's approval, she was pleased that Denise seemed interested in establishing an easy rapport with her future son-in-law, Thia was appalled to find herself scrutinizing every expression and analyzing each gesture, searching for signs of hypocrisy on both their parts.

What's in it for them? the skeptic in her wanted to know, while the realist warned her not to study Luc too closely, because she was certain to find traces of whatever she was looking for, and the romantic argued that she loved Luc too deeply to be influenced one way or the other, no matter what she found.

Luc threw his head back and laughed at something Denise had said, and he looked so vital, so rugged and appealing with his gypsy-dark eyes and white flashing smile and the silvery hair at his temples gleaming in the lamplight, that simply looking at him made Thia's heart skip a beat.

What if you are just another asset to him? she asked herself. *What if he does see you as a socially adept hostess who can be relied on to use good table manners? What if your primary function in his life will be to dress up and look decorative and expensive when the occasion calls for it? Why not admit how flattering that is and be satisfied? Isn't that enough?*

The romantic in her insisted that it wasn't enough but dared to hope for more, and the realist knew that she wanted Luc so much that she would settle for whatever she could get. And in the end the realist had the last word, for Denise was standing beside Thia's chair, speaking to her. Thia's musings ground to a sudden stop, and she looked up at her mother inquiringly.

"Did you say something to me?"

"I did, but you were worlds away." Although Denise clucked her tongue reproachfully, a smile twinkled in her eyes. "I asked if you'd care to come to the powder room with me."

Thia rose and followed after her mother as, taking her agreement for granted, Denise began weaving her way between the tables. She nodded to several acquaintances and called a greeting to a close friend, but once in the powder room she glanced about hastily, as if to assure herself that she and Thia had the place to themselves. Then she seated herself on one of the velvet-cushioned benches in front of the mirror.

"You've hardly spoken all evening," she observed softly as she removed her compact from her evening bag. "Is something wrong?"

"No," Thia replied without conviction. "Except—well, naturally I'm anxious for you and Luc to get along."

"Naturally," said Denise. "But tell me, Cynthia, would it have made any difference to you if we hadn't hit it off?"

"Yes, Mother, it would. You may find it hard to believe, but your approval means a great deal to me."

"Well, for whatever it's worth, you have it." Denise fluffed the feathery hair at the back of her head with her fingertips before she closed the compact and turned her attentions to her lipstick. Almost as an afterthought, she added, "I'm surprised you'd give any credence at all to my opinion."

"Mother! I know we don't always see eye to eye, but what a thing to say—"

"It's the truth, Thia. In case you haven't noticed, I'm not a terrific judge of men."

Thia sank down onto the bench beside her mother. "If you're thinking of Daddy—"

"It's not just your father, darling. Take Luc, for instance. Way back when you and he were in high school, I thought he'd never be anything but a ruffian, and now look at him! Then there's Hoagy Jantzen. After your father and I were divorced, I set my cap for him. I wasted some of the best years of my life yearning after that man. I made a laughingstock of myself with my friends, and it's only lately that I've tumbled to the fact that he's attracted to young women—"

"But you're still young."

"Maybe by your standards, and certainly by mine, but not by Hoagy's." Smiling at her own foolishness, Denise dropped the tube of lipstick into her bag. "According to him, any female on the shady side of puberty is over the hill, so you can see what an idiot I've been."

"No, Mother. Not an idiot. Naive perhaps, but not an idiot."

"Call it what you will, Thia. The truth is, where men are concerned, I've got two strikes against me as it is. I've been wrong before, and I could very well be wrong about Luc."

"Whatever you think, I wish you'd tell me," Thia urged impatiently.

"Honestly, darling!" Denise stared at her daughter incredulously. "I can't believe you're interested in hearing my opinion of Luc."

"I am, though. Not necessarily as your daughter, but as one woman to another."

"But you've always been so self-sufficient. That's why I always encouraged you to become a career woman."

"Are you sure it wasn't because I was such an ugly duckling?"

"You were not an ugly duckling, Cynthia Jean, but at times you came dangerously close to being a silly goose!" Denise chided her astringently. "No, it was your damned independence that made me decide you'd never marry. Why, even when you were a tiny little thing just learning to walk, you wouldn't let me hold your hand."

"It's mostly a front, Mother."

"A front?" Denise repeated blankly.

"You know—when in doubt, fake it. Behave with confidence. Bluff your way through."

"But why?"

"I guess in the beginning I thought that acting as if I were in complete control would be the same as being in control."

"And now?"

"Now?" Thia smiled ruefully. "Maybe it's habit."

"And maybe you're more in control than you care to admit."

"Yes," Thia murmured. "Maybe I am."

"Too much independence can be awfully lonely," said Denise.

Thia's gaze shied away from her mother's and fell upon her ring. Beneath the pink-tinted lights that circled the mirror, the diamond sparkled brilliantly, burning with a thousand tiny blue-white flames. "And frightening," she amended shakily.

"And frightening," Denise agreed. She covered Thia's hand with her own. "I wish I'd known this before, dear. I might have been able to help you."

"Then help me now, Mother. I love Luc so much, it scares me."

Despite Denise's calming touch, Thia's hand had curled into a fist. Her face was pale with tension, and seeing this, Denise nodded knowingly.

"Yes," she said. "I can see that you're afraid, and I think I know why. It's because loving someone puts you in jeopardy. It gives the man you love a certain power over you. He can hurt you simply by not returning your love—"

"That's it, Mother! That's what I'm afraid of."

"Well, you needn't be. I'm convinced Luc loves you."

Sensing the qualification in her mother's tone, Thia prompted, "But?"

"I think," Denise began hesitantly, "that he's as reluctant to admit he's in love as you are, Cynthia. And I also think you're going to have to be prepared to understand a lot and forgive a lot more."

After a momentary pause, Denise went on more strongly, "Luc Domini is a man who desperately needs to prove something to himself, and until he succeeds, everyone and everything else will have to take a backseat to that need."

"Including me?" Thia inquired huskily.

"Yes, my darling daughter. Including you. Maybe even especially you. If they marry at all, men like Luc often choose to marry women who have outside interests of their own. I suppose it's because their work leaves them precious little time to entertain their wives."

Denise gave Thia's hand an encouraging pat as she added, "Unless I miss my guess, there'll be times when you'll feel horribly neglected. You'll have to have the wisdom of Solomon and the patience of Job, but I expect when all's said and done, you'll find Luc is worth it."

Suddenly Denise could not bear Thia's intensity. Her mouth drooped wearily as she got to her feet, and after giving herself a last critical look in the mirror, she smoothed her skirt over her hips and collected her evening bag.

"I'm glad we had this little chat," she said brightly. "But now I'd suggest we get back to the table before Luc decides we've deserted him."

Later that night, as Luc drove toward Denise's house, Thia basked in a warm glow of contentment. She was pleased by the way the evening had gone, and grateful to Luc for being so sweet to her mother.

Her spirits soared to a record high when they said good night to Denise, and Denise offered her cheek for Luc's kiss. But a few minutes later, her heart sank when she learned that Luc had to leave for Portland the next morning.

"Another board meeting," he explained as he drove through the soft summer darkness in the direction of the nursery. "You'll be happy to hear that we're considering moving the corporate headquarters to Stratford."

"How long will you be gone?" asked Thia.

"It's hard to say. I'd like to be back by Thursday, but it all depends on how well the meeting goes. If the board votes to relocate, I could get hung up for an extra day or two."

"Will you be back in time for the dance?"

"Wouldn't miss it." Luc slanted a grin at Thia as he parked near her front door. "I'll see you Saturday for sure, honey."

Thia would have reminded him to telephone, but thoughts of her conversation with Denise made her hesitate. *If he cares for you at all, he won't need the reminder to call,* an inner voice cautioned.

Better not press him, she decided. Besides, as Luc helped her out of the car, he seemed abstracted, as if his mind had already leaped ahead to the work week and was sifting through the business decisions he must make.

If only we could have some time alone, Thia thought wistfully. Aloud, she said, "I wish I could ask you to come in for a nightcap, but Celia's such a light sleeper—"

"That's okay." Luc caught both her hands with his and drew them to his shoulders. "Maybe next weekend..."

The rest of his words were inaudible, absorbed by her mouth as he kissed her. But even while he held her in his arms, Thia felt a new distance opening up be-

tween them, and she wished he were not so understanding about their shortage of privacy.

Every time they seemed to be on the brink of recap-
turing the emotional intimacy they'd shared the afternoon they'd made love, she sensed Luc's withdrawal,
and it filled her with despair. She was jealous of the
long hours he devoted to his business, and she wondered if he ever envied the attention she gave the nursery.

Of course, what she really wanted was some sort of
reassurance that he cared for her, but she couldn't
muster the courage to ask him outright if he loved her.
A tight knot of panic gathered in her throat as she
asked herself, *What if he said he doesn't love me? What if
he feels nothing more than fondness for me?*

I'd marry him anyway, Thia realized, *and live on hope.*

"See you Saturday?" Luc whispered.

"Saturday," she promised.

She longed to cling to him, to hold him close and
never let him go, but instead her arms slipped away
from his neck. She stood in the shadows on the porch,
watching him walk toward the Porsche with his lithe,
springy stride, and she missed him even before he had
climbed into the car and driven away.

The time between this evening and next Saturday's
Founders' Day Dance seemed to stretch out endlessly.
But Thia had more than enough work to keep her busy.
And somehow she would get through it.

Chapter Ten

For reasons only indirectly connected to Luc's absence, by the time the nursery closed on Wednesday afternoon, Thia had cause to revise her assessment. How could she possibly survive the week when she wasn't even sure she could survive the next five minutes?

"First I had to replace the irrigation system. Then the cooler in the greenhouse went out. Then it was an outbreak of personnel problems, and now the transmission on the van's acting up," she told Celia. "I don't know where I'm going to find the money for the repairs, yet there's no way I can get along without the truck, so I'm caught between a rock and a hard place!"

Pausing for breath, Thia looked at her engagement ring and thought how ironic it was that Luc should have given her a diamond worth a small fortune while, with every passing day, the nursery seemed to move a step closer to bankruptcy. Perhaps the business had already passed the point of no return....

"If the bank doesn't come through with the loan I applied for today, I don't know where to turn next," Thia went on, "and if one more thing goes wrong—and it probably will!—I swear I'm going to throw in the towel."

"Maybe that's not such a bad idea, Sis, at least for tonight," Celia said mildly, glancing about the living room. "It would do you a lot of good to get away from this place for a while."

"But Luc might phone!"

"And, if you'll pardon my bluntness, he might not!"

"Be as blunt as you like," Thia returned bitterly. "I can take that, but I'm not sure I can forgive your honesty."

Celia repressed a sigh and tried a softer approach. "Look, Thia, even if Luc does call, it won't do any harm for him to be the one cooling his heels, wondering where you are for a change. If you ask me, he needs to learn that two can play that game."

"Are you implying that he takes me for granted?"

"No," Celia replied flatly. "I'm saying it straight out."

Thia frowned, but she had to admit that Celia's accusation was justified. Luc had not found the time to call till after ten o'clock on Monday night, and last night he hadn't called at all.

"You're right," she agreed glumly, "but we're going to be married, Celia. We're supposedly adults, and I don't believe in playing silly games—"

"Don't take me so literally. All I'm saying is that you need a break. For God's sake, Thia, you need to do *something* to take your mind off the nursery, even if it's only for a few hours."

"And what do you suggest I do?"

"Well, I've always found that treating myself to a really scrumptious addition to my wardrobe works wonders for my morale. How about going shopping for a dress for the dance?"

"After all I've told you about the difficulty I'm having meeting expenses, I shouldn't have to explain that I can't afford a new dress.''

"*Au contraire,* Thia! Now that you're engaged to Luc, you can't afford not to get one. He's a man of some prominence, so he has to present a certain image to the public, and as his future wife, so do you.''

"Get off the soapbox, Celia. That's a crock and you know it.''

Celia frowned at this flippant response, and it was her severity that restored some brightness to Thia's eyes.

"Anyway," Thia continued, "I have a whole closetful of clothes that I brought home from Portland. Some of them are practically new, and no one here in Stratford has seen most of them—''

A smile had supplanted Celia's frown. "Are they still in style?''

"They should be.''

"Then what are we waiting for?'' Celia cried gleefully, starting toward Thia's bedroom. "Let's take a look.''

An hour later they had nearly exhausted the supply of clothes in Thia's closet with their impromptu fashion show, and most of the garments were strewn across the bed. As Celia inhaled and sucked in her stomach so that she could close the zipper on the dress she was trying on, she said, "Doesn't this take you back? Remember how we used to play dress-up?''

Thia smiled at the breathless note in her sister's voice. "One thing I recall," she said, "is how much I envied you when we were younger.''

"Do you mean that?'' Celia asked.

"Well, sure I do. I envied you—along with most of the other girls in my class. I'm surprised you need to ask, Celia. You were so pretty and popular.''

Celia sat on the edge of the bed next to Thia and hugged one of the pillows to her chest. "I didn't feel pretty," she said. "I didn't feel enviable either. In fact, I used to wish I could trade places with you."

"With me? But why?"

"Because you never seemed to need anyone or give a damn whether the other kids approved of you."

"I did, though," said Thia.

"I know that now, but back when we were in high school—well, you know how teenagers are."

"Yes, Celia. I do."

"Anyway, I just wanted to tell you that I envied you every bit as much as you envied me. Maybe even more."

"Is that why you told Mother I was seeing Luc?"

Celia nodded and nervously smoothed her hands over the pillow slip. "I realize it's no excuse, but I had no idea how important Luc was to you, Thia, and I can't begin to tell you how ashamed I was afterward. I mean, I just wanted you to know—"

"Hey, Celia. It's forgotten. Nuff said?"

"Nuff said," Celia agreed. "But now I have another confession to make."

"What is it?"

"I'm afraid I've popped a seam on this dress."

Thia smiled and replied philosophically, "Oh well, I never really liked it much."

Celia got to her feet and began wriggling carefully out of the snug-fitting cocktail dress. Her face was intent as she replaced the dress on its hanger and inspected the damage she'd done to it. When she was satisfied that the tear could be mended, she put the cocktail dress away in the closet and collected the garments that were hanging from the back of the closet door.

All business, she turned to Thia and said, "At least we've narrowed the possibilities for the dance down to these two."

"Oh?" said Thia innocently. "Is that what we've been doing?"

But this time Celia did not rise to the bait. As if without interruption, she declared, "Naturally, you'll want your costume to make a statement, and either of these should do that, so all you have to do now is decide what sort of statement you want to make."

Although Thia tried to look properly impressed, she couldn't help grinning. "Sounds fantastic," she said, "but exactly what are my choices?"

"You can be youthful and bridelike or a woman of the world."

"And that's it?"

"That's it," Celia answered sternly.

"Are you sure I can't be a Dream Girl or a Movie Queen?"

Celia shook her head. She would not return Thia's smile, and Thia thought, *My God, she's really serious about this!* Wondering what had happened to her sister's sense of humor, she inquired hopefully, "How about a floozy with a heart of gold?"

"Sorry," said Celia. "We're fresh out of floozies— unless you want to change your mind and buy something new."

"No, I can't do that."

"I have a little money set aside. I could lend it to you—"

"No!"

"Then you have your choice of looking demure or sophisticated. Which one strikes your fancy?"

Neither, Thia answered silently, but she knew that a

negative response would never satisfy Celia. Not when she was in one of her imperious moods.

Sighing resignedly, Thia rolled onto her stomach, propped her chin in her hands, and studied the dresses Celia was displaying.

In her social-butterfly days, the frothy confection of black lace and organza had been her favorite. It was as comfortable as an old friend, because she'd had several memorable evenings wearing it and had come to regard it as her "lucky" dress. She had worn it often, and invariably it had made her feel outgoing, confident of her own attractiveness, and yes, sophisticated.

But did Celia honestly believe that the other selection was demure?

If she does, thought Thia, *she couldn't be more mistaken.*

Oh, it looked demure enough, but in this case appearances were deceptive, and she was surprised that a woman with Celia's clothes sense hadn't recognized that fact.

Bemused, Thia glanced from the peppermint-pink shift to her sister. Celia's grave expression told her that Celia hadn't been joking when she'd called the dress "demure," and Thia covered a smile with her hand as her gaze returned to the simple little nothing of a dress.

On the rack, on its hanger, or if its wearer remained absolutely motionless, the silk-jacquard frock looked modest, artless, and thanks to its color, sweet enough to make your teeth ache.

However, when Thia had first tried it on she had discovered that the bias-cut fabric did magical things for her figure. It floated and hinted and clung to her with her slightest movement so that, in its own inimitable and not too subtle way, the dress was a masterpiece of seduction.

In one sense it was artless, because its design made it impossible to hide anything. By bits and pieces, one curve at a time, it molded itself to her body, now revealing this graceful line, now that provocative roundness, and a moment later, that enticing dimple.

She had bought the dress on a whim, against her better judgment, and on the one occasion she had worn it, she'd made quite a dramatic impact on the men at the party she'd attended, although she'd done nothing more suggestive than inhale and exhale and take a few steps from one group of guests to another.

And this was the dress Celia called demure?

If Thia had had to define it with one word, the word she'd have chosen was "Wicked"!

Laughter bubbled up in her throat and threatened to escape as she wondered what it would be like to wear such a dress to a dance.

No doubt she'd create quite a stir. With the help of such a sensational outfit, she might even be the belle of the ball. But while that prospect would have delighted her in her wallflower days, now she was more discriminating.

She wanted to stir only one man. She wanted Luc to see her in a new light, to shock him into a greater awareness of her. She wanted to bewitch him, titillate his senses, fire his passions, shatter his control—

"Well?" Celia rattled the hangers and shook the dresses impatiently. "Which one will it be?"

"The black, I think," Thia decided.

"Excellent choice," Celia approved, and Thia nodded regretful agreement.

The black dress was certainly flattering, and probably it would be wise to save the other one for a private showing; to wear it just for Luc.

She envisioned his reaction if he were to see her in the peppermint-pink dress, and she could almost feel his hands caressing her through the silk. Her skin tingled as she imagined him removing the dress.

Thia remembered Luc kissing her, touching her, making love to her, and this led to thoughts of her own response. She imagined herself seizing the initiative, doing wild, seductive things that would drive Luc out of his mind, and in that instant she would have given everything she possessed for the nerve to throw caution to the wind and indulge the wanton side of herself, just for one night.

Chapter Eleven

A carnival atmosphere had overtaken Stratford. Overnight, as if by magic, the streets nearest the plaza had sprouted souvenir stands and booths selling corn dogs and hamburgers, cotton candy and soft drinks, pretzels and beer. Jugglers and acrobats, clowns, mimes, and other free-lance performers had found their way into town to entertain the Founders' Day crowds.

Thia closed the nursery early on Saturday. Business had been slow all week and there hadn't been a single customer all morning. She could only assume that everyone in town had gone to the centennial parade. And after the parade they would attend the barbecue and band concert in the park. And when the last dignitary had made the last flowery speech, the townsfolk would go on to the special presentation of *As You Like It,* or to the springboard diving exhibition or the bicycle races or the baseball game. The list of activities offered something for everyone and would continue all day and half the night.

When Thia made her delivery to the florist shop, Kate reported that she had a record number of orders to fill, but it was not surprising that on this centennial weekend no one was in the mood for gardening—including Thia.

As she loaded plants into the loaner van the Chevy garage had provided and drove toward the Warwick Inn, she wished that she were free to attend more of the festivities, but she knew she'd be too busy with the decorations to make it to anything but the dance.

Harry Lawlor, the shop teacher at the high school, had volunteered to supervise construction of the platform Thia had requested and install the lily pond and fountains. Aided by several of his students, he was just finishing up when she arrived.

"You've done a fabulous job," she told them.

It required only the smallest stretch of the imagination to see that they deserved the compliment. By daylight the artificial turf looked as plastic as it was. But by night, with the fountains splashing and the hundreds of miniature lights they had strung through the potted shrubs shining like stars through the foliage, the incline would look lovely.

Harry and his students stayed on to help Thia unload the van and rig up the standards for the hanging baskets. Even with their help, however, it was after six o'clock before the last plant was in place. While Thia floated gardenias on the lily pond, the boys cleared away the debris, and Harry swept the pathway that formed the main entrance to the ballroom.

"Do you think we should have roped off the path?" Thia asked.

"Nope. This platform's plenty solid." To illustrate how safe it was, Harry walked across the slope, stamping his booted feet with every step he took.

Thia arranged the last of the gardenias and stood up

to admire their handiwork. "I'm glad you thought of using that floor tile," she said to Harry.

The shop teacher leaned on his broom and squinted at the walkway, eyeing the herringbone brick pattern of the linoleum that covered it.

"Yep," he agreed laconically. "Looks good."

They tested the lighting and the fountains, and loaded the carpenters' tools and excess plumbing supplies into Harry's truck and the leftover lumber into the van, completing their chores in companionable silence.

The first of the musicians came trooping in with their instruments just as they left the ballroom, and Thia hurried home to grab a bite to eat and change clothes.

She found a note from Celia on the coffee table. "Luc called," it read, and beneath the message was a long row of ditto marks and the hastily penned comment, "Must be love! As you can guess from the number of times he called, he missed you a whole bunch last week. Says he'll pick you up at eight."

The last line made Thia bolt for the shower, for it was already seven fifteen. But halfway to the bathroom, she slowed to a walk.

"No, dammit," she muttered rebelliously as she stepped out of her jeans. "This is one night when I will not be rushed."

Tonight she was going to be seeing Mickie Lloyd for the first time in fifteen years. There would be other people at the dance she hadn't seen since high school, and she was going to take the time to look her best. If she wasn't ready when Luc got there, he'd just have to wait.

As it turned out she kept Luc waiting only ten minutes, and when he saw her in her lacy black dress, he seemed to think that she was worth waiting for. His dark eyes glowed with appreciation as he drew her into the warm circle of his arms and kissed her hello.

After a brief, tantalizing greeting, his mouth settled over hers with an urgency that told her more eloquently than words how much he had missed her during the past week, and she held on to him with her arms around his waist and returned his kiss with all of her own pent-up longing.

When the kiss ended, Luc rubbed his cheek against hers and said softly, "I—uh—I brought you a posy."

He released his hold on her to retrieve the white corsage box from the end table, and he seemed hesitant, even shy, as he opened the box and presented her with a spray of tiny, honey-colored orchids with ruby throats.

Thia gasped at their perfection. "Oh, Luc, how beautiful!"

"Do you really like them?"

"I love them. I can't tell you how much." Cradling the orchids close to her face, she inhaled their delightful perfume. "And they even have a fragrance."

Luc touched her cheek. "I was afraid giving you those would be like carrying coals to Newcastle."

She looked at him inquiringly. "Because of the nursery?"

Luc nodded.

"But the main reason I decided to take over the nursery is that I love flowers more than anything. And no one ever gives them to me...." At Luc's grin, she added, "Well, hardly ever."

Luc fastened the wristband so that the flowers lay against her lower forearm. They felt cool and velvety next to her skin, and they made her feel exotic and beautiful.

"They're not the right color for your dress," Luc said briskly, studying the overall effect, "but I chose them because they remind me of you."

"Oh, Luc—"

At a loss for words, Thia threw her arms around Luc and gave him a fierce hug, and when she moved away from him, her eyes were bright and her smile radiant.

Confronted with such naked gratitude, Luc chuckled self-consciously and pressed a kiss into each of her palms.

"I hoped you'd be pleased, Thia mia," he said, "but I had no idea you'd be this pleased."

It had occurred to him that Thia was more deeply touched by his gift of flowers than she had been by her engagement ring, and all at once he knew that she would never be contented with the superficial, that it would take more than material possessions to satisfy her. In this respect she challenged him as no other woman could, yet at the same time her emotional transparence seemed to invite an exchange of confidences.

Luc found her candor intriguing, endearing, and more than a little frightening. After a lifetime of keeping his own counsel, he doubted that he had it in him to share himself with anyone. He'd never intended to give anyone that degree of power over him, and although he loved Thia, and Lord knew he wanted her, the idea of trusting her with his innermost self filled him with dismay and an unfamiliar yearning. . . .

He was tempted to be completely open with her, dammit! Tempted enough that he recognized the potential danger and cautioned himself, *Take it easy, fella. If you're not careful, she'll have you totally defenseless.*

Aloud, he said abruptly, "We'd better be going, honey. Celia wants us in the receiving line."

Thia nodded, puzzled by his unexpected mood swing, and Luc smiled at her. But the smile did not reach his eyes.

Wondering at the change in him, she said absently, "Give me a minute to freshen my lipstick, and I'll be ready."

They stood next to Mickie Lloyd and Austin Cooke in the receiving line. Thia and Mickie met one another with squeals and hugs, while Austin and Luc looked on indulgently.

"My golly, look at you!" Mickie cried, her vibrant face wreathed with smiles. "You're gorgeous!"

"You always were good for my ego," Thia laughingly replied.

"It was mutual, kiddo. You believed in me when no one else did. There was a time when you were the only one who didn't make fun of me for wanting to be a singer."

"Well, you've certainly shown all of 'em how wrong they were!" Thia exclaimed. "Will you be singing for us tonight?"

"Try 'n' stop me," said Mickie. "Later—"

The band began tuning up just then, cutting short their conversation. Within minutes the first group of revelers had taken to the floor, and when the musicians struck up a medley of Glenn Miller tunes, more dancers came into the ballroom.

Thia smiled and offered pleasantries and shook hands with the most recent arrivals, but with one part of her mind she registered the fact that Mickie had linked arms with Austin Cooke.

As soon as the dance had gotten officially underway, they had been surrounded by well-wishers and autograph seekers, and now and again Mickie whispered some comment to Austin, but it was some time before Thia recognized that there was quite a lot more than affection between the striking brunette singer and the debonair, eminently distinguished Shakespearean actor.

Austin was at least twenty years Mickie's senior, but there was a kind of tender protectiveness in the way she touched his hand and tipped her head close to his, and when Austin Cooke looked at Mickie, his expression became almost worshipful.

After half an hour or so the band segued into its second set, and when the opening bars of "Stardust" swirled around them, Austin led Mickie onto the dance floor. By then it was obvious to Thia that, despite the difference in their ages, Mickie was very much in love with Austin Cooke. And it was also obvious that the feeling was mutual.

As he drew Mickie into his arms, Austin looked at her as if she were infinitely precious to him, and Thia experienced a twinge of emotion that felt suspiciously like envy.

Involuntarily, she glanced at Luc and wondered if he would ever look at her the way Austin looked at Mickie. Would he ever love her that much?

Grasping at straws, Thia told herself, *If Luc smiles at me in the next ten seconds, I have nothing to worry about.*

Smile at me, Luc, she pleaded silently. She willed him to turn toward her, but he was too preoccupied to glance her way. He was deeply engrossed in conversation with a stocky, bullet-headed man who reminded her of Daddy Warbucks in the *Orphan Annie* cartoons, and from the snippets of dialogue she overheard concerning "interest rates" and "amortization" and "return on capital," she assumed he must be a business associate of Luc's.

"It's Cynthia Sommers, isn't it?"

The question came from just behind Thia. She recognized the man's softly modulated voice even though she could not immediately place his face. His shock of sandy hair was vaguely familiar, as were his sea-blue eyes and perfect profile, but try as she might, Thia could not recall his name.

"You don't remember me, do you?"

"No," said Thia. "I'm sorry, but I don't."

The man's chuckle told Thia that his confidence was not even slightly dented.

"Good," he said smoothly. "That gives me the advantage."

Thia stole another glance at Luc, and when she saw that he had been surrounded by a new cluster of party goers, she smiled into the man's blue eyes and said, "I may not recall your name, but I'm sure you already have more advantages than you know what to do with."

"Oh, but I do know," the man replied. "For instance, I plan on using this one as leverage to persuade you to dance with me."

"You don't need leverage for that. All you need to do is ask."

"Well, in that case..." the man clicked his heels together and bowed gallantly over her hand. "May I have the pleasure of this dance, Miss Sommers?"

"You may, Mr.—" As he swept her into his arms, Thia studied the man's clean-cut features, but his identity still eluded her. "What is your name?" she asked.

"Barry Crippen. We met at Vernon's ordination."

"Good grief, so we did! I didn't recognize you without your—"

"Without my vestments?"

Flustered because she had been flirting with a minister, Thia missed a step, but Barry only laughed. When he saw that she was blushing, he pressed his cheek to hers and led her in a series of dizzying spins.

"Vernon's not here tonight, is he?"

"He's in Eugene," Barry said dryly. "You can relax, Cynthia."

"Call me Thia," she said, and Barry happily went along with her request. Now that the ice between them was broken, they talked together easily while they danced, until halfway through the band's rendition of "String of Pearls," when Craig Bleier, whom Thia had known since grade school, cut in.

After that Thia danced with a lot of men. Some were old acquaintances and some were relative strangers, but all of them claimed to be admirers. They complimented her so outrageously that her popularity might have gone to her head if only Luc had been among her partners.

But Luc spent more time talking shop than with her. Finally, when the bandleader introduced Mickie's number, Thia sought Luc out.

The house lights were dimmed and the spotlights were trained on Mickie. During her performance, Luc and Thia held hands under the cover of the darkness, and when Mickie sang of lost love and loneliness, Luc's grasp on Thia's hand tightened possessively. Her fingers were numb long before Mickie's song ended.

"Dance with me, Luc," she invited huskily once Mickie had taken her bows and the band was playing a romantic ballad.

Luc smiled sheepishly and let go of her hand. "I wish I could, Thia, but I never learned how to dance."

"Oh." For a moment she looked at him with consternation, then she wound her arms about his neck and moved her hips in time to the music so that her thighs brushed provocatively against his. She felt him tense and gave him a light, cajoling kiss on the lips. "It's easy," she murmured. "I'll teach you—"

"Some other time," Luc said shortly.

He pulled away from her, and Thia realized she had committed two separate blunders. Not only had she embarrassed Luc by embracing him in public, she had also forced him to admit the gap in his social education, and although she didn't pursue the issue, Luc's wounded pride had formed a barrier between them.

She tried to redeem herself by responding graciously as Luc introduced her to several of his colleagues. She put up such a convincing front that Luc didn't notice that her display of charm was forced. He seemed pleased that she had acquitted herself so well, but she felt like a fraud. She wished they could leave.

Celia drifted by, smiling as she danced in Brad Scofield's arms, and Thia couldn't help thinking that if Luc were to take her home now, they would have the house to themselves. Her pulses leaped at the thought of being alone with him, but talk had turned to business again, and Luc did not seem at all inclined to leave.

She caught a glimpse of Kate and Kenny Mulholland as they strolled past the French doors on the terrace. She waved at them, but for the moment they had eyes only for each other.

Mickie didn't stay long after she had finished her number. It was only ten thirty when she left, and while she waited for Austin Cooke to claim her wrap, she spied Thia and made a beeline to her side.

"Come see us tomorrow," Mickie urged.

Wondering if Mickie's "us" meant that she and Austin were a twosome, Thia hastily agreed. "Where are you staying?" she asked.

"The Wayfarer." Already on her way to the door, Mickie added, "Come for lunch. I'll order something from room service and we'll have a good ol' gossip."

Thia smiled and waved at her friend, but her smile faded when Mickie reached Austin Cooke and the actor leaned upon Mickie as if he hadn't the strength to support himself.

It was only for an instant. In the blink of an eye, Austin had regained his usual dignified bearing. If he hadn't looked so weary, Thia might have thought she'd imagined the incident.

Chapter Twelve

The formal announcement of Thia and Luc's engagement appeared in Sunday's paper. When Mickie let Thia into the Presidential Suite at the Wayfarer that afternoon, she demanded, "Why the heck didn't you tell me you're getting married? If I'd known, I'd have included your fiancé in my invitation."

Thia threw up her hands to ward off the rolled-up newspaper Mickie was brandishing and replied, "I hardly had the chance to tell you anything last night."

"You're right," Mickie allowed, somewhat mollified. "We didn't have much time last night. But today's a whole new ballgame, and you're not leaving here till you've told me all about Luc Domini."

"That," said Thia, "could take forever."

"Somehow I knew you'd say that." Mickie laughed and unfurled the paper. "This announcement reads like a Horatio Alger story that's been edited by E. F. Hutton."

"That's my mother's doing. When she puts her mind to it, she can be awfully thorough."

"But I'll bet your mama doesn't know everything about the man."

Mickie punctuated her comment with a wink, and much to her chagrin, Thia blushed.

"Aha! Just as I thought!" Mickie tossed the newspaper aside and consulted her dainty, diamond-studded wristwatch. Her eyes shone gleefully when she looked at Thia. "You'll have to stick to the highlights, because Austin's due back at three, but you've got about two and a half hours—"

Now it was Thia's turn to cry, "Aha! I thought there was something more than professional courtesy between you and Mr. Cooke."

Mickie didn't blush. She only smiled, and a trace of sadness dimmed the sparkle in her eyes as she said, "You always could see right through me, Thia Sommers."

"You can't hide love, Mickie. But I won't tell anyone if it's supposed to be a secret."

"Well, we're not ready to go public yet. My fans would have a fit if they found out we're having an affair, and Austin's fans would think he's gone completely bonkers. But we've been together for almost a year now. We've kept the press from finding out we're cohabiting, but the way we feel about each other isn't any secret."

"But something is," Thia observed quietly.

Although Mickie quickly turned away, Thia saw her blink back tears. "It's such a lovely day," Mickie remarked shakily. "I had the waiter set up our table on the balcony. Why don't we eat before our lunch gets cold? I went ahead and ordered the salmon for both of us. I hope you don't mind."

Puzzled by the abrupt way Mickie had changed the subject, Thia replied, "Salmon's fine."

"Then my reputation is safe." Mickie managed a

semblance of a laugh. "You'll never believe this, kiddo, but in certain circles, I'm known as quite a hostess."

"Why wouldn't I believe it?"

"Well, you know. In the old days I wasn't very social. Hell's bells! I was barely even housebroken."

"We were children, Mickie. No one's a great hostess at twelve."

"No, I suppose they aren't."

Mickie led Thia onto the balcony, and for the next two hours they sat at the luncheon table with its snowy linen, gleaming crystal, and silver chafing dishes. They drank most of a bottle of wine, but neither of them ate very much, and they hardly noticed the view of the mountains because they were too busy talking.

Thia began by answering Mickie's questions about Luc, and before long she found herself confiding in Mickie.

"My mother says to give Luc time. She says he has to prove something to himself. And my grandmother says he needs to be loved, but I don't think either of them realizes how self-contained Luc is, or how devoted he is to his work. Even when we're alone together something comes between us. It's as if part of him is holding back, watching and analyzing—"

"Always?" Mickie probed.

"No, not quite always," said Thia. "There was one time when he let down his guard and I felt really close to him. But mostly there's this—I don't know. This *distance* between us."

"That must be hard for you," Mickie murmured sympathetically.

"It is," Thia said with feeling.

"How do you account for Luc's remoteness?"

"What do you mean?"

"I hate to be the one to suggest this, Thia, but is it possible there's another woman?"

"I wish it were that simple."

Mickie expressed her surprise at Thia's reply by raising her eyebrows, and for a moment Thia was silent. Then she went on. "Sometimes I think that Luc doesn't care for me in a—a husbandly way. Then again, I think maybe he's a workaholic. Maybe it's just that his business comes first with him. And that scares the dickens out of me, because if his corporation is my rival, I don't have any idea how to compete."

"If there's not another woman, I don't think you need to compete," Mickie said slowly. "From what you've told me about Luc, I think he's testing you, kiddo, and probably himself as well. Furthermore, I think your mom and grandma are pretty darned astute. Given time and lots of loving, Luc will come 'round."

"Will he, Mickie?"

"I'd stake my life on it," Mickie replied emphatically.

Thia stared into her wineglass without really seeing the clear, light rosé. "If only I could be sure—"

"Listen, girl, have I ever given you a bum steer?"

"Not that I recall, but—"

"But me no buts, Thia. I'm right this time, too. I can feel it in my bones. Besides, I think I know what makes Luc tick."

"Do you, Mickie? Honestly?"

"Scout's honor," Mickie replied firmly.

"Tell me how you know."

"Well, Luc and I have certain things in common—"

"Such as?"

"Such as having our fathers run out on us. Such as

watching someone close to us turn into a lush. Such as growing up on the wrong side of the tracks. Believe me, Thia, it was no picnic. In my neck of the woods one of the first lessons a kid had to learn was not to trust anyone. And some of the things that happened to me when I first got into the music business reinforced that lesson. It's kind of a vicious cycle, because unless you're willing to rely on others, they can't show you how reliable they can be."

To illustrate her point, Mickie swirled the wine in her glass, setting off a miniature whirlpool, and Thia nodded. "I see what you mean," she said, and Mickie produced a tight little smile and took a sip of wine.

"Anyway," said Mickie, "by the time I met Austin, I was certain that the only one who gave a damn about me was me. It seemed as if everyone I ran into was out for what they could get. I mean, they all wanted a piece of the action. And I was suspicious because Austin was such a gentleman. All he did was treat me like a lady—me! Mickie Lloyd! He even calls me Michelle...."

Thia opened her mouth to comment, but Mickie rushed on. "I know a little bitty thing like that might not amount to anything to someone like you, kiddo, but it was enough to make me wonder what the heck he was after. It took ages, but finally it dawned on me that Austin simply is a gentleman. Treating women like ladies is as natural to him as breathing!"

Thia nodded thoughtfully. "I'm pretty sure I understand what you're saying, Mickie. As long as I'm honest with Luc—"

"That's it," Mickie cried. "Honesty, Thia. Even if it hurts. 'Cause it's for sure Luc's gonna know if you're putting him on. Honesty and patience—"

"And lots of loving," Thia finished, supplying the

last ingredient in Mickie's prescription. Smiling, she added, "I think I can swing that."

Mickie laughed and topped off the wine in Thia's glass. "Then you'll do okay, kiddo."

They talked about lighter topics after this. Mickie mentioned Austin's name so often that it became obvious to Thia that the actor was her friend's favorite subject.

Shortly before Austin was due to return, Mickie complimented Thia on the way the ballroom had been decorated, and Thia found herself telling Mickie about the nursery's financial woes. The bank had not approved her loan, and she was at her wits' end. The business was running on borrowed time, and she didn't know what to try next.

"What's your basic problem?" Mickie asked.

"Money," Thia replied flippantly, choosing to downplay her worries. "There's never enough of it at the end of the month."

"But what causes the shortfall?" Mickie persisted. "Is it cash flow or bad debts—"

Recognizing that Mickie was serious, Thia broke in, "The basic problem is that I'm undercapitalized. After Granddad's death, the business went downhill, and I didn't have enough of a cushion when I took over from my grandmother to see me through till the nursery started turning a profit. Then I discovered that Gran had deferred a lot of maintenance. I've had to invest in more repairs and new equipment than I'd counted on."

"Have you thought of taking in a partner?"

"Naturally I have, but the business is on such shaky ground. It's not what I'd call an attractive investment."

"Not unless you found a high roller who has the option of writing the loss off his taxes if the nursery goes under."

Thia smiled. "Now you sound like Luc."

"Have you discussed this with him?"

"No."

"Well, don't you think you should?"

Thia shook her head. "He's always so concerned with his own business interests."

"And when you're with him, you don't want to talk business."

"Not if I have the choice."

"Damn!" Mickie frowned. "I wish I was in a position to help you out, but I've got the meanest, tightfistedest financial adviser in the world—"

"That's just as well, Mickie," Thia broke in. "I couldn't let you take that kind of risk even if your adviser would."

"Which brings us back to Luc."

Thia pressed her lips together so that the generous curve of her mouth assumed a distinctly stubborn cast, and Mickie sighed and glanced pointedly at Thia's engagement ring.

"Look, kiddo," she said, "maybe I'm stating the obvious, but diamonds like that one don't come from Cracker Jack boxes."

"No," said Thia. "They don't."

"Then I'm right in thinking that Luc could solve your money problems with one stroke of his trusty pen?"

"He could," Thia replied stiffly. "If I asked him to, he probably would. But the cost might be too high."

Mickie looked at her sharply. "In other words, you're afraid he'll think you're marrying him for his money."

"Yes—no!" Thia drew in a deep, ragged breath. "I guess what bothers me is that I have no idea what he'd think."

"Are you sure there's not an element of pride involved?"

Before Thia could respond to Mickie's question, they heard the scrape of a key in the lock of the hall door, then the sound of the door opening, closely followed by Austin Cooke's resonant voice calling, "Darling, are you decent?"

Her face luminous with happiness, Mickie replied, "'Course not, you dope. If you're lucky, I never will be. Why do you ask?"

"Because I've brought a young lady home with me—theoretically speaking, that is."

"Cool it, Austin. You've already succeeded in arousing my curiosity. Who is she?"

"Sally Irwin."

"The little blonde who plays Hotspur's wife?"

"The very same."

"Well, for Pete's sake, why are you hiding her out in the hallway? Bring her in."

Chuckling at Mickie's rejoinder, Austin entered the suite. He slouched against the doorjamb for a moment, as if to orient himself, and when he saw Mickie and Thia sitting on the sunlit balcony, he came toward them.

"Am I interrupting anything earth-shattering?" he asked as he sauntered across the room.

"Not really," Mickie answered lightly. "We've solved just about all the really important world problems. How was rehearsal?"

"Ghastly!" Austin declared with a dramatic roll of his eyes. His knees seemed to give way beneath him with the force of his criticism, and he collapsed into the chair next to Mickie's before he continued. "It was positively wretched, darling, but keep your fingers crossed. It's generally a good sign when a dress rehearsal stinks!"

As Austin spoke, he smiled at Thia, who had gotten to her feet.

"Hello again, Cynthia."

"Hello, Mr. Cooke," Thia replied respectfully.

A pained expression crossed Austin Cooke's aristocratic features. "Please, my dear, if you're too impressed to call me Austin, a simple 'your excellency' will do."

"Ignore him, Thia," Mickie teased. "His head's three sizes too big for his hat as it is." She made a face at Austin and saw that he had confiscated her empty water goblet and was pouring the last of the wine into it. Suddenly serious, she inquired, "Should you drink that?"

"It's not for me, dear heart. It's for Sally." With this reminder, Austin glanced toward the open hall door. He frowned when he saw that the doorway was empty and called, "Come out, come out, wherever you are."

His frown changed to an encouraging smile when a fair-haired young woman timidly poked her head around the edge of the door. The woman moved so that she stood in the open doorway, nervously juggling a pile of scripts that she cradled in her arms.

"Come in, Sally," Austin coaxed. "Don't be shy."

At his urging, Sally stepped into the room, but she stumbled on the threshold, which caused several of the scripts to slide off the stack onto the floor. As she knelt to pick them up, she remarked diffidently, "You have company. Maybe we should rehearse later."

"Nonsense," Austin returned crisply. "Come in, child, come in. Your scene with Hotspur needs work, and my fellow thespians are always welcome to join the fun at the Austin Cooke School of Overacting, wherever it may be. Am I correct, Michelle?"

"Invariably," Mickie acceded dryly. "But you're Falstaff. Why can't the actor who's playing Hotspur coach Sally?"

"It wouldn't serve much purpose," said Austin. "This is his maiden performance too."

"Well, in that case I suppose you'd better work with her."

At Mickie's confirmation, Austin flashed a jubilant smile at Sally and offered the goblet of wine to her, but Mickie held up one finger, indicating that she intended to qualify her permission.

"You have till five o'clock," she said, and for Sally's benefit added the explanation, "After that Austin will want to rest till the performance."

Sally agreed with alacrity, but Austin's face fell. His voice took on a playful, wheedling note as he bargained, "That's not nearly enough time, dear heart. After all, Stratford is one of the most prestigious Elizabethan theaters in the country, and we owe it nothing less than our best."

When Mickie only looked at him, completely deadpan and obviously unmoved by this appeal, Austin turned to Thia. Seeking fresh ammunition, he inquired, "You're coming tonight, aren't you, Cynthia?"

"I wouldn't miss it for the world."

At Thia's fervent reply, Austin grinned engagingly and said, "Do I detect a frustrated actress beneath that lovely exterior?"

"Goodness, no!" Thia exclaimed. "There's only one thing connected with performing I've ever had a yen to do, and that's one of those marvelous scenes where the characters have a rip-roaring fight and throw things and break a lot of dishes—"

Thia faltered into silence when she saw that Mickie

was staring at her as if she had never really seen her before.

His eyes twinkling with amusement, Austin remarked, "That's hardly what I'd call typecasting. You strike me as being a dyed-in-the-wool lady, terribly well-bred and not at all the sort to scream and throw things."

"I know," Thia agreed. "Maybe that's why I'd enjoy cutting loose and playing that kind of role, but other than that, my only interest in the theater is as a fan." Smiling, she concluded, "An extremely dedicated fan."

"Well, if you're dedicated, you must come backstage after the performance tonight. Perhaps we could have supper together."

"Yes, Thia, let's!" Mickie seconded Austin's invitation. "And bring Luc with you."

"I'll have to check with him," said Thia, "but if he hasn't anything planned, it's a date." Her voice was husky with eagerness as she told Austin, "Now I'll look forward to tonight even more. I've always been an admirer of yours."

"There, Michelle! D'you see?" Austin cried. "She's looking forward to seeing the play, and if your old chum's going to be in the audience, we must be perfect. Better than perfect!"

Mickie's shrug said that she knew when she'd been outfoxed. "You have till six," she compromised good-naturedly. "What's more, I'll even cue Sally so that you can concentrate on critiquing her."

"Will you , darling? How deliciously cooperative of you." Austin kissed Mickie on the forehead, rewarding her for relenting. Then he cast an expressive glance at Sally and said, "Prepare yourself, young lady. You're in for a rare treat. There's something about the way Michelle caresses the consonants and lingers over the vowels as if she's reluctant to let them go that gives remarkably sexy overtones to Shakespeare's lines."

Mickie fluttered her lashes at Austin and said, "Thanks, darlin'. I take that as a compliment," and Sally relaxed enough to smile.

By the time Thia made her good-byes a few minutes later, the ingenue had abandoned her attempts to balance the pile of scripts and was sitting on the balcony railing, sipping her wine and listening to Austin's suggestions as to how she might interpret her character, hanging on his every word and looking at him with wide-eyed adoration.

"Isn't he sweet with her?" Mickie said as she accompanied Thia to the elevator.

"Yes, he's very generous," Thia agreed.

Mickie nodded eagerly. Her eyes were misty with emotion as she said, "And that's just one reason why I love him so much."

Chapter Thirteen

Thia arrived home to find a message from Luc waiting for her, breaking their date for the evening. The prospect of seeing Austin Cooke's performance no longer seemed so appealing, and her shoulders drooped dejectedly as she thumbed through the Yellow Pages, searching for the Wayfarer's number.

She only hoped Mickie would not hear the dejection in her voice as she told her friend, "Luc had to go back to Portland. Some sort of problem has developed with one of the subcontractors who's slated to start the remodeling at the inn."

"Are you still planning on coming to the play?" Mickie inquired.

"Yes." Thia straightened her spine with the sudden determination to salvage what she could of the night's entertainment. "I said I wouldn't miss seeing Austin, and I meant it. I just wanted to let you know that Luc and I won't be having supper with you."

"It's probably just as well," was Mickie's subdued response. "Since it's opening night, Austin's likely to be totally wiped out after the play. Maybe we can work something out for next weekend, though."

They made tentative plans to get together after Austin's play closed the next Saturday, but as Thia hung up she had a nagging feeling that Mickie had left much unsaid, just as earlier that day Mickie had sidestepped giving a direct response to Thia's comment about the air of secrecy surrounding Mickie's relationship with Austin. The more Thia thought about it, the more certain she became that there was something vitally important that Mickie was not telling her.

She was still puzzling over Mickie's oddly maternal attitude toward the actor as she dialed her mother's number. When Denise answered, Thia invited her to the play.

"Luc's been called away," she explained, "so I have this extra ticket."

"How very odd," said Denise. "I thought only doctors and plumbers had to cancel dates because of emergencies."

"So did I, Mother, but Luc's teaching me otherwise."

To her own ears, Thia's laughter was a poor parody of amusement, but it must have sounded genuine to Denise, because she replied, "I must say you're taking it well."

Her mother's sympathy was very nearly Thia's undoing. The truth was, she was bitterly disappointed that she would not be seeing Luc tonight. She felt like weeping, but it would be disloyal to complain to her mother. And besides, she knew that crying wouldn't solve anything.

Maybe nothing will bring you closer to Luc, a treacherous inner voice cautioned, but Thia swallowed her tears and said bravely, "If I'm taking it well, perhaps it's because I've decided to follow your advice."

"Have you, Cynthia?" Denise was touchingly pleased

and surprised to hear this, but not so surprised that she neglected to ask, "Which advice is that?"

"To be patient," said Thia. "To give Luc time."

"Good for you, darling."

Denise offered the praise in a bewildered tone that made it clear she had no recollection of ever having given any such counsel to her daughter, and Thia thought, *Dear Lord! What good is my mother's advice if she can't even remember giving it to me?*

She had a sudden hysterical desire to giggle, and when Denise suggested that they meet at the theater, Thia agreed and said a hasty good-bye.

Her mother had sounded so delighted, Thia didn't tell her that asking her to the play had been an afterthought. When she had discovered Luc was out of town, her first impulse had been to offer Luc's ticket to Celia. But Celia was out somewhere with Brad Scofield, and she'd phoned Denise primarily because it seemed a shame to waste an excellent third-row center seat. So now, on top of the other emotions that seethed within her, she had to cope with a sizeable portion of guilt.

Thia had not been fibbing when she'd told Austin Cooke she was an admirer. She thought his talent was nothing short of awesome, and *Henry IV, Part I,* was her favorite of Shakespeare's histories. In the past she had seen Austin in the roles of Hal and Hotspur, and that evening, seeing him portray the classic buffoon Falstaff, she was impressed by his versatility.

Austin was physically wrong for the part, yet within moments of his entrance the audience forgot that the self-indulgent braggart was in reality Austin Cooke decked out in a costume cleverly designed to give his slender elegance the appearance of Falstaff's corpulence.

It was a demanding role, the more so because the inveterate scalawag was so well loved, but Austin brought to it his own brand of resilience, an irrepressible exuberance, and a keen comedic sense. He was, quite simply, suberb.

After the performance Thia and Denise went backstage, where they found Mickie guarding the door to Austin's dressing room.

"I'm sorry I can't invite you in," Mickie said. "Austin's too tired to receive visitors. I hope you understand."

"Of course," said Denise.

Thia hastened to add her agreement, and said, "We just wanted Austin to know how much we enjoyed the play—especially his performance."

Mickie smiled as if she were the one being complimented. "He was awfully good, wasn't he?"

"He was brilliant," Thia said quietly. "I hated to see the play end."

As Thia and Denise turned to leave the theater, Mickie called after them, "Would you like to come again Wednesday night?"

"Would I!" Thia exclaimed. "I only wish I could, but the house is sold out."

"You're forgetting, kiddo, I have connections," said Mickie. "I also have a recording date in Portland, so I'm not going to be here, but I'll leave a ticket for you at the box office."

If Thia had not seen the play on Sunday, she would have been entranced by Austin's Wednesday-night performance. As it was, however, she saw certain differences that were more mystifying than enjoyable.

The changes were barely discernible; so subtle that the rest of the audience didn't seem to detect anything out of the ordinary, and at first Thia thought she might be imagining things. But Act III, Scene 3 began with Falstaff's seriocomic lament, "Bardolph, am I not fallen away vilely since this last action? do I not bate? do I not dwindle?" And by then Austin's speech was noticeably slurred.

Thia wondered whether Austin might be experimenting. Had he chosen to play the part with broader humor so that he could emphasize Falstaff's drunken devotion to fleshly pleasures? Was that why he staggered occasionally? Was that why his gestures seemed vaguely uncoordinated? Or were these new bits of business unintentional?

She remembered Mickie's reaction when Austin had poured the wine for Sally. "Should you drink that?" Mickie had asked, and this recollection brought more serious possibilities to mind.

Could it be that Austin had been drinking? Did he have a truly Falstaffian weakness for the bottle? Was this secret vice responsible for the hint of sadness in Mickie's eyes?

Thia tried to dismiss these thoughts. She told herself that she was being uncharitable, that any number of things could account for the slight tremor in Austin's step as he made his exit. Above all else, he was a professional. Even if he had a problem with alcohol, surely he would not drink before a performance.

When the play was over, the audience applauded so enthusiastically that the cast took several curtain calls, but the crowd reserved its highest tribute for Austin Cooke. They gave him a standing ovation, and Thia got to her feet and applauded with the rest, but her enthusiasm was dampened by concern for Mickie.

Although Luc was spending yet another week in Portland, even when Thia was hundreds of miles away he couldn't get her out of his mind. In the midst of business meetings she dominated his thoughts, and when he tried to sleep at night, she invaded his dreams.

He tried jogging and swimming and racquetball, and when the dreams intensified, he took to staying awake later and later, getting so little rest that he could scarcely see straight, let alone think straight. He became haggard and short-tempered. On Tuesday he had lunch with Mickie Lloyd, and Mickie told him things about Thia's business problems that made him even more irritable.

On Wednesday morning the head of the legal department remarked that Luc seemed to have lost interest in the inn and in other projects that were still in the planning stages, and by Thursday even the women in the steno pool had noticed how distracted he was.

In all his calculations, Luc had never foreseen that falling in love would have this effect on him, but then he had never suspected that he was a latent romantic either.

Neither had the Domini Developers comptroller, Herman Dowd, and he was astonished when Luc came into his office on Friday afternoon and said that he needed to talk to him about a personal matter.

"I'm honored that you'd want to confide in me, Luc," Dowd replied. "But perhaps you should consult a younger man—someone closer to your own age."

"Not about this." Luc closed the door to the outer office. Declining Herman's offer of a chair, he waved to the older man to remain seated and wandered to the windows. He stood there, gazing out at the city's skyline, as he added, "Unless I'm wrong in thinking you've been married longer than any of the others."

"From that I assume there's a woman involved," said Dowd.

Luc nodded.

"Then I'm even more flattered that you'd approach me. But I must warn you, Luc, where females are concerned, I'm no expert, even if I have been married a good many years."

"You must be fairly knowledgeable, Herman. Your wife is the most serene woman I've ever met."

"Yes, she is," Herman agreed, "and while I can't take the credit for that, I think I can safely say that Evelyn has been happy with me."

"So you must be doing something right."

"And you'd like to know what that might be."

"That's right." Luc swung away from the windows and looked at the accountant. "You see, I'm getting married in November—"

"Are you?" Herman smiled as if this explained everything. "Congratulations, my boy!"

"Thanks, but the truth is, I don't know— That is, I'm not sure—" Luc flushed. "Oh, hell! What I'd like to know is, what makes a good marriage work? And how does a man keep his wife satisfied? I mean, what in Heaven's name do women want?"

Herman leaned back in his chair and folded his hands beneath his chin. "If I had the answer to those questions, Luc, I'd be a billionaire. But can't you ask your fiancée?"

"Thia," said Luc. "Her name is Thia, short for Cynthia. And believe me, I've tried, but there's no way I can ask her."

Dowd studied Luc above his tented fingers. "In that case, there is one piece of advice I might give you."

"Yes," Luc prompted. "Go on."

"I think you'd agree that my wife is quite a lovely woman."

"Certainly I would."

"Well, thirty-five years ago, when I first met Evelyn, not only was she a knockout, but she was also clever and sweet and fun to be with. As you might guess, she had many suitors, and several of them were richer or smarter or better-looking than I was. To be frank, I never could figure out what she saw in me, and finally, after we'd been married a few years, I asked her about it."

"What did she say?"

"That I have many qualities she finds endearing." Herman chuckled. "Modesty's one of them, so obviously I can't list them all. And she also said that I have one asset that's more appealing and much more important to her than all the rest—"

"What is it?" Luc asked impatiently.

The older man would not be rushed. He paused, smiling expansively, before he replied, "Imagination, my boy. Evelyn says it's the most powerful force in the universe!"

As the week wound down, Thia's concern for Mickie displaced her worries about the nursery. It even kept her from constantly thinking of Luc. But at Saturday night's performance, she was so distracted by Luc's presence that she gave considerably less than her full attention to the action onstage.

It seemed that all Luc had to do was hold her hand and she could think of nothing but him. She was so keenly aware of him as he lounged into the seat next to hers in the darkened theater that she wouldn't have noticed had Austin chewed the furniture or turned cartwheels across the stage, and she knew that the play had gone well only because of the thunderous applause the audience gave it.

Relieved for her friend's sake, Thia thought, *Mickie will be so very pleased.* She didn't notice that Austin had not taken his curtain calls along with the rest of the cast until Luc pointed it out to her.

In a speculative undertone that was intended for her ears alone, Luc inquired, "Do you suppose Austin's ill?"

"Why—what makes you say that?" Thia stammered with alarm.

"His final exit was a bit shaky. And Mickie made some comment about this being his 'swan song.' At the time I thought it was just a figure of speech—"

"Mickie said that?" Thia broke in sharply. "When did you talk to her?"

"We met for lunch on Tuesday."

"In Portland?"

"Naturally in Portland. That's where I've been all week."

The icy disapproval in Luc's voice made Thia want to shiver. She apologized stiltedly, saying, "I didn't mean to sound suspicious, Luc. It's just that I had no idea you and Mickie had met—"

Luc squeezed her hand, effectively silencing her. "Forget it, Thia. Just now I've got a hunch something's wrong. We'd better get backstage."

Even as he spoke, Luc started moving down the aisle toward the entrance to the wings. Towing Thia along in his wake, he shielded her with his body as he shouldered his way through the throngs of people heading toward the exits.

The corridor leading to Austin's dressing room was

crowded too, and Thia clung to Luc's hand and tried to keep pace with him. Her concerns had returned full-blown now, and they assumed frightening proportions when Mickie opened the dressing room door to Luc's knock.

"Thank God it's you, Luc. I've been waiting for you. We're going to need your help."

Mickie's voice quavered and her face was white and strained. As she stepped aside and motioned them into the dressing room, Thia saw that Austin was sprawled on the studio couch, lying with one arm hanging limply to the floor and the other shading his eyes from the harsh glare of the overhead light.

While Thia stood just inside the door, immobilized by alarm, Luc crossed to the sofa in two long strides and sat on his heels at the older man's side.

"How are you doing, Mr. Cooke?" he asked.

Austin responded with a hoarse guttural sound that was midway between a groan and a laugh. "I've been better," he said weakly, "but at least I made it through the bloody play."

"You sure did, buddy," said Luc.

With some effort, the actor moved his arm and focused on Luc. "Do I know you?" he inquired.

"You remember Luc Domini, Austin," said Mickie. "You met him at the dance."

Austin mumbled something in reply, but he had covered his eyes again, and his voice was muffled by the flowing sleeve of his costume.

Mickie rushed to kneel beside the couch. Taking Austin's hand, she gently lifted his arm away from his face.

"What is it, darling? What did you say?"

Austin gave her a tremulous smile. "I said it's time to go home, Michelle."

"Yes, my darling. Right away."

Austin sighed wearily and closed his eyes.

"Does he need a doctor?" Luc asked softly.

"No. No doctor," Mickie answered.

Although she had agreed that they should leave the theater, she seemed incapable of carrying out Austin's request. She continued holding his hand, pressing it to her bosom, and she appeared to be approaching a state of shock.

"Medication?" Luc tried again.

"No," Mickie replied dully.

"Have you a car here?"

The take-charge note in Luc's voice finally registered, and Mickie nodded gratefully.

"Where is it?"

"Near the loading dock. It's the white Seville."

"The keys—"

"They're in my bag." Mickie cast a harried glance toward the coat rack, and Luc spotted her shoulder bag draped over one of the hooks. He handed the purse to her and she fumbled through the contents, found her keycase, and passed it to Luc.

"Thia," he said, "why don't you and Mickie go on ahead in my car."

"No!" Mickie cried. "I want to ride in the car with Austin."

Austin's eyes flew open. "I don't want that flock of vultures in the hall to see me. Not in this condition."

"Vultures?" Mickie echoed blankly. "They're your fans, dearest."

"All the more reason why they mustn't see me," Austin countered with surprising strength.

His obstinacy seemed to fuel Mickie's uncertainty, and seeing that her resolve not to leave Austin was weakening, Luc reasoned, "It's going to be easier for Austin if you let Thia drive you back to your hotel, Mickie. That way you can have his room ready for him—"

"Luc's right," Thia spoke up, casting what she hoped would be the deciding vote in favor of Luc's judgment. Without waiting for her friend's agreement, she put one arm around Mickie's shoulders and guided her toward the corridor.

"Come along now," Thia said gently, and Mickie automatically moved toward the door, but at the last moment she hesitated.

"How long will you be?" she asked Luc.

"We'll wait for the crowd in the hall to thin out, then we'll be right behind you. You have my word I'll have Austin back at your hotel in no time, so try not to worry." Turning to Thia, Luc inquired, "Can you handle a stick shift?"

Thia answered with a nod of her head, and when Luc tossed her the keys to the Porsche, she astonished herself by fielding them perfectly. She was trembling inside and trying desperately not to show it, but Luc must have sensed how shaken she was. Before she and Mickie left the dressing room, he gave her a reassuring hug and whispered, "Don't you worry either, Thia mia."

Mickie alternately wept and babbled incoherently during most of the drive to the Wayfarer, but by the time Thia had parked Luc's car in the hotel garage, Mickie had begun to regain her composure.

"Give me a minute to pull myself together," she pleaded. "I don't want the hotel staff to see me crying."

She dried her eyes and powdered her nose, freshened her lip gloss and put on a brave front, but once she and Thia were alone in the privacy of the Presidential Suite, her frantic pacing betrayed her anxiety.

"What's taking them so long!" she cried.

"Austin was in costume, Mickie. Luc's probably helping him change. And it was still fairly crowded backstage when we left."

Mickie nodded, accepting the logic of Thia's arguments, but she continued pacing until her anxiety began to infect Thia.

"Why don't I order something for us to drink?" she suggested.

"If you want something, go ahead," Mickie replied dispiritedly.

"Maybe some tea?"

"Whatever," Mickie acceded, and Thia dialed room service and placed the order.

Luc and Austin still had not arrived when the tea was delivered to the suite, and although Mickie was dry-eyed, she was more on edge than ever.

"Drink this," Thia directed, passing Mickie her cup. "It will help you calm down."

Mickie sipped the hot, fragrant beverage obediently, but she didn't sit down, and at last Thia said, "Maybe it would help if you talked about it."

"Nothing will help," Mickie replied shrilly. "It's hopeless, Thia. It's a rotten, lousy, can't-win situation."

"What is, Mickie?"

"This—this illness of Austin's. It seems that the less medical science knows about treating a disease, the more names they give it, and this one has more than its share. The most technical is amyotrophic lateral sclerosis, but it's also known as ALS, Lou Gehrig's disease, creeping paralysis—you can take your pick what to call it, but by any name it's killing Austin, slowly but surely—"

"Oh, Mickie! Are you sure?"

"Positive." Mickie sagged into a chair. She seemed peculiarly detached as she went on. "Austin's doctor made the diagnosis about two years ago, and there's no mistake. It's been confirmed."

"But can't they do something to stop it?"

"Not a thing, Thia. There is a new drug they're experimenting with. They say it's effective in most cases, but it wasn't in Austin's."

"Well, if they're studying the disease, maybe they'll discover other ways of treating it."

"Sure," said Mickie. "Maybe."

"Did you know Austin was sick when you—when he—"

"When we fell in love?" Mickie supplied the ending of Thia's question. "Yes, I knew. Austin was terribly up-front and self-sacrificing about it. As a matter of fact, he tried to talk me out of moving in with him by giving me a description of how the disease would affect him. First progressive weakness, then paralysis and wasting of the muscles. He warned me that we might not have much time, that eventually he'll be completely paralyzed." Mickie slammed her teacup onto the lamp table at her elbow and pounded the edge of the table with her fist. "Lord, Thia! At the end he won't even be able to talk!"

"Oh, Mickie." Thia spoke in a cracked whisper as she sank to her knees in front of her friend and took Mickie's hands in hers. "I wish I could help you. Really help you. Saying I'm sorry isn't enough, and I realize it isn't much comfort, but I am sorry."

Mickie returned the pressure of Thia's fingers. Her face was taut and determined as she said, "I know you are, kiddo, but you needn't be. After the way I fell apart tonight, you probably won't believe this, but the truth is, Austin and I are luckier than most couples—"

"Please, Mickie, don't do this. You don't have to hide your feelings from me."

"But I mean it, Thia. Honestly I do. You see, so many people wish their lives away. They exist in the future or they get hung up on the past, and they never figure out that all there is is now. And the weirdest thing of all is that a lot of them have to lose the one they love before they recognize how much that loved one meant to them. But this is something Austin and I have known from the start. We may not have much time together, but we make every minute count. And ALS spares the intellect, Thia. When Austin's bedridden, when he can't move or talk or eat, he'll still be Austin. And that's enough for me."

Saying this seemed to have a tranquilizing effect on Mickie. She sat quietly in her chair drinking a second cup of tea while Thia went into the bedroom, turned down the bedcovers, and located Austin's pajamas and robe.

"Thanks, kiddo," Mickie said when Thia returned to the living room. "What Austin's going to need now is rest. I was afraid doing the play would be too much for him. I was scared that he wouldn't have the stamina to make it through rehearsals, let alone three performances."

"But he did, Mickie, and he was magnificent."

"It meant so much to him to play Falstaff. He said he wanted to go out with a bang, and whether it was a successful bang or a flop, he wanted his last performance to be memorable."

Mickie swallowed convulsively, as if she were forcing back tears. "He told me he got a standing ovation Wednesday night. I wish I'd been there to see him, but I didn't think I could stand watching Austin if it hadn't gone well. I was too big a coward to stick around."

"You saw the play tonight, though."

"Only Act One," Mickie replied with a rueful shake of her head. "That's an improvement over last week, but after that I hid out in Austin's dressing room."

"Well, at least he had the satisfaction of knowing you were in the theater."

"He's also getting a heap of mileage out of teasing me for being such a fraidycat." Smiling crookedly, Mickie added, "He's so damned much fun, Thia."

"I noticed." Although Thia was smiling too, Mickie's features were blurred by the tears in her eyes. For a moment both women were silent, each of them overcome by sorrow that the life of a man so vital, so gifted and giving, should be cut tragically short.

It was Thia who broke the silence. "Where will you go from here?" she asked.

"Back to Portland, I suppose," Mickie answered stoically. "Austin says 'the show must go on.' He insists that I have to finish cutting my album, but after that I don't care what he says or what kind of offers I get, I'm not leaving him again. If the Queen of England wants me to do a command performance, I'll tell her, 'Sorry, Liz, some other time.'"

"Yes," Thia murmured. "I can hear you saying just that. But what will you do?"

In the same calm way, Mickie replied, "If I have my way, we'll go to Austin's place near Carmel. We'll admire the sunset in the evening and count the stars at night, and during the day Austin will work on his memoirs and we'll just be together. And if anyone wants to see us, they'll have to come there." Brightening, she suggested, "Hey, Thia! Maybe after we're settled you and Luc could come for a visit."

"Maybe we could at that, Mickie. I've never been to Carmel, but I've heard it's beautiful."

"It's fabulous, kiddo. Austin's house overlooks the Pacific, and there are redwoods all around. Everywhere you look, there's another fantastic view, and there's something that's very peaceful about it."

Now that she had warmed to her topic, Mickie went on to describe the grandeur of the California coastline in great detail. She was telling Thia about the sea lions that frolicked in the rockbound cove near Austin's home when Luc and Austin finally arrived.

As they entered the suite, Austin was leaning heavily on Luc's strong supporting arm, but he smiled at Mickie and waved off her assistance when she would have hurried to help him.

"Luc and I are doing perfectly well on our own," he said. "I'm already feeling much improved."

"Are you sure you're all right?" Mickie inquired anxiously.

"Certainly. Or I will be after I've had a chance to rest."

"He needs rest about as much as I need a hole in the head," Luc contradicted Austin with a grin. "He's a hard one to keep in line. On the way back to the hotel, he even tried to talk me into stopping off to see the floor show at Corky's Tavern."

Mickie looked at Austin as if he were a rambunctious ten-year-old and she his suspicious mother. "What kind of floor show?" she asked.

"Terpsichore," Austin replied proudly. "D'you hear how the word flows trippingly from my tongue?"

Mickie frowned. "Oh, I hear it, all right, but it sounds like so much Greek to me."

"It is Greek," said Thia.

"Give the little lady a big cigar," Austin cried in a carnival barker's voice.

"So what does it mean?" asked Mickie.

"It refers to the muse of dance," Austin replied. "In a word, dancers."

"*Exotic* dancers," Luc qualified. "Austin did his damndest to persuade me that if he's well enough to say 'Terpsichore,' he's well enough to watch the strippers, but I wasn't buying."

If Luc had thought Mickie would find this story amusing, he was mistaken. She was visibly irritated as she muttered, "Well, of all the—"

"Michelle, dearest," Austin interjected smoothly. "Before you say anything you'll regret, I must point out that it's amateur night."

Somewhat reassured by his good humor, Mickie demanded, "What does that have to do with the price of ouzo in Athens?"

"It's simply that I feel duty bound to offer my encouragement to any aspiring performer."

Austin's smile made him look almost angelic, and Mickie laughed relievedly. "You're incorrigible, Austin," she cried. "You really are too much! Here I've been worried sick about you, and all the while you've been having a high old time with Luc. Whatever in the world am I going to do with you?"

"Well, for starters how about letting Luc get me into bed. Then you can play nurse to your heart's content." By now Austin was panting with exertion, but he was also an actor to the core. He even dramatized his weakness by falling against Luc and crying, "Lay on, Macduff."

As Luc half carried him through the door to the bedroom, Austin grinned at Thia, and a few minutes later, when Luc called that Austin was ready to receive visitors, Mickie and Thia found the actor looking very much his debonair self, if a bit pale, clad in silk pajamas and safely in bed, propped up by the pillows at his back.

Anticipating Luc and Thia's departure, Austin said, "I'm sorry we had to cancel out on supper."

"So am I,' Luc replied. "This might sound strange, but it's been a pleasure all the same. Maybe the four of us can get together some other time."

"And under less trying circumstances," Austin amended gravely. "It's been a pleasure for me, too, and before you leave, I'd like to thank both of you for not leaping to the conclusion that I'd been drinking or something equally antisocial."

"Don't mention it," Luc returned briskly, as if his understanding were of no consequence.

"But I must," Austin insisted. "You've no idea how many people relish assuming the worst about me, especially since I happen to be a celebrity."

This disclosure made Thia feel about two inches high, for she had been concerned that Austin's problem might be too great a fondness for alcohol. But as they drove away from the hotel and she told him of her fears, Luc dispelled her pangs of conscience by asking her two simple questions.

"Did it give you pleasure thinking Austin Cooke might be a drunk?"

"No."

"Did it make you feel superior?"

"Of course not! I was terribly worried—"

"The defense rests," said Luc. His brusqueness made it plain that he had little tolerance for needless remorse, and for a time neither of them spoke.

Thia thought about Luc's gentle camaraderie with Austin. She remembered the patient way he had dealt with Mickie's near hysteria, and she wished that he would show the same degree of patience with her. She was so caught up in her reflections about the evening that she paid scant attention to the route Luc was taking. It was not until he pulled into the parking lot of Pete's Hideaway that she became aware of her surroundings.

"If it's all the same to you, Luc, I'd rather not have dinner here."

Luc glanced at her as if he understood her reluctance to be with crowds of people; as if he shared it.

"I've heard they have a special picnic supper. How about if I order one of those? We could take it to your place."

Thia shook her head. "Celia's there," she replied huskily. "If we show up with a takeout dinner from Pete's, she'll ask scads of questions."

"She knew we were going to have supper with Mickie and Austin?"

Thia nodded.

"Damn!" Luc scowled and leaned his head against the seat back. His hands clenched about the steering wheel.

"We could go to your motel," Thia suggested.

"That's no good either. I don't like the idea of taking you to a motel room to begin with, and the desk clerk's a nosy son of a—"

"Then let's go to the park."

"At this hour? No way." Despite his harsh denial, Luc's expression softened. He turned and opened his arms to her, and as she eagerly went into them, he added, "Lord knows it's been too long since we've been together, and I want you, honey, so much it hurts, but a midnight roll in the grass is not what I had in mind."

"Well, I don't care where we go as long as we can be alone."

"I feel the same way, Thia mia."

Luc's voice was as warm as the summer night, as soft and tender as the kisses he scattered across her forehead, her cheeks, the side of her neck. With the same gentle insistence, his lips moved to her eyelids and tasted the saltiness of tears.

"You've been crying."

At Luc's observation a ragged sob escaped Thia. She ignored the bruising pressure from the gearshift knob, which was gouging her leg, and burrowed into him, digging her fingertips into the fine weave of his dinner jacket and burying her tear-streaked face in the hollow of his shoulder.

"Mickie's tough, honey." Luc ran his hands over her back in a rhythmic, soothing motion. "She'll be okay. She has a lot of inner strength."

"I know she does," Thia murmured hoarsely. "It isn't that I'm worried about her, and I'm not grieving for Austin either."

"Why the tears then?"

"It's just— Oh, Luc, I don't know."

Luc drew her closer, as if he would absorb her sudden paroxysm of weeping with his own body, and encouraged by his sympathy, Thia whispered, "I envy them, Luc."

"Envy them!"

She felt Luc tense, and in the next instant his hands clamped about her shoulders and pushed her away from him. She saw the perplexity in his eyes as he declared, "I swear to God, Thia, sometimes I can't figure you out. How can you possibly envy Mickie and Austin when there are so many things against them? There's the age difference, and they have to be constantly on the lookout for fans, and they're barely a step ahead of the press getting wind of what's going on. At this point Austin has problems with impotence, and to top it all off he's dying—"

Luc uttered the last word in an abrasive growl, and when he lapsed into silence Thia stared at him uncertainly, not knowing how to explain. It was easy enough to admit to herself that she coveted Mickie's closeness to Austin, that she longed to create the same loving unity between Luc and herself. But how she could say this to Luc without sounding selfish or critical or, worst of all, self-pitying?

At last, dragging her gaze away from his, she answered with inadequate repetition.

"Still," she said softly, "I envy them."

The wistful tilt of her head revealed more than her reply. It required little insight for Luc to read into her comment the things she had censored. This unwanted knowledge made him uneasy, and he moved away from Thia and sat with his forearms propped against the steering wheel, staring stonily through the windshield.

What the devil! he thought. When he looked at the situation from Thia's angle, he envied certain aspects of Mickie and Austin's relationship too. Being completely open with Thia, withholding nothing, laughing and loving with her and letting the chips fall where they might, would be the closest thing to heaven in this cold, uncaring world.

But he was accustomed to being a loner, and doing his bit so they could reach this rarefied plateau would require some radical changes on his part. It would require an emotional investment he might be incapable of making, particularly when he knew very well that Thia was prepared to accept less than her ideal.

Oh, he was willing to follow Herman Dowd's recommendation and try to be more imaginative, and he would gladly share his material possessions with her. He would also give her more of his time. Might as well. Fighting against his desire to be with her was like trying to fight his way out of quicksand. The more he struggled, the deeper he sank.

The past couple of weeks had proved that. He could have spent twice as much time in Stratford, but he'd purposely stayed away. He'd needed to find out what it would be like without her, and he had discovered that it was sheer, unadulterated torture. His own private hell.

Without Thia he felt as if he were missing some essential part of himself. She had become an obsession, and his loss of control was staggering, but the idea of losing his autonomy threw him completely off-balance.

The subconscious urge for self-preservation made him wonder what would happen if it turned out that he could never share his most intrinsic self with Thia. What if pride prevented his taking all she had to give?

The answer, when it occurred to him, eased his discomfort.

For as long as they were together, they would have a little bit of heaven.

We should be content with that, Luc told himself fiercely. *It's sure as hell more than most people have.*

So why, having reached this conclusion, did he feel as if he'd struck a bad bargain?

He looked at Thia and saw that she was watching him, her amber eyes wide and unblinking, fascinated by the play of emotions his thoughts had etched upon his face. He immediately schooled his features to conceal his emotional tug-of-war, and although she was disturbed by the enigmatic change in him, she was not surprised by it.

Neither was she surprised when Luc changed the subject, shifting her thoughts away from Mickie and Austin by saying, "We could take our dinner to the Kirby house."

"You signed the lease?"

"With an option to buy. Hoagy Jantzen brought the papers to the motel this morning, and he'd made enough compromises for me to decide to go along with the deal. I trust that's acceptable to you."

His formal phrasing and cool, impersonal smile seemed to indicate that he was merely paying lip service to an apology. Thia bit back an angry retort, but Luc felt her slipping away from him.

"It's a lovely house," she said distantly. "I only wish you'd consulted me about it."

"I did consult you, Thia. Have you forgotten that you went through the place with me?"

Luc's sardonic question brought them full circle, back to the stalemate of cross purposes and conflicting feelings from which they'd started. Thia might have protested that there was a difference between touring the house with him and making a commitment to a year's lease, but since he had presented her with a *fait accompli,* it would be pointless to belabor the issue.

And the last thing she wanted was to spend their little time together arguing, so she tried to hide her disappointment. She smiled, she hoped graciously, and let the matter drop.

Chapter Fourteen

A full moon rode high in the sky, washing the landscape with silver, but on the grounds of the Kirby estate the heavy growth of pines kept the light from penetrating.

Thia shivered with anticipation as she walked with Luc toward the front door. The house had no near neighbors and the night was very quiet, almost unnaturally so. Not a passing car, not a birdcall or the hum of an insect or the tiniest of breezes, disturbed the silence. Their footfalls were muted by the mossy path, and even her voice was hushed as she inquired, "What happened to your flashlight?"

"The batteries are dead," Luc said softly.

Thia sighed. "I wish they weren't. This makes me feel like we're breaking and entering or doing something else we shouldn't be doing."

Luc chuckled. "That's part of the fun."

"But it's so dark." Thia stumbled over a tree root that marred the otherwise even surface of the path. She might have fallen if Luc hadn't steadied her, and exasperated by her own clumsiness, she muttered, "I'll bet the electricity hasn't been turned on."

"You'd win," Luc replied amiably. "The utility company won't get around to it till Monday."

"Well, how will we find our way around?"

"Pete's provided us with these."

Balancing their box supper with one hand, Luc removed two tall white candles from the basket and handed them to Thia with what would have been a flourish had she been able to see them more clearly.

"If you'd like to take the basket, I'll carry you across the threshold."

Luc's casual offer both tempted and disturbed Thia. After thinking it over briefly, she said, "Thanks, but no thanks. I don't think it's legal till we're married."

"Neither is going to bed together, but we've done that, so why not this? Seems to me it would be a mighty fine way to kick off our own private housewarming."

"To begin with, I didn't know this was supposed to be a housewarming, and as to your carrying me inside...." Thia shook her head helplessly. "I don't know, Luc. Maybe I'm superstitious, or maybe it's just that I'd like to preserve some traditions, but I can tell you one thing. If you expect me to be consistent, you're going to be disappointed."

Luc laughed outright at this response. He was still laughing as he unlocked the front door and led her into the house, where the darkness was so nearly total that it seemed palpable. They crept across the foyer as stealthily as two naughty children, moving toward the silvery pool of light that spilled into the hallway from the library. Thia found that she was holding her breath until they reached the end of the hall and discovered that the library was bathed in moonlight. It looked tranquil and inviting.

Luc lighted the candles, and as they spread out their supper on the moon-dappled carpet near the lozenge-shaped windows, she was impressed all over again by the room's pleasing proportions and handsomely detailed woodwork. Inspired by the romantic combination of candle glow and moonlight, she could envision how lovely the library would look when it was furnished. She imagined how cozy it would be to sit with Luc by the fireplace, watching the merry leap of flames up the chimney, exchanging warm caresses and sweet kisses. She imagined how exciting it would be to climb the stairs to the bedroom and lose themselves in an embrace....

Somewhat belatedly, Thia recognized the direction her wayward thoughts had taken and hastily refocused them.

Perhaps a tuxedo sofa would be the most appropriate choice for this room, along with pair of Eames chairs at either side of the hearth, and a sturdy oaken table near the bookshelves. With the addition of a couple of occasional chairs, some good reading lamps, a mantel clock, and a few other odds and ends, the library would be charming.

If Luc had seen fit to ask her opinion before he'd signed the lease, she would have been delighted with his choice of home for them, but as it was, she could summon up only token appreciation. And when, inevitably, their conversation turned to the house, Luc couldn't help knowing this. She could tell that he was puzzled by her grudging acceptance of the status quo, and hurt when she suggested that Celia supervise the renovations.

"I thought you'd want to take care of that," he said.

Choosing her words carefully, Thia explained, "It's not that I don't want to do it, Luc. I just don't have the time. Naturally Celia would go over everything with me—with both of us. She'd give our preferences top priority, and we'd have final approval.''

Luc gave her a long, probing look. Then, shrugging, he said, ''If you don't have the time, I guess that's the way it'll have to be.''

He passed Thia her plate and filled one for himself, and they sat so close together that their shoulders touched while they sipped Perrier from champagne flutes and sampled pâté and lobster salad and fragrant, piping-hot dinner rolls and an assortment of cheeses and fresh fruits. But both of them were too encapsulated in their own thoughts to do justice to the elegant picnic supper, and their conversation had dwindled away to nothing long before Luc began packing the leftover food into the basket.

Thia felt the gulf between them widening, and she despaired. Earlier Luc had said he wanted to make love to her, but their disagreement over the house had come between them, and she was certain that at any second now he would suggest they leave.

But she didn't want to go home. She wanted to be with Luc. She needed to be close to him.

It might have been desperation that made her behave so seductively, or perhaps it was only the moonlight. She knew only that she felt unreal, as ephemeral as moonbeams. Even her movements were languorous and dreamlike as, guided by instinct, she slipped Luc's dinner jacket off his shoulders and loosened his tie.

She felt him stiffen with momentary surprise at her boldness, but when she kissed him, his mouth was as hot and eager as her own, and as she lay back against the carpet and pulled him down beside her, she touched the tip of her tongue to his and murmured soundlessly against his lips, ''Hold me, Luc. Love me.''

"I do, Thia mia. I will."

His whispered reply was barely coherent, but the rough urgency of his hands as he stripped her of her clothing and caressed the soft, honeyed skin beneath made her head reel with desire for him. They kissed again and erotic waves of sensation coursed through her, each more intense than the one before as his mouth left hers to explore the trail his hands were blazing upon her fevered body, his tongue teasing and taunting, savoring the sensitive bend of her elbow, the satiny slope of a shoulder, the burgeoning ripeness of a nipple.

While her trembling hands undid the last of his shirt buttons and moved to his belt buckle, his hands continued their knowing glide. He drew her stockings off slowly, ceremoniously, pausing to place a tantalizing flurry of kisses across the arch of her foot and along a slender ankle and calf to the back of her knee. At last his searching mouth found the moist, velvety flesh of her inner thighs, and the sweet torment of his probing tongue sent her passions soaring.

"Luc!" she gasped, but the hammering thud of her heart obscured her voice.

Her body had become a finely tuned instrument of pleasure, hips arching to Luc's caresses, moving restlessly in response to his slightest variation of rhythm. Her toes curled into the carpet and her hands clutched at his head to draw him closer, fingertips alive to the coarse, springy texture of his hair.

Every fiber of her being yearned for him, was attuned to him. Each individual nerve ending was vibrating, singing with need.

Once more she cried his name, and this time he must have heard her because he released her to tear off the rest of his clothing. In less than a minute he was as naked as she, and as unashamed. He stood over her proudly, yet he was as unconscious of his arrogance as he was of how beautiful he looked with his lithe, graceful body limned silver by the moonlight, and when he dropped down beside her and folded her in his arms, she welcomed him with abandon.

He positioned himself above her and she felt him pressing against her softness, seeking entry. She wound her arms and legs around him and met his hungry demands with her own wild cadence. Beneath his hard caresses her body liquefied and flowed into his, so that she lost the essence of herself in the fiery starburst of heat that signaled release, and suddenly she was floating, spinning, cushioned in his arms yet deliciously suspended in space and time, and she clung to him and cried out because their union was so sublime, so perfect, and she did not want it to end.

Gentling her with caresses and whispered love words, Luc rolled onto his back, holding her close so that she lay on top of him while her breathing slowed and she drifted back down to earth.

"Now *that's* what I call a housewarming," he growled.

Thia laughed, but her eyes darkened soberly as she murmured, "Oh, Luc, I wish we could always be like this."

Luc's chuckle rumbled out from deep in his chest. "Insatiable little thing, aren't you?" he teased, and she tangled her fingers in his hair and gave it a light, punishing tug.

"You know what I mean!"

"Yes, Thia mia, I think I do." He cupped her chin with his hand and tipped her face toward his. "You'd like us to have more time together, wouldn't you?"

She nodded. "I'd like that, too," he said, "and I'll see what I can work out, but I'm afraid, for the next few months, it's going to be difficult."

"It's not just the time, Luc."

"Then why don't you tell me what it is?"

Although Luc was as close as ever, she sensed that emotionally part of him had retreated, and she swallowed hard, trying to dislodge the hot lump of tears in her throat. Had he intentionally misunderstood her? Didn't he realize that she needed more than his physical presence? And if he didn't, how could she explain it to him?

"Well," she began slowly, "even when we're together, we're not really together. There's a part of you that I can't touch—"

"Do you resent my work?" Luc interjected brusquely.

"No!" Thia answered without hesitation. "Truly, I don't. Oh, sometimes I feel a little jealous because I know how terribly important your company is to you, and I wish you'd tell me more about it. As it is, I feel shut out of a major part of your life."

Luc had already withdrawn emotionally, and now he withdrew physically. After putting Thia away from him, he got to his feet and began climbing into his clothes, and she followed his lead.

"You're guilty of the same thing," he said quietly.

She confronted him warily, holding her dress to her bosom. "How do you mean?"

"When Mickie and I met for lunch last Tuesday, she told me about the problems you're having at the nursery."

"She had no right!"

"She had every right, Thia. She's your friend and

she was worried about you. And anyway, I've suspected all along that things weren't going well for you. I had hoped you'd take me into your confidence, maybe ask for my help.''

Luc was already tucking his shirttail into the waistband of his slacks. Envying his nonchalance, Thia hurriedly stepped into her dress and struggled with the hard-to-reach zipper. Irritation made her clumsy, and halfway up the track the zipper snagged on the dress fabric and refused to budge. Nevertheless, she lifted her chin proudly as she retorted, ''Since Mickie told you everything else, surely she must have told you why I didn't approach you.''

''She did.'' Luc nodded and crouched down to tie his shoes. ''I can sympathize with your pride, Thia, and I can understand your reasoning, even if I don't find it flattering, but there's something you have to understand too.''

''Oh?'' Thia gave the zipper another surreptitious tug. ''What's that?''

Now that Luc was dressed except for his jacket and tie, he noticed she was having trouble with the back zipper on her dress. He spun her around and began untangling the snarl she had created before he replied, ''Simply that I'd never have asked you to marry me if I'd thought you were a gold digger.''

''Well, thanks for that, at least,'' Thia said stiffly. ''Since you've brought it up, why *did* you ask me to marry you?''

''Because I— Dammit all anyway, Thia! You know how I feel about you.''

''Sometimes a woman needs to hear the words, Luc.''

''Do you think I don't know that? Don't you realize

that every time I see you, I want to tell you how I feel?"

Thia spun around and stared at him with disbelief. "D-does that mean you love me?"

"What else would it mean?"

Despite his surly response and grim expression, Thia would have thrown her arms about Luc and kissed him, but before she could, he turned her around and resumed working at the zipper.

"Now you've really gotten the damned thing all fouled up," he muttered.

"You were saying you love me, Luc. Don't change the subject."

"What else is there to say about it?"

As if to underscore his fast-waning patience, Luc gave the zipper a sharp yank. Surprisingly it slid free, but before he could finish zipping Thia's dress, she had turned so that she could watch his face as she suggested, "You could tell me why you've never said it before."

"I thought I had."

"Well, you didn't. I'd have remembered."

Luc's eyebrows drew together in a frown. He started to spin Thia around again, but this time she resisted, saying, "Please, don't. I'm beginning to feel like a top."

Luc's sense of humor asserted itself. His lips twitched into a smile as he conceded, "Okay. So maybe I never told you how I feel about you, but I took you out to Ramsey Slough and showed you the shack and the clippings. What did you think all that was about?"

"Just what you said at the time, Luc. That it was supposed to resolve my doubts about being your first choice."

"Holy Christ! Are you always so blasted literal?"

"Yes, my darling. Especially with you."

She smiled into Luc's dark eyes, and when the bleakness in them warmed and gentled, just as she'd hoped it would, she looped her arms around his neck and kissed him softly on the mouth.

"Look, Thia," he said uneasily, "what I was trying to say before is that I haven't had much experience with sharing my feelings, so it may take a while before I get the hang of it."

"I can wait, Luc, if only you'll let me share my feelings with you." He raised a quizzical eyebrow at her, and she went on. "You once said that I'm reserved, and you were right. I'm not overdemonstrative, and I promise to restrain myself. I won't rape you in public or take any liberties you'd find too embarrassing, but sometimes, even if we aren't alone, I'd like to hold hands with you or kiss you—"

Luc silenced her with a kiss. "It's a deal," he agreed huskily, "on one condition."

"What's that?"

"I know you see the material things I can give you as a poor substitute for attention—"

"Oh, Luc! Is that how it seems to you?"

"Hear me out," he said sternly, but the way he smoothed the silky tendrils of hair away from her forehead and framed her face between his hands was not at all stern. "What I'd like to propose is this: I'll try to share your feelings if you'll let me help get the nursery back on its feet financially."

For long moments Thia was silent, thinking that somehow Luc had managed to make what should have been a loving commitment sound like a business merger. But if his proposition was less than she'd hoped for, it was better than nothing. And maybe he was right. Maybe both of them needed to learn to take what the other had to offer. At least it was a beginning.

Besides, how could she deny him anything when she loved him so much? Her knees had turned to jelly just looking at him, because he was so damned sexy with his hair all tousled.

"I'd like to make a stipulation or two of my own," she murmured.

"Let's hear 'em."

"Unless we're going someplace formal, I wish you wouldn't wear a necktie."

Luc smiled. "I could go for that."

"And unless it's chilly, I'd rather you didn't wear a jacket."

"You got it. But I'm warning you, I draw the line at going barefoot."

Thia's eyes lighted up. "Would you consider going without underwear?"

"I will if you will."

To round out his answer, Luc gave her a wicked grin and a pinch on the bottom. Thia pinched him back, and suddenly they were in each other's arms and both of them were laughing.

"Is it a deal?" asked Luc.

Thia stared at him incredulously. "You mean you'd actually go without underwear?"

"Good Lord! You really do take me literally." Luc hugged her. "No, not that. The other. I help you with the nursery—"

"And I get to kiss you in public."

Luc's hopeful grin compelled a favorable response,

but the way he was holding her was even more compelling.

"Yes, my darling." Thia sighed blissfully, relishing this enticing form of persuasion. "We'll try it your way."

Chapter Fifteen

They tested their agreement the next day. Luc spent most of the afternoon at the nursery, going over the books, touring the greenhouse and fields, checking the inventory and inspecting the equipment. He even examined the personnel records.

As he and Thia strolled through the greenhouse on their way back to the office, he remarked, "I seem to recall that your grandparents used to do quite a bit of landscaping."

"They did, and it was one of their more profitable ventures. But they had the necessary heavy machinery to handle major plantings, and Grandpa to operate it."

Luc paused to take a last thoughtful look around the garden shop before he followed Thia into the office and seated himself in the visitor's chair beside the desk. Although the shop was quiet now, earlier in the day it had been open for business and he'd noticed that a steady stream of customers had kept both Thia and Penny Burgess busy. Most of the transactions had been small, but where there was such a brisk flow of sales, there had to be potential for growth.

While he contemplated ways and means of tapping into this potential, Luc picked up a file folder from the in basket and leafed through the stack of unanswered letters, memos, and telephone messages it contained. When he'd finished, he saw that Thia was watching him, her face taut with expectation.

"Well?" she asked anxiously. "What's the verdict?"

In an effort to allay her nervousness, Luc lounged back in his chair and propped his feet on the corner of the desk. "Things are critical," he said, "but not entirely hopeless. In other words, I have some good news and some bad news."

"Don't bother with the kid-glove treatment, Luc. Give me the bad news first."

"Okay, honey, if that's the way you want it. In the first place, your assessment of the situation was right on target. You are undercapitalized. In order to avoid bankruptcy, you're going to have to make a sizeable investment in new equipment, and to justify that kind of investment, you're going to have to expand your business."

"That's what I told Hoagy Jantzen, but he wasn't at all impressed."

"No, he wouldn't be. Not when you're a relative newcomer to running a nursery. But I think you have part of the solution right here." Luc tapped the edge of the file folder against the palm of one hand as he went on. "In reading through this, I noticed that in the past week you've had several inquiries about landscaping."

Thia stirred uneasily, leaning forward in her chair and folding her hands on the desktop. She studied her tightly clenched fingers as she replied, "Most of the inquiries came from people who admired the decorations at the Founders' Day Dance. I hate to refer them elsewhere, but I don't see how I can do anything else. I simply don't have the wherewithal to take on full-scale landscaping jobs, so if that was supposed to be the good news, I don't see the point."

"The point, Thia, is that there's more than one way to skin a cat. As I see it, you have two choices. You can let me provide the backing so that you can either lease or purchase the machinery you need to branch out—"

"No, Luc," Thia broke in. "I know I agreed to accept your help, but I can't let you assume that kind of risk."

"Not even if it would give me pleasure to do it?" Luc asked soberly.

"No," she said, adamantly shaking her head. "I'm sorry, Luc, but not even then."

She glanced at him from beneath her lashes, concerned that he might be angered by her refusal; but if he was upset, he hid it well. There was a hint of finality in the way he tossed the folder into the in basket and got to his feet, but except for the spasmodic leap of a muscle along his jaw, his face was impassive, his manner all business.

"So be it," he said. "Then the option you're left with is subcontracting part of the work." Luc folded his arms across his chest and watched the spark of interest in Thia's eyes grow into guarded enthusiasm as he explained, "What you have to do is find a heavy-equipment operator who has the machinery and the expertise to do the excavating and grading and leveling while you supply the plans, the plants, the contacts, and the know-how."

"And we split the costs?"

"And the profits," Luc qualified.

"I've wondered whether an arrangement like that might be possible, but would our prices be competitive?"

"There's no reason why they shouldn't be. Since you'd be under no obligation to subsidize the contractor's expenses when he wasn't on a job for the nursery, your fee could be a real bargain."

"Sounds feasible," Thia murmured.

"It is," said Luc.

"But where will I find this paragon to do the grading and leveling and excavating?"

"You can leave that to me."

"Does that mean you already know of someone?"

"Sure do, and he's tailor-made for the job. He's from Medford, he's recently gone into business for himself, and next week he's going to be working at the inn. I'll ask him to stop by and see you—"

That was as far as Luc got before Thia raced around to his side of the desk and hugged him. Between the fervent kisses she gave him, she cried, "Oh, Luc, I'm so relieved and so very grateful! How can I ever repay you?"

Luc's response was instantaneous and intense. She felt the passionate surge of his arousal as his arms went around her and crushed her close, as he rubbed his bearded chin against her temple and raggedly inhaled the sweet fragrance of her hair. He nuzzled the side of her neck, and when an excitement that rivaled his own rippled through her, he chuckled and said, "Don't worry, Thia mia. Given the proper incentive, I'm confident you'll think of something."

Their mouths met and clung in a long, deeply searching kiss, and his hands played over her, caressing her boldly through her clothes and then tunneling beneath, making deliciously intimate forays that left her gasping with desire.

"Luc, my darling," Thia whispered breathlessly.

"That's the right incentive, but it's not what I'd call proper."

It was some time later before they resumed their discussion about the nursery, and when they did get back to it, it was a loving give-and-take of opinion in which they engaged. They disagreed over only one thing: what to do about the van.

Luc insisted it should be replaced with a new one, and Thia countered that she'd rather make do with the old one until her cash position had improved. Finally, Luc suggested a compromise, saying that he would go along with her preference if she'd let him pay for the repairs the van needed.

"We'll leave it to the mechanic," said Luc. "If he says the van's safe for you to drive, you can keep it. Otherwise I'm buying you a new one, like it or not."

Since he was genuinely concerned for her safety, Thia accepted his ultimatum. Swallowing her pride left a bitter taste in her mouth, but that same evening, when they went out for pizza, she exercised her end of their bargain by kissing Luc in front of dozens of onlookers at Emilio's, and she discovered that this sort of revenge could be very sweet indeed.

On the surface it appeared that their agreement had gotten off to a promising beginning, but in reality it soon deteriorated into a battle of wits.

Underneath they hadn't changed. They were still the same stubborn, strong-willed people, and as summer turned into autumn, it seemed to Thia that in certain respects she and Luc were poles apart and pulling in opposite directions, painfully tearing each other apart.

She thought of him constantly and wanted only to be

with him—to see him, touch him, talk with him—but they had little time together.

With construction underway at the inn, Luc had gotten involved with negotiating options to purchase land for a shopping center project near Salem, which meant that he was often out of town during the work week. But even if he hadn't had to travel, the nursery's newly instituted landscaping service required so much of Thia's time and attention that she had little energy left for anything else. And more often than not, the occasional free hour she had was given over to helping Celia with redecorating the Kirby house.

And she still thought of it as the "Kirby" house. Sometimes she slipped and referred to it that way in her conversations with Luc, too. Although the work was progressing beautifully and with every passing week the house reflected more of her personal tastes, she couldn't quite believe that it would soon be home to Luc and her.

She was not always good-natured about the demands Celia made upon her, especially if she happened to be deep in thought, trying to solve a drainage problem or figure out whether to terrace a slope or rely on plantings to minimize erosion. There were moments when, thankful as she was for Celia's help, as much as she appreciated her sister's conscientious attention to the task of renovating the house, Thia believed that she never wanted to see another paint sample or swatch of fabric as long as she lived.

Then there were the wedding plans. Ostensibly, Denise had assumed command of those arrangements, but what this amounted to was that she called several times a day to badger Thia into asking Vernon to officiate, to add a name to the guest list, or to nag Thia about selecting the invitations, the music, the flowers—her mother's list of complaints seemed endless.

After one particularly vitriolic exchange with Denise, Thia told Luc, "This formal wedding is so complicated. Sometimes I wish we could just elope."

Over the next several weeks the arguments with her mother continued, and after each argument Thia repeated her wish, but Luc never took her seriously.

There were bright spots, of course. Celia's reliability for one. She had taken over the morning delivery of cut flowers to the florist shop. Between them, she and Kate kept that arm of the business running smoothly, and Thia greatly appreciated this, since she had kept her promise to herself and insisted that Duffy retire.

The old man had left under protest, and after a few days of having him constantly underfoot and continually grumbling about the way she kept house, Velma Langtry wanted Thia to change her mind and take him back on a part-time basis. And she just might. She had hired a high school boy to help out with some of Duffy's duties, but she missed the old man's expertise.

The Mulhollands were another bright spot. On the night of the dance, Luc had made an offhand comment that a chef as talented as Kenny should write a cookbook, and when the remark got back to Kenny, he actually started writing one.

A radiant Kate told Thia, "I've never seen him this committed to a project. He's at the typewriter at least four hours a day, and the rest of the time he's trying new recipes and perfecting the old ones. All of a sudden he's all grown up—well, he is most of the time. And I don't know whether to laugh because of my husband's turning into such a class act, or cry because I miss the happy-go-lucky little kid he used to be."

Thia was happy for the Mulhollands. She was pleased with the gains the nursery had made and gratified by Celia's growing sense of responsibility, but when she was alone in her room at night, these bright spots were cold comfort.

She missed Luc. She felt incomplete without his arms about her, and she counted the hours until she could be with him. Yet with both of them so busy, they seldom saw each other, and when they did, Luc rarely came to the house empty-handed.

On one evening he brought Thia perfume, on another a topaz pendant on a fine golden chain, on still another a costly leather handbag.

"I feel like a kept woman," Thia said to Celia. "It's as if he's trying to buy me."

"You're a certifiable idiot," Celia replied unsympathetically. "You should thank your lucky stars that Luc's so generous with you."

After this Thia kept her feelings to herself, but she didn't thank her lucky stars when Luc continued to shower her with small but expensive presents. Instead, she thanked him by showering him with affection in public.

Embarrassed, Luc counterattacked. In early September he invited Thia to accompany him when he traveled to Portland for the quarterly meeting of his board of directors. Thia hesitated until Luc reminded her that she'd said she wanted to know more about his company, and then, delighted that he was willing to share this facet of his life with her, she agreed.

In the next phase of his strategy, Luc lulled her into complacency by not bringing her a gift when he picked her up for the drive to the airport, and she rewarded him by behaving with ladylike decorum while he showed her through Domini Developers' corporate headquarters and introduced her to the office staff and board members.

When it was time for the meeting, she volunteered to wait for Luc in his office.

"Are you sure you don't want to join us in the boardroom?" Luc inquired. "You'd be more than welcome."

"I'm sure," she replied, and she meant it. Luc had told her the day's agenda was more or less routine, and she honestly preferred not to intrude.

In a way, seeing Luc in this supercharged environment was a revelation. The world of high finance seemed his natural element, and the way the others deferred to him made her realize how important he was.

She was also a bit overwhelmed by the firm's offices, which occupied the penthouse of an imposing glass-and-steel tower that overlooked the Willamette River. This far above the city streets the very atmosphere reeked of money. She thought that even the clouds that drifted by the windows of Luc's private office had a faint greenish tinge, and there was something about the ankle-deep carpets, abstract paintings, and high-tech glass and chromium furnishings that made Thia want to walk on tiptoe and speak in whispers.

For four and a half years she had worked in an office similar to this one, yet she had never felt completely comfortable in it. Thia felt uneasy now, but she was determined not to show it.

She was seated on one of the modernistic, suede-upholstered cubes near the desk, glancing through the latest issue of *Fortune,* when one of the secretaries appeared, bringing her coffee in a silver pot on a silver tray. The older woman poured the aromatic blend into a cup as fine and fragile as eggshells and waited until Thia had pronounced it excellent before she withdrew, quietly closing the door to the outer office behind her.

An hour later Thia had finished her coffee and exhausted the supply of magazines. Feeling a bit more relaxed, she began exploring the office, and that was when she discovered the little alcove containing the scale models of Domini Developers' current projects.

She recognized the Warwick Inn project immediately. A single-story, L-shaped addition would house an indoor pool and sauna, a gymnasium, and massage cubicles. Part of the lobby would be given over to a complex of beauty salons, where the guests could pamper themselves with facials and manicures, scalp and hair treatments, and lessons in applying cosmetics, and the ballroom would become an aerobic dance studio. Only the shell of the original building would remain when construction was finished and Fountain of Youth Health Spas had moved in, but the design preserved the stately dignity of the place. Perhaps it even enhanced it.

The other model was of the proposed shopping center in Salem. Built on three levels, with the usual gamut of specialty shops, boutiques, and huge department stores, it was unique in its use of natural light and in the way it blended into its hillside location.

Thia was still engrossed with this model when Luc came into the alcove along with Stan Huxley, the architect responsible for the shopping mall.

"Is your meeting over already?" she asked.

"Just about," Luc replied. "We're taking a lunch break."

Gesturing toward the scale model, Stan inquired, "What do you think of my baby?"

"It's fascinating," said Thia. "The detail is incredible."

Flattered, Stan beamed at her and launched into a long-winded and highly technical discussion concerning the specific construction problems the shopping center project posed, but Thia didn't hear a word of his monologue.

She was acutely aware of Luc standing beside her: of his strength, of the patient way he was listening to Stan. She was profoundly affected by the quiet authority Luc exuded, and stirred by the touch of his hand, which rested lightly at the small of her back. Deep inside her some tiny core of resistance crumbled, and she felt a rush of sweet, aching tenderness for him.

God, but she loved him so much! More than life itself. Yet all too often lately, she had reduced her love to a childish game of one-upmanship. She had been so busy salving her own wounded ego that she hadn't given a thought to Luc's feelings, and what made her selfishness insupportable was that she not only loved Luc, but she also admired him. She respected his shrewdness and marveled at his accomplishments. And in a moment of blinding insight, she understood his need to govern his own destiny.

He had risen so far, so fast. In a comparatively short span of years he had fought his way to the top of the heap, and he had done it on his own, with honesty, imagination, and the unflagging determination to succeed.

If needing him had made her feel that she was opening herself to the pain of rejection, needing her must make him feel exquisitely vulnerable. If she'd been frightened of admitting how much she loved him, if it had been difficult for her to jeopardize her independence by committing herself to him, the act of loving commitment must be infinitely more difficult for him.

From the first moment she'd seen Luc, she'd been drawn to him. He'd excited and challenged her. And if she had always been attracted by his single-mindedness, if she had always admired his proud sense of purpose, did she have any right to ask him to change? Did she truly want him to change? And if she did, to what extent?

On the night of their housewarming, Luc had admitted he loved her. He hadn't actually said the words, but he had given her his commitment. And she had demanded proof of his affection. Perhaps, when all was said and done, if she demanded less, Luc would give her more. Perhaps someday he would feel secure enough to give her all the love he had to give, and if it meant a lifetime of waiting, that was a promise worth waiting for.

An increase in the pressure of Luc's hand upon her back made Thia realize that Stan's lecture had drawn to a close.

Glancing at his watch, Luc said, "Our reservations are for one o'clock. We'd better be going."

Stan laughed and rubbed his pudgy hands together. "By all means. I wouldn't want to miss lunch at the Concourse."

From his cherubic appearance, Thia assumed that Stan didn't miss any meals. She decided that she liked the roly-poly architect, and she exerted herself to respond to his genial small talk as the three of them left Luc's office and took the elevator to the ground floor. As they walked across the vestibule toward the street,

Luc offered Stan a lift to the restaurant, but Stan declined, saying, "I have a couple of errands to run on the way back to the office, so I'm going to need my car."

He winked at Thia as he spoke, and she wondered if he was being diplomatic. Had he guessed that she longed to be alone with Luc?

A taxi pulled in to the curb and they parted company with Stan. During the ride to the Concourse, Luc took Thia's hand and held it close to his thigh so that the cabdriver couldn't see his innocent display of affection.

Bringing her up to date on his plans, he said, "We'll be hosting a party of eight for lunch."

Thia realized she was about to make her debut as his hostess. "Would you give me a rundown on our guests?" she asked.

"You met them this morning," Luc replied. "Except for Irene Dalton, they're all members of the board."

"And Irene is your secretary?"

"*Executive* secretary," Luc corrected her dryly. "She manages the office—even does some of the hiring and firing. If you ask her, she'll tell you she's the one who really runs the firm, and there are times when I think she may be right. Lord knows Irene's the only one who can figure out the filing system, on top of which she has a memory that runs on overdrive and a mind like a computer."

Thia thought she sounded formidable. Aloud she said, "Has she been with you long?"

"From the beginning. To be frank, I'd never have gotten the firm off the ground without her." Grinning, Luc added, "Don't tell Irene I said that. She's bossy enough as it is."

Thia nodded and smoothed the palm of her free

hand over her skirt. When she recalled the stylish but austere woman Luc had introduced her to that morning, she began to feel a bit apprehensive. Obviously Luc attached a great deal of importance to Irene's judgment. *Meeting her is like meeting his mother,* thought Thia. *What if she doesn't approve of me?*

During lunch, Thia discoverd that she needn't have worried. Irene Dalton might run Luc's office according to her own iron-clad rules, but when she stepped away from her managerial duties, she was like a mother hen with one chick—and Luc was that chick. However, once Luc was comfortably settled in his chair at the head of the table, Irene proved to be more democratic. She fussed over everybody, including Herman Dowd, the dapper, silver-haired accountant who was a dozen years older than Irene and twice as dignified.

Admittedly, she subjected Thia to a thorough scrutiny and a rapid-fire interrogation, but by the time the waiter served the entrée, she seemed to approve of Thia as Luc's fiancée, and Thia breathed a bit easier.

Lunch turned out to be surprisingly festive, and the rest of the day passed uneventfully. It was late that evening and Thia and Luc had returned to the nursery before Thia learned that the trip to Portland had been a diversionary action. Luc had lured her away from home, and he'd arranged, without her knowledge or consent, to have the house painted in her absence.

Celia ran onto the porch and waved a greeting to them when Luc parked his car near the walk. "Isn't this a lovely surprise?" she cried. "Doesn't the house look terrific?"

Too stunned to comment, Thia climbed out of the car and stood staring at the freshly painted bungalow.

She had trusted Luc, dammit, and he had betrayed

her trust. It was bad enough that he insisted on bringing her luxurious presents when he knew very well that she couldn't afford to return the gesture. But this—this gift could be classified as a necessity.

Because he had enough pride for ten men, he must realize how humiliating this sort of thing was, yet he'd made her feel like a pauper. He'd made her feel incompetent. He was forcing his financial assistance upon her, and it was the last straw!

The silence had become conspicuous, and Celia rushed to fill it. "This was so considerate of you, Luc," she said. "I can't believe how charming the house looks. It was getting pretty rustic, but now—well, I'm really looking forward to staying on here after you and Thia are married, and I just know you're going to be the dearest, sweetest brother-in-law a girl ever had!"

While Luc tried to look modest and Celia's thanks went effusively, interminably on, Thia started toward the front door. Earlier in the day she had resolved to put an end to her childish games, to call a truce and accept Luc's gifts without reprisals, but at this moment she was shaking with fury over Luc's deception, and her noble intentions were temporarily forgotten.

She had reached the porch when Celia said uneasily, "For Heaven's sake, Thia, aren't you going to thank Luc?"

Reminded of her vow, Thia stopped in the doorway, but she didn't turn around. Her spine was so rigid that every line of her body conveyed outrage and injured pride, and her voice was frosty as she said, "Just now I'm speechless with surprise. But don't worry, Celia. Luc knows exactly how I feel, and I give you my word that eventually I'll think of an appropriate way to thank him."

On that chilly note, without saying good night to

Luc, without so much as glancing in his direction, Thia marched into the house and straight through the living room to her bedroom. It took all the self-control she possessed to keep from slamming the hall door behind her, but she closed it gently and collapsed onto the edge of the bed, promising herself that somehow she would find a way to repay Luc for his duplicity.

Various possibilities came to mind, but none of them seemed stringent enough, and before another minute had passed, her anger had turned inward and she was appalled that she had seriously considered getting even with Luc.

She loved him, and even if she had been the most vindictive person on earth, she could not have borne hurting him. But she couldn't bring herself to thank him, either. Not with any degree of sincerity.

She curled up on the bed and lay staring into the darkness, biting her lip to hold back the tears that threatened to fall, praying for enlightenment and listening to the low murmur of voices from the living room that told her that Luc and Celia were talking. She wished they would talk a little louder so that she could hear what they were saying. She felt certain they were discussing her, but pride kept her from moving closer to the door so that she might eavesdrop.

Luc finally left a quarter of an hour later. She heard him say good night to Celia and get into his car, and before the soft growl of the engine had disappeared down the drive, Celia closed the front door so forcibly that it shook the whole house. Her steps were heavy with determination as she stormed along the hall to Thia's bedroom, and she stopped just outside. After knocking sharply at the door, she threw it open and switched on the lights.

While Thia blinked in the sudden brightness, Celia

glared at her and cried, "I hope you're satisfied, Thia Sommers. You may be too proud to admit it, but Luc Domini is the best thing that ever happened to you, and if you can't see how much he loves you, you're not looking very hard. He has to love you, or he wouldn't put up with your stiff-necked pride, and you're doing your best to blow it! Well, let me tell you, I'm fed up with you, even if Luc isn't!"

"Stay out of this, Celia," Thia responded shortly. "You don't know what you're talking about."

"The hell I don't! You're forgetting I've been there. Do you think I learned nothing from my marriage?"

Thia was more astonished than offended by her sister's angry outburst. She automatically sprang to her feet, preparing to defend herself more vigorously, but before she could find her voice, Celia shouted, "Don't say anything, Cynthia Jean. For once in your life just listen, because I am about to do you a big favor. I'm going to give you some priceless advice, and I hope you have the good sense to follow it."

Celia paused for breath, and when she went on, her voice was a trifle less shrill. "If you love Luc, if you value his love at all, take what he gives you and try to be content with it. And if you're not content, at least tell him why. There are no perfect people in this world, but Luc's about as close to perfect as they come, and if you'd stop crying for the moon, maybe—just maybe— you'd realize that you've already got a ticket to paradise right in the palm of your hand. Don't throw it away, Thia. I'd give anything for the chance you've got!"

Having spoken her mind, Celia turned on her heel and stalked along the hall to her room, and Thia made no move to stop her. She had acknowledged the elements of truth in Celia's accusations, and she no longer felt the least bit combative. On the contrary, she felt introspective.

As she got into her nightgown and crawled into bed, she thought about her grandmother's letter, and she knew that while Elvira Sommers had been right in most respects, she had been wrong about one thing. It was as selfish to insist upon being the one to do all the giving as it was to be only a taker.

She thought about Mickie and Austin and remembered Mickie saying something about people having to lose the person they love before they recognized how much the loved one meant to them.

But mostly she thought about Luc. She understood the insecurity that made him feel he must bind her to him with expensive presents, because she herself was none too secure. She understood his need to prove himself because, thanks to her years as a wallflower, she had the same need. And she knew that what she had to do now was to think of some way to convince Luc that she understood; that he didn't have to prove anything to her.

Thia slept very little that night. Sometime after midnight she dozed off for a while, but she slept only long enough to have a dream.

In her dream she was standing at the end of a long wooden pier, watching a ship sail away from the harbor. Away from her. She saw puffs of smoke belch from the smokestacks before she realized that she had been left behind, and then she began jumping up and down and waving her arms and crying, "Come back! Please, come back! Wait for me!"

The passengers on the ship stood in an unbroken line by the railing, smiling and waving farewell to her, but no one made any effort to stop the vessel, and she knew that the ship would not come back.

Never had she felt more bereft. She awoke in a cold sweat, her heart pounding. Had she missed the boat with Luc?

The question kept her awake. Soon her mind was racing, devising and discarding ways to show Luc how much she loved him. And since she couldn't turn off her thoughts, eventually she surrendered to them.

At two A.M. she began cleaning and reorganizing the kitchen cabinets. From four to six she rearranged the furniture in the living room, and at six thirty a bleary-eyed Celia staggered into the kitchen and found her slumped over a cup of coffee at the breakfast counter, emotionally drained and physically exhausted, yet exhilarated because she had finally decided on a plan of action.

Yawning and pushing the silky spill of blond hair out of her eyes, Celia poured herself some coffee and sat next to Thia. Neither of them spoke until she had finished her first cup and refilled her mug. Then, nodding toward the living room, Celia remarked, "I see you didn't sleep much either."

Thia smiled wanly and shook her head, and Celia cleared her throat and stirred sugar into her coffee.

"Look," she began stiltedly, "I'm sorry about last night. I got carried away—"

"It's all right, Celia," Thia interjected. "Your phrasing might have been a touch melodramatic, but you told me some things I needed to hear."

"Not very tactfully, though."

Thia smiled again, this time with more conviction. "Some things can't be said tactfully. And besides, you were talking about more than Luc and me, weren't you?"

Celia laid her coffee spoon aside. "You're right, of course. Lately I've been doing a lot of thinking about Ross and me, and I guess seeing you with Luc last night reminded me of my own mistakes."

"You've never stopped loving Ross, have you, Celia?"

"No, I guess I haven't. Before Brad left for Washington, he asked me to marry him and I turned him down."

"Is there a chance you and Ross might reconcile?"

"I don't know." On a note of rising hope, Celia added, "Maybe. It's what I want, and I think Ross wants it too. But first I have some growing up to do."

Thia gently touched Celia's hand. "I think you've already done a lot of growing up."

"I think you have too, Thia, but there's one thing I simply have to tell you."

"Oh?" Thia was taken aback, but she quickly recovered and prepared herself for another bout of recriminations. "It's a good thing my skin is getting thicker by the minute," she said. "Fire away."

Celia grinned, easing the sudden tension between them. "Please don't take this personally, Sis, but I really detest the way you've rearranged the living room furniture."

"So do I." Thia laughed relievedly. "Oh, Celia, it's absolutely awful."

Chapter Sixteen

After they finished their coffee, Celia helped Thia restore the living room; and while they moved the furniture about, Thia confided in her sister, outlining the strategy with which she hoped to win Luc's confidence. In the small hours of the morning her scheme had seemed straightforward and logical, but in the clear light of day the flaws became glaringly apparent, and she began to have doubts.

"So what's your opinion?" she asked Celia anxiously. "Do you think it will work?"

Celia sat in the wing chair, her chin in her hand, frowning contemplatively while she considered Thia's plan. "It might," she replied at last. "If the whole thing doesn't backfire. If Luc doesn't think you're being sarcastic. If he doesn't think it's just your way of having the last word."

Thia flopped down on the sofa. "How demoralizing! I was afraid you'd say something like that."

"Well, you wanted my honest opinion, didn't you?"

Thia nodded.

"And after the way you've been acting, you couldn't blame Luc for being skeptical, could you?"

"No, I couldn't," Thia allowed soberly.

"After all, people don't change overnight—"

"You've made your point, Celia!"

"Have I?"

"Yes! Apparently you think my plan is silly."

"Oh, I wouldn't put it that strongly. But I do think you should be careful how you go about it."

Thia smiled ruefully and tucked her feet under her, sitting tailor fashion. "And naturally you have some suggestions."

"Naturally I do," Celia agreed breezily. "That's what big sisters are for."

"Well? Are you going to tell me what they are or make me guess?"

"Of course I'm going to tell you. Just give me a moment to think."

Rising, Celia crossed to the windows and stared out at the sun-drenched yard. After what seemed an eternity but was actually a matter of minutes, she said, "To begin with, you'll need to set the scene, so how about starting the evening with a romantic dinner for two in your new home. A meal, by the way, that you have lovingly prepared with your own two hands—"

"Yes, I think I get the picture."

"Soft lights and sweet music and cozy domesticity— and you wearing something slinky and seductive—"

"I have just the thing," Thia murmured, thinking of the wicked peppermint-pink dress.

"Does it make a statement?" Celia asked.

"It most certainly does. It says, 'what you see is what you get.'"

"All right! Then after dinner—"

"You don't have to spell it out. I can manage dessert on my own."

"I'm sure you can," Celia said mildly. "Which

brings me to the moment when you present Luc with his gift—and this is the part that bothers me. I can appreciate the significance of your giving him something expensive and utterly useless, but men being what they are, I'm not certain Luc will understand what you're getting at unless you add an inscription."

"An inscription? But what could I say?"

Celia shrugged one shoulder and turned to face Thia. "That, my dear sister, is up to you. All I can tell you is that it should explain what you're doing in a very personal way. Maybe you could use a quote from a poem."

"Maybe," Thia said doubtfully.

"Which brings me to my last point," Celia continued hesitantly, her eyes avoiding Thia's. "How are you fixed for cash? I mean, if you need a loan to pay for Luc's present—"

"Thanks, Sis, but I can swing it. I have two landscaping jobs billed out, so I should be able to pay myself a salary again."

"But that means you'll have to wait till the end of the month."

"I'd probably have to wait that long anyway. It's going to take a while to have Luc's gift made."

"That's true," Celia admitted. "But what'll you do in the meantime?"

"Apologize profusely and love Luc like crazy." Thia was smiling confidently, but silently, she added, "And keep my fingers crossed."

Thia did apologize, and Luc accepted her apology. She kept her fingers crossed too, but for the next two weeks she had little opportunity to love Luc like crazy. He was in Portland most of that time, and although he telephoned almost every night, long distance proved to be a poor substitute for being with him.

By October first, however, Thia was ready to put her plan into operation. She had ordered the gift from the same jeweler who had sold Luc her engagement ring, and she had agonized over the inscription, searching through anthologies of poetry and reading *Bartlett's Familiar Quotations* until the fine print swam in front of her eyes. She spent one Friday evening in the Card and Candle Shop on the plaza, reading the verses on the greeting cards, and she discovered that there really was a card for every occasion—except this one.

After that experience, she decided to compose her own inscription.

Once upon a time she had supported herself with her facility with words, but now, when so much depended on saying just the right thing, she couldn't string two words together gracefully. She had so much to say and so few lines to say it in, and she was writing pure drivel.

She wrote and rewrote, then started all over again, and she was unhappy with the final result. It was corny instead of clever, and not at all lyrical, but it had one virtue: It delivered the message she wanted Luc to receive.

The Kirby house was ready too. The new appliances had been installed, making the kitchen a gastronome's dream, and the master bedroom was sumptuously decorated in a modified Art Deco style, all rounded corners and flowing lines and spaciousness, awash with seafoam green.

On the second Saturday in October, Luc stopped by the nursery on his way from the airport to the inn. The garden shop was full of customers, so he took Thia into the greenhouse, where they ducked behind a convenient evergreen clematis to kiss hello.

"Do you know what day this is?" he asked.

"The thirteenth—"

"That's right." Luc folded her body to his with breathtaking ardor. "If things had been different, it might have been our wedding day."

He claimed her lips hungrily, as if he wanted to ravish her. His tongue was probing and plunging, seeking out the deepest, sweetest recesses of her mouth, and she wound her arms around his waist and pressed closer to him and opened her mouth wider, responding with a need born of desperation.

Why had she objected when Luc and Celia had chosen this date for the wedding? At the time she'd thought she had sufficient reason to ask for a postponement, but now it seemed foolish, especially when she heard footsteps approaching along the graveled pathway between the beaches.

Luc was trembling as much as she as they sprang apart, shaken by a spasm of longing and painful frustration, dissatisfied with the stolen kisses and hurried embraces of the past month.

Before she left Luc to offer her assistance to the customer who had invaded their trysting place, Thia inquired huskily, "Are you going to be in town for a while?"

"Just for tonight, I'm afraid," Luc answered roughly. "I have a meeting in Salem at ten tomorrow morning—"

"But it's Sunday!"

"I know, hon, but this should be the wrap-up. After this week we'll have finished the preliminaries for moving our main office to Stratford, and the shopping center project should be off the ground."

"I see." Thia wanted to weep with disappointment. She decided she could not wait any longer, and hastily suggested, "Let's have dinner at the house this evening. I want to show you what we've done with it."

Luc's gaze moved over her face, finally settling on the tender curve of her mouth. His dark eyes smoldered with desire, and his hand shook as he touched her cheek. "It's a date," he said.

Thia's heart skipped a beat and her breath caught in her throat. "Then I'll meet you there, Luc," she whispered. "About seven o'clock?"

Luc chuckled. "I can't wait that long, Thia mia. What's wrong with six?"

Thia laughed. "Six is fine." As he turned to leave, she added, "And Luc, bring your toothbrush."

Luc's only answer was a roguish grin, but it spoke volumes. It promised her an evening of intimacy and ecstasy. It fed her own excitement and made her wonder how she could possibly wait until six o'clock to see him.

Although the rest of the day seemed to drag, it was filled with hectic preparations for the evening. Early in the afternoon Thia went shopping. She had planned to keep the dinner menu simple, but she had to go to three different supermarkets to find the thickest steak, the freshest salad greens, the most luscious hothouse strawberries.

At the last store she visited she added to her shopping cart the ingredients to make Belgian waffles for breakfast. After paying for her purchases, she took the groceries directly to the Kirby house and stored the perishables in the gleaming new refrigerator. Then she rushed back to the nursery to load the van with candles and masses of flowers, her tape deck and a selection of cassettes, the necessary dishes and utensils, and bed linens and towels.

She packed her overnight bag, carefully including her sheerest nightie, the perfume and pendant Luc had given her, and the pièce de résistance—the sexy peppermint-pink dress.

With her packing out of the way, she had only one more chore to do before she left the nursery. She began to have second thoughts while she gift wrapped Luc's present, and during the drive to the house tormenting questions buzzed through her mind.

Would Luc think she was mocking him? Would he understand that the gift was her way of saying that she would meet him halfway—more than halfway? Would he think she'd been inspired or simply an extravagant fool when she'd chosen to spend hundreds of dollars on a golden key with an acrylic tag? Was the inscription too sentimental? Was it silly? Dear Lord! What if he laughed at her?

Her misgivings multiplied while she scattered bouquets of flowers throughout the house and made the bed with lavender-scented sheets and laid a fire in the bedroom fireplace.

Thia felt on edge all afternoon, as if she were racing a clock whose hands refused to function, but by five fifteen she had showered and changed into her dress and finished applying her makeup. She sipped a glass of wine while she wandered from room to room, checking that everything was as it should be.

George Benson sang softly from the stereo, and the table looked lovely with its centerpiece of coral-colored tea roses and baby's breath. The candles were ready to light, the salad was crisping, the potatoes were scrubbed and ready to bake, and the steak was ready to slide under the broiler.

Only Luc's gift worried her. She had displayed the foil-wrapped parcel prominently, putting it by his place at the table. It was the first thing she saw when she went into the dining room, and every time she saw it, she felt a little less confident that giving it to Luc early in the evening was the right thing to do.

She was torn by indecision until Luc arrived. He was twenty minutes early, and when she heard his car in the drive, her courage completely deserted her.

Acting on impulse, she grabbed the package, ran upstairs, and hid it beneath her pillow. She knew she was only postponing her moment of truth, and she felt like the world's worst coward as she hurried back to the foyer to meet Luc, but the moment he opened the front door, she forgot her cowardice in the joy of being with him.

Tonight he was devastatingly attractive in a dark-blue cable-knit sweater worn over an open-collared shirt and gray slacks. Just seeing him made her heart swell with love for him. His face was ruddy from the chill autumn wind, his eyes were warm with desire, and his smile eclipsed the sun, which was setting behind the mountains.

When he saw her, his grin broadened, and he held up his toothbrush as if it were his ticket of admission.

"The rest of my stuff's in the car," he said, "but I thought you'd want to check this out."

She would have run to his arms, but he held her a small distance away from him so that he could look at her.

"You're wearing the perfume I gave you," he said at last, "and the necklace."

Thia stroked the topaz pendant with loving fingers. "I never thanked you properly for this, Luc, but it's beautiful."

"It is on you," Luc said gently. As he drew her close, he added, "I like your dress. When I dream about you, if you're wearing anything at all, it's usually something like that." He kissed her, and his hands moved over her with thinly disguised excitement, telling her just how effective the dress was.

Thia went onto her tiptoes and melted into his embrace, returning his caresses with her own and trailing moist feathery kisses along his jaw.

"I hoped you'd like it," she whispered close to his ear. "Tonight I intend to do everything I can to please you."

"Everything?" Luc asked with mock alarm.

"Everything," she repeated solemnly.

"That's funny. I had the same idea about you."

A throaty laugh escaped Thia. "Ah, but I said it first, so tonight's my turn."

To show Luc how eager she was to please him, she traced the outline of his ear with the tip of her tongue and slipped one hand between them to touch him more intimately. His subdued groan and the way he buried his face in the side of her neck encouraged her to move her body against his with a pliant sensuality that left him in no doubt as to her intentions.

Tantalized beyond endurance, Luc groaned outright and hauled her even closer, molding her softness against him until Thia's fast-mounting passion matched his own throbbing excitement. His voice was raspy with desire as he said, "What if I insist it's my turn?"

"I'd say you're mistaken."

"And what if I say pleasing you would give me the greatest pleasure?"

Thia caught the fleshy part of his earlobe between her teeth and gave it a playful nip. "Then I'd say, 'Sorry, but that's against the rules.'"

Luc cupped her chin with one hand and planted a kiss on the tip of her nose. He suppressed a grin and tried to look reproachful as he said, "Tell me honestly what you're up to, Thia mia. Are you trying to pick a fight?"

"Of course I am, darling." With a sexy sidelong glance at Luc, Thia stepped away from him, swinging her hips seductively as she sauntered toward the living room. "Did you think I wore this dress and spent the whole afternoon shopping and fixing dinner just so we could end the evening making love?"

Chuckling, Luc hurried after her, peeling off his sweater and tossing it over the back of a chair as he went. He captured her hand in his and swung her around to face him as he said, "Let's see if I've got this straight. We're playing by your rules, but it's my evening—"

"That's right, Luc." She lifted his hand to her mouth and kissed it, then rubbed her cheek against his knuckles. "Tonight your wish is my command."

Enthralled, Luc leaned closer to her and drawled, "Suppose I want to begin by making love?"

Thia widened her eyes innocently. "Don't you even want to see the house?"

"I'm dying to see it. Show me the bedroom."

Luc started toward the stairs, tugging her along behind him, and despite the laughter in his voice, Thia sensed his urgency. She followed him gladly, but halfway up the stairs, she couldn't resist asking, "What about dinner?"

"What about starting with an appetizer?"

This time Luc's actions belied the levity in his reply. Stopping in midstride, he swept her off her feet and into his arms, gathering her possessively close and cradling her against his chest. As he strode down the hall, Thia pouted up at him, pretending to be offended.

"Is an appetizer all I am to you? I thought I qualified as the main course, at least."

"Thia, you know damned well you're manna for the soul, a feast for the eyes—"

"What about the rest of your body, Luc?"

He paused to nudge the bedroom door open with his knee before he replied, "You are a veritable ten-course banquet."

He deposited her in the fading square of sunlight at the center of the bed, and she lay where she had landed, watching him from beneath her lashes and holding her arms up to him.

For a moment he stood staring down at her, arrested by her radiance, marveling at how soft and lovely and desirable she looked with her hair lying in a silken tangle across her forehead and the dusky-gold sunset honeying her skin and shining from her eyes.

It was strange, he thought, that when they were apart it was her delicacy he remembered. But whenever they made love, she surprised him by being ripe and lush—even lusty.

"Luc," she sighed. "Have you any idea how much I love you?"

She barely breathed the words, but he heard the longing in her voice and dropped down on the bed beside her. As he sank back against the pillows, he muttered thickly, "Show me, Thia mia. I'm starving for you."

Luc seemed content to let her be the aggressor, and although she had thought that once they were in the bedroom he would seize the initiative, she did not need a second invitation.

She saw bemused expectation in his eyes. She saw that he was silently debating whether he should take a more active role, but in the end he remained passive as she unbuttoned his shirt and loosened his trousers, neither assisting nor opposing her. His acquiescence challenged her, and she rose to the challenge.

She strove to define the dimensions of her love for him with her warm mouth and eager hands, with questing fingers and seeking tongue, with whispered endearments and the tantalizing press of her soft flesh against his hardness. She kissed him on the mouth, shyly at first, brushing his lips with hers gently from side to side, coaxing his lips to part. And when his arms went around her and his mouth opened, she molded her lips to his and deepened her explorations as tenderly as if this were Luc's first kiss and she were some pagan goddess of seduction. She felt the gliding response of his tongue, and withdrew slightly, enticing his pursuit, and while their tongues dueled sweetly for supremacy, her hands began their own assault on his senses, stroking his shoulders and the sinews of his arms and his smoothly muscled chest. She cherished every inch of him, caressing the lean angles of his body slowly and with beguiling thoroughness, yet she taunted him by avoiding the more intimate contacts that would bring his pleasure to the breaking point.

At last Luc's hard-won control snapped. He cried her name harshly, then again with entreaty, and guided her hands to his body, and for a timeless time she was oblivious to everything but him. Her reactions were instinctive, her only concern finding new ways to heighten his sensations.

She heard his ragged breathing and the heavy drumming of his heart, and her own excitement spiraled. His face was suffused with passion, his pupils dilated, his lips drawn back in a taut grimace of ecstasy. She touched him and knew that he was fully aroused, and she felt proud that she could excite him so.

"Thia," he groaned. "Do you see what you do to me?"

His fingers were searching frantically for the zipper at the back of her dress, and she rose on one elbow and angled herself across his chest to help him.

"Tell me how to please you, Luc," she whispered. "Show me what you want."

The dress slid off her shoulders and his hands were hot and impatient as they roved over her, finding the fastener on her bra and flinging the lacy scrap aside, eagerly groping for the rounded warmth of her breasts, lingering to fondle the sensitive nipples and tease them to saucy peaks before he stripped off the rest of her clothing.

Within a matter of seconds she sat astride his thighs, wearing nothing more than the topaz pendant, which nestled coolly in the satiny hollow between her breasts, and the perfume he had given her, which mingled with the musky odor of desire, and a smile that was loving and jubilant and mysterious.

"More," Luc muttered. "I want all of you."

His hands underscored his demand, clutching at her hips and telling her that he could wait for her no longer, fitting her to him so that he could fill the hungry void inside her with a bold, seeking thrust. And she gave him what he wanted with a delectable eroticism that drove him to the brink of rapture again and again, then brought the release of a shattering climax that touched his very soul.

They did not get around to eating the dinner Thia had so lovingly prepared until ten o'clock. Luc ate ravenously. He praised her abilities as a cook outrageously and tried to be properly appreciative of the progress Celia and Thia had made with redecorating the house, but it was obvious that what he really wanted to do was take Thia back to bed and make love to her again. Since she wanted the same thing, this was the highest praise he could have given her.

In less than an hour they returned to the bedroom, and when Thia folded back the bedcovers, Luc found his present. But by then he was not at all interested in opening it.

This time he assumed command of their lovemaking, and their coming together was gloriously uninhibited and intensely satisfying. Afterward they lay with their limbs entwined, too contented to move; and gradually, with Luc still inside her, they drifted into sleep.

The soft gray light of dawn had filtered into the bedroom when Thia awoke. She felt the mattress dip and reached out for Luc. When her hand encountered the crisp emptiness of the sheet on his side of the bed, she opened her eyes and saw that he was standing by the night table, clad only in the towel he had wrapped about his hips after his shower.

He was sorting through the clothing he had discarded so hastily the night before, emptying the pockets of his trousers, and for a few seconds she lay looking up at him, admiring the proud, sculptured lines of his body and inhaling the clean, early-morning fragrance of his after-shave.

She spoke his name quietly, and he turned to her and

smiled. "I'm sorry," he said, bending down to kiss the corner of her mouth. "I didn't mean to wake you."

"I'm glad you did."

She wrapped her arms around his neck, shivering as the cold morning air fanned over her skin, and he pulled her closer, sharing his body heat with her.

"Stay, Luc," she pleaded. "Don't leave me just yet."

Luc glanced regretfully at his watch. "I'm afraid I have to, honey. My plane leaves in an hour and a quarter."

"What time is it now?"

"Almost five forty-five."

She touched his cheek and smoothed back the unruly lock of hair that had fallen across his brow. "Can't you stay a few minutes longer?"

She shivered again, and his gaze left her face to wander over the lissome nakedness the slipping blankets had exposed.

"Well," he said thoughtfully, shoving back the bedclothes so that he could see more of her, "maybe a few minutes longer."

Even as he yielded to her request and to his own urges, Luc pulled off the towel and slid into bed beside her, and although he had to be at the airport by seven, he made love to her as if time had ceased to exist.

Thia was sleeping when he finally left the house, and when she awoke for the second time that morning, the pattern of light and shadow in the bedroom told her that it must be close to eight o'clock. She opened her eyes reluctantly and stretched, luxuriating in the bone-deep contentment that pervaded her body. But her euphoria was short-lived.

The present! She had completely forgotten about Luc's gift.

Her eyes flew open and she sat up abruptly, then leaped out of bed, pulling the pillows with her, flinging them away and stripping the blankets and sheets off the mattress, anxiously looking for the parcel.

But the gift was gone and Luc was gone, and she was chilled by the certainty that he had taken it with him.

Dear Lord! He would open it on his own. She would not be there to explain what she'd meant by giving him the key, and she could not rely on the inscription to make him understand.

Her fingers felt numb with fear as she hurried into her clothes. She had no idea what she was going to do once she was dressed beyond vague, formless plans of going to the airport and following Luc to Salem. If only she could be with him, perhaps she could make him see that she had given him the present with the best of intentions. After all, wasn't it the thought that counted, rather than the gift?

She was trying to work out the worst of the tangles in her hair when the telephone rang, startling her so that she dropped the hairbrush. While the brush skidded beneath the bureau, the phone rang again, and she stared at it dumbly, too horrified to answer.

Although Celia knew where she had spent the night, Thia was certain that it was Luc who was phoning, and when she worked up the courage to answer on the fifth ring, she learned that her assumption was correct. The caller was Luc.

"Hello, Thia," he said, and though she tried, she could not gauge his mood by his tone of voice.

"Wh-where are you?" she stammered. "Are you calling from Salem?"

"No," Luc answered without inflection. "As a matter of fact, I'm in Stratford."

"Stratford? But why? Did you miss your plane?"

"Not exactly. The truth is, I changed my mind about the trip."

"B-but you'll miss your meeting."

"Yeah," Luc acceded flatly. "Well, I guess you could say that something more important came up."

Thia wondered what could be more important to Luc than his meeting, and she dreaded the possibility that it was her gift, but before she could ask, Luc spoke up.

"Look, Thia," he said briskly, "I'm calling from the Copper Kettle Cafe on the plaza, and I thought maybe you'd like to join me here for breakfast."

"Yes," she replied reflexively. "Yes, of course I would, Luc. But please, don't keep me in suspense. Tell me why you decided not to go to Salem."

"Well, I—uh—I opened my present."

Suddenly, Thia's hands were slippery with perspiration. She closed her eyes, envisioning the baroque golden key with its beveled acrylic tag.

"And?" she prompted feebly.

"I read the inscription," Luc replied.

In her mind's eye Thia saw the ornate tracery of Gothic letters on the clear plastic, and even as the message she had composed sprang sharply into focus, Luc began reciting the inscription.

"My love's not for sale—
you can't buy it."

Thia cringed with embarrassment, but before she could interrupt, Luc recited the rest of her doggerel.

"It's yours for the taking—
please try it.
And just for a start,
here's the key to my heart:
Say you love me—
or if you can't say it,
imply it."

As Luc concluded, Thia thought she detected amusement in his voice—and something else as well. But at
that moment in time, she was barely rational and she was
incapable of defining his emotions. She wished she
could see him, because she knew that he was waiting for
her to make some comment, and the silence between
them was deafening.

It was Luc who ended the silence. "Thia," he said
softly, "I just wondered— That is, I get the impression—"

After these uneasy starts, Luc hesitated. Thia heard
his deep intake of breath, and when he went on, a hint
of shyness had crept into his voice.

"What I want to ask is, have you changed your mind
about our bargain? I mean, have you switched sides?"

"Yes, my darling," she cried. "Oh, yes! I've switched
to our side."

Luc's low-pitched laughter seemed to indicate that
this was the answer he'd hoped to hear.

"How soon can you get here?" he asked.

"Give me ten minutes," she replied. "Maybe less."
How could she stand waiting even one minute to see
him? "Unless— Would you like to come back to the
house? I could fix waffles—"

"No," Luc cut in firmly. "I'd rather you came here."

His answer burst Thia's fragile bubble of elation, and feeling somewhat deflated, she agreed. "If that's what you want, Luc, I'll be there before you know it."

She worried about Luc's surprising preference while she belted her coat and collected her handbag and got into the van.

Why in the world would he choose to meet her in public when they had the privacy of their own home at their disposal? She had thought he'd understood what the key represented. He'd asked about her change of heart, and based on that flimsy evidence, she'd jumped to the conclusion that he'd found her sincerity convincing. She had even dared to hope for a corresponding sign of compromise from him, and now her hopes were dashed.

"The only thing you've accomplished," she muttered, "is to make a fool of yourself."

She spun the wheel angrily and turned into the stream of traffic on Siskiyou Boulevard with a squeal of tires that seemed to second her opinion of herself. Realizing that she was speeding, she eased back on the accelerator and tried to concentrate on her driving. But before she'd traveled another mile, a new thought had occurred to her.

From the very beginning she had recognized that Luc's business was all he really cared about. Later she'd been afraid that his business was all he'd let himself care about, and now it appeared that her fear was well-grounded. At least until the time came when he allowed himself to trust her.

Thia scowled as she pulled into a parking slot near the Copper Kettle, worrying that Luc might never feel sure of her love for him, but when she approached the entrance to the cafe, her scowl disappeared.

Luc was waiting for her just inside the dining room, and after one look at his face, she knew that the key had convinced him and won his trust. The way he held his arms out to her said this more clearly than words, and he looked younger, happier, more carefree than he ever had, even when they were in high school.

Thia felt as if she were walking on air as she went into his arms. At first he simply held her, and then he pressed an envelope into her hand.

He kept one arm about her shoulders while she studied the airline logo stamped in one corner of the envelope.

"What's this?" she asked dully.

"Open it and see."

She did as Luc instructed, and found that the envelope contained a pair of tickets on that afternoon's excursion to Reno. She stared at the tickets, shaking her head with disbelief.

"The flight doesn't leave until two," said Luc. "You have plenty of time to pack and do whatever else you need to do."

Confused, Thia looked at him warily. "What made you decide to skip your meeting?" she asked.

"Well, I was at the airport and I saw this travel poster for Nevada, and I got to thinking that it's too nice a day to spend in some stuffy office. And Herman and Irene can wind things up as well as I can—"

"But why Reno, Luc? Did you get a sudden urge to gamble?"

"No. Actually I thought it would be fun to take a week or so off—especially if I can talk you into coming with me. If you're worried about the nursery, I already checked with Celia, and she said she and Penny can handle things—"

"Yes, I'm sure they can. But why Reno, Luc?"

"It—uh—it just seemed like a good idea at the time. I thought we might catch some shows and rent a car and drive over to Tahoe for a few days, maybe even go on over to the coast and see Mickie and Austin."

Thia swayed on her feet with shock, and Luc put his other arm around her to steady her.

"This is a dream, isn't it?" she said.

"No, honey, you're wide awake. At least, I hope you are."

"But I can't believe this is happening."

"Believe it, Thia. It's real." Luc smiled self-consciously and shuffled his feet, but his arms about her tightened as he said, "If you'd still like to elope, we could get married in Reno."

Thia's first inclination was to say there was nothing she'd like better, but then she remembered how important it was to compromise and inquired breathlessly, "What would you like, darling?"

"I just want to be with you," Luc said gravely.

Miraculously, before the sound of his voice had died away, he kissed her. Right in front of the waitresses and busboys and fry cooks, not to mention the entire breakfast crowd that frequented the Copper Kettle Cafe, Luc kissed her.

And it was not a dutiful peck on the cheek he gave her, but a lingering kiss on the mouth. A tender kiss. A loving kiss. A lover's kiss.

It was a long time before he released her, and when he did, under the cover of the whistles and applause their audience gave them, he told her, "I love you, Thia mia, more than I can say. I always have and I always will."

His whispered declaration of love was barely audible,

but she sensed that part of him wanted to shout it from the middle of Main Street so that all of Stratford could hear. And as he led her to their table by the windows, he smiled at her, and she knew that finally, irrevocably, Luc Domini had come home.

HARLEQUIN *Love Affair*

Now on sale

STARSTRUCK   *Anne McAllister*

Any man who attempted to turn an interview into a seduction, then had the nerve to invite himself to dinner, deserved exactly what he got. Liv James couldn't help feeling that actor Joe Harrington, America's heartthrob, deserved a good dose of reality—Liv's kind of reality. That included a hyperactive rabbit cavorting in the back of her van, a slightly charred casserole and, of course, the children.

Five of them. If the casserole didn't poison him, the commotion would deafen him. . . . It must have been the novelty he loved, Liv decided. But as time passed and Joe began to talk of settling in Madison, Liv prayed the novelty would wear off before she got in too deep!

SEASON OF DREAMS   *Robin Francis*

It was ironic that the Stratford, Oregon, Centennial Celebration was to be held at the Warwick Inn. The old hotel had been recently purchased by Domini Developers and was to be decorated by Sommers Nurseries. Once, Thia Sommers and Luc Domini had been outsiders in the town, and both had fled after high school. Thia's love of plants had called her home to take over her grandmother's nurseries. But Luc Domini had become the kind of successful, polished businessman who usually buried an unhappy past.

His return mystified Thia—until she learned that he had come back for her!

THE GLORY RUN   *Anne Henry*

Once Emily Williams had been a fleet-footed golden-haired girl who existed for the sheer joy of running. Despite her eight-year hiatus from competition, Coach Keith Lancaster had only to see Emily on the track to know that she still possessed the heart of a runner and the grace of a gazelle. Once Emily had been the Texas state champion. With Keith's help, she could be the best in the world.

But time had changed Emily, endowing her with a woman's heart. She needed much more than determination and his help to win. She needed Keith's love.

Next month's titles

NO SAFE PLACE   *Barbara Bretton*

For too long, Stefanie Colt had skated on thin ice. Unable to walk the streets of New York without casting nervous glances over her shoulder, unable to contemplate her responsibilities at work without feeling a cold dread, Stefanie felt that her memories were slowly consuming her. It was only a matter of time, Stefanie knew, before she became totally paralyzed by fear.

Helping people like Stefanie was more than Dan O'Conner's business—it was his obsession. He knew of no other way to exorcise his own very private demons. . . .

ADAM AND EVA   *Sandra Kitt*

St. John was everything Eva Duncan had been promised. Almost. Lush, warm, exotic and spectacularly beautiful, it was not quite the picture of serenity and tranquillity it was cracked up to be. That was Adam Maxwell's fault. If he had confined his ill humour to her, Eva could have tolerated the neighbouring marine biologist. But having flown down to the island with his adoring young daughter, Eva bristled whenever she heard him ordering the child about.

For his daughter's sake, someone had to stand up to this man. Gathering her courage, Eva was determined to do just that, despite the consequences!

SOMEONE ELSE'S HEART   *Zelma Orr*

Over the years, Andy Timmons had developed a sixth sense for danger. A pilot in her family's Colorado-based charter service, Andy discovered that her keen instincts enabled her to chart a course around pea-soup fogs and treacherous winds—and thus avoid mishap.

Andy's instincts told her to give Scott Rawlings a wide berth. Scott, who soon became a regular customer, didn't like flying, and his loud misgivings were enough to distract any pilot. Unable to avoid Scott, Andy tried to ignore him, but it was just not enough to avert catastrophe!

These books are
already available
from

HARLEQUIN
Love Affair

THE OTHER HALF OF LOVE
  Jacqueline Ashley
THE DREAM NEVER DIES
  Jacqueline Diamond
DAYDREAMS Rebecca Flanders
PROMISE ME TODAY
  Cathy Gillen Thacker
WHEN LOVE ISN'T ENOUGH
  Kathleen Gilles Seidel
CHEROKEE SUMMER Anne Henry
WINTER'S BOUNTY Muriel Jensen
MISPLACED DESTINY Sharon McCaffree
DARE TO DREAM Modean Moon
MEASURE OF LOVE Zelma Orr
THE LAST KEY Beverly Sommers
MIX AND MATCH Beverly Sommers

If you experience difficulty in obtaining any of these
titles, write to:
Harlequin Love Affair, P.O. Box 236,
Croydon, Surrey CR9 3RU

These two absorbing titles
will be published in October
by

HARLEQUIN
SuperRomance

SILVER HORIZONS by Deborah Joyce

Minta Cordero, FBI undercover agent, had been
ordered to take a vacation and stay out of trouble.

She chose the Cayman Islands in the Caribbean. So
did Brad McMillan who was conducting top-secret
tests on his underwater robot. From the moment
they met, and even after they fell in love, Minta
suspected Brad was involved in something danger-
ous.

When she learned the devastating truth about him,
Minta was forced to make a choice. Either turn in
the man she loved, or turn her back on justice.

THROUGH NIGHT AND DAY by Irma Walker

There was a saying that the Pelente men loved only
once, and when Mayi Jenners married Laurens
Pelente, she knew it would be forever.

They would spend their lives in a fairy-tale village in
the high Pyrenees, the Basque country Mayi readily
adopted as her own. When the letter came, she saw
her dreams shatter.

Laurens didn't want to believe the startling revelation about his wife, but as head of the Pelente
household he could not ignore it. So Mayi set out to
win back the love—and trust—of her proud husband.

Harlequin ◈

Accept 4 gripping Love Affair titles absolutely
FREE

Share in the bittersweet passions of heartbreak and joy in Love Affair romantic novels.

Here are stories every woman will understand, stories that explore the hearts and minds of men and women caught in the tender trap of love. By becoming a regular reader of Love Affair romances you could enjoy six thrilling new titles every two months and a whole range of special benefits too:— your very own personal membership card, a free monthly Newsletter packed with exclusive book offers, recipes, competitions, a monthly guide to the stars, plus extra bargain offers and big cash savings.

And by way of introduction we will send you 4 superb Love Affair romances free — turn over the page for details.

Complete the coupon below and send it back today and we will send you 4 Introductory Love Affair Romances, yours to keep FREE.

At the same time we will reserve a subscription to Harlequin Love Affair for you. Every other month you will receive six of the latest novels by leading Romantic Fiction authors, delivered direct to your door. You don't even pay for delivery. Postage and packing is always completely Free. There is no obligation or commitment — you only receive books for as long as you want to.

What could be easier? Just fill in the coupon below and send it to:—
HARLEQUIN READER SERVICE, FREEPOST, P.O. BOX 236, CROYDON, SURREY CR9 9EL

Please Note: READERS IN SOUTH AFRICA write to:
Harlequin Ltd., Postbag X3010, Randburg 2125, S. Africa.

FREE BOOKS CERTIFICATE

To: Harlequin Reader Service, FREEPOST, P.O. Box 236, Croydon, Surrey. CR9 9EL

Please send me, free, and without obligation, four Love Affair romances, and reserve a Reader Service Subscription for me. If I decide to subscribe I shall receive, following my free parcel of books, six new Love Affair titles every two months for £7.50 post and packing free. If I decide not to subscribe, I shall write to you within 10 days. The free books are mine to keep in any case. I understand that I may cancel my subscription at any time simply by writing to you. I am over 18 years of age.

Signature _____

Please write in BLOCK CAPITALS.

Name _____

Address _____

_____ Postcode _____

SEND NO MONEY — TAKE NO RISKS.
Please don't forget to include your Postcode.

EP16L